# MESSAGE IN A BULLET

## A Raymond Mackey Mystery

### Book 1

Owen Thomas

**For Marlo**

# ONE

He's an old hump, this one – sitting alone in the sewing room. Trying not to think about the heat.

Hard to do since that's all the rusted rotary in the corner wants to talk about. Every time the fan makes another pass, it creaks, then rattles out a complaint about the heat not caring about the time. Nine o'clock in the evening and the temperature thinks it's high noon. It's like watching Bogart and Bergman in some old movie where the sound isn't keeping up with the lips. Only hotter.

Nothing to be done about it except to try to pretend it's not a problem. Try to pretend he's not living on the surface of the sun.

So he keeps sweating and drinking and looking at the crime scene photos.

His shoulders are hunched into a pool of tired yellow light that glazes the top of the battered desk – saw-blade scars and screwdriver wounds and smears of old grease like black bloodstains – with a kind of luminous syrup. The light dribbles from a garage-sale desk lamp with a cracked plastic shade, craning its segmented silver neck obnoxiously over the back of the typewriter. Like maybe the lamp wants to see the crime scene photos too.

The desk is the same heavy, oak monstrosity. Jimmy Kline had helped him move it up two flights of stairs from the garage where it had long served as a shelter for luggage underneath and a platform for tools and a second-hand gun safe on top.

That was the last time he'd seen Jimmy, sitting on the stairs, sweating and panting as they'd downed the last two beers and traced the deep triangular sheetrock wounds they'd just punched into the wall.

They hadn't talked much. It was a conversation of heavy breathing and grunting and swearing. Jimmy never liked him and he'd never liked Jimmy. Nothing like marriage and grief to bring people together; to get the heavy furniture where it needs to be.

And the desk – the erstwhile tool-bench, luggage-cozy – had needed to be up in the goddamned sewing room. Five years now and this guy's no-account brother-in-law was in the wind, probably living out of his car to evade process or off scamming the daughters of the well-to-do. Florida, if he had to guess. Miami. Jimmy was Chicago-born and -raised, he and his sister both. But all Jimmy ever talked about was Miami.

Nothing quite like death to free a person.

But wherever Jimmy was, dead maybe, or in jail, or married with two kids and selling life insurance, who the hell knew or cared, wherever Jimmy was, the desk was still up here, crammed into the corner beneath the window so this guy, this miserable pathetic hump, can look out over the neighborhood after a hard day's work and nurse an Old Forester and bang away on his vintage, dirty-turquoise Smith Corona Corsair. The desk had needed to be in the sewing room because the sewing room could no longer be a sewing room. The very sight of the sewing room would kill him. The white Singer sewing machine, and the rosewood credenza full of supplies, and the little cream-colored love seat, and the antique rocker with the hand-embroidered "I've Got Your Back" pillow. All that was gone now.

Because the very sight of the room full of those things, her things, would have killed him. One more glance inside as he passed down the hall to the guest bedroom where he now slept would have been a bullet to the brain. It would have killed him.

So. Just the desk, then, and the lamp and the Smith Corona and the Old Forester and the extra, suddenly worthless, dining room chair that had desperately needed to stop moping down in the dining room and come up where it could do some good. Those things and now the rusty fan too, shaking its head and bitching about the heat. The sewing room had needed to be a different kind of room. A home office.

Except that it would always be the sewing room. Her sewing room. The best he could hope for was a sewing room pretending its damnedest to be something else. A home office. It was a cheap, dime-store disguise at best. But he supposed it had worked. He was still alive.

Philippa leaps up onto his lap, purring. The fan is quick to warn against this, worried about the fur and the extra heat. But he doesn't care. Phil always has a place. She rubs the top of her head against the back of his hand until he sets down the photos and dips a finger into his glass. Phil sniffs and takes the drop of Old Forester. He massages her soft tiny head until she closes her eyes and stretches out. Somewhere deep inside her white softness, she starts to vibrate contentment. His legs are uncomfortable. He needs to uncross and re-cross. But he holds his position. For Phil's sake.

He gives her another drop, then takes a drink for himself and trades the glass for the photos. One at a time, he takes one off the top of the pile and brings it up to his face. He spends five, six seconds on a photo, then picks up the next.

The two dented, green garbage dumpsters jammed up against each other.

Next. The concrete loading dock behind Al's Super Electronics.

Next. The broken metal fence running along the north end of Al's all the way to the sidewalk.

Next. On the other side of the fence, the hulking eight stories of dirty brick that keep the tenants of the Chandler Belle Vista Apartments out of the weather, which, according to the pictures, looked to be mostly dreary with a fifty percent chance of gloom.

Next. A photo of nothing, foggy whiteness mostly. A blurry overexposure, quaintly anachronistic in today's photo-perfect society. But incompetence never goes out of style. He wads it up and drops it in the trashcan under the desk. Phil watches, cocking her head like the discarded ball of paper might be a flying mouse or a discarded scrap of chicken.

Next. The tiny, black iron balcony on the seventh floor. That's where the body had come from. Back when the body was still a person.

Next. Another shot of the broken fence. A closeup. Rough landing.

He spreads the photos out on the desk. He wants to look at them all in a row, so that they tell the whole story.

Not a real story. Well, *partly* real. *Based on* reality. But at the end of the day, an imagined story. The kind of story that this washed-up lump of a guy, this has-been, sad-sack hump, will spin up into a novel that he will send off to fifty agents who will each react exactly like the guy who, having opened his front door to find a burning paper bag at his feet, has started frantically stomping at the flames. And after all the fires have been put out and all the shit-covered shoes have been tossed out onto the lawn and all the front doors have been slammed, this guy will sigh and self-publish and then, inevitably, start on another story that is not real. Well. Not entirely.

Because the photos on the desk aren't photos of an actual crime scene. This guy took them himself, one random Saturday afternoon when he was driving home from the grocery store. He picked a place that looked promising, a place that had once actually been a crime scene, pulled out his not-so-smart knock-off cellphone, waited for people to get out of the way, hauled his thick bag of bones out of the driver's seat, snapped a dozen shots, drove home, put away the groceries, connected to Wi-Fi, queued the photos to his inkjet printer, waited, added photo paper, requeued the photos, waited, changed the ink, waited.

And then out they came.

But the question is why. Why do all this.

Because our guy here learned that the story comes easier if he worked it just like an actual case. Worked it just like he always had. Visit the scene. Stoop under the yellow tape. Take it all in, left to right, right to left, up and down, as someone in a white contamination suit busies about taking a billion photos with a real camera. Talk to people. Canvas. Press the flesh. Hand out cards. Then go back to the scene a dozen times, only without the yellow tape and without the red-and-blue lights and without the body that used to be a person. Scratch your head. Take your own damn photos with your own crappy cellphone camera because you sense something is missing that the first billion professional photos failed to capture. Go back to the landfill of a desk with your name plaque on it, pour another cup of weak coffee and make some calls. Stare at the photos. Go home, take the photos with you. Put on Billie or Ella or Sarah or Dinah and stare at the photos until your head hurts. Start in with the Old Forester. Stare at the photos some more, until you can almost bring them to life. Try to figure out what happened.

Try to answer how the person had become a body.

That's why he took those photos.

Well, *me*. That's why *I* took those photos.

That's me there in the sewing room that's trying to be a home office, bullshit writing den, sitting behind that monstrous, raggedy-ass desk. Me. Ray Mackey. Those are my photos. That's my late wife's cat in my lap. And that's my half-empty glass of Old Forester that I drink these days like mother's milk, two bottles a week easy. Because Phil, and Old Forester, and my memories of Marlo, and the latest story coalescing in my head, and this long, hellishly hot summer that will never end ... these are the only things that keep me from freezing to death in Chandler, Illinois in the middle of August.

It used to be the job that saved me. The work. Figuring out how a person becomes a body. That's how I survived for the first year-and-a-half after Marlo. I practically lived at the Chandler Police Department. No, not practically. Let's be honest; I *did* live there. Slept many a night on that awful breakroom couch. Long quiet nights of working and sleeping and drinking until the sun came up and busted through those windows, splitting my melon into little painful bits. When I wasn't out working the streets or killing time in my car, I stayed secluded in the northwest corner of the clamorous, glass-and-tile fluorescent box that was the homicide division, hooked into an IV of coat-pocket bourbon and unanswered questions about why people are dead.

No. Not why. How.

I can't answer the why. Never could. Fuck if anyone can answer the why.

I'm retired now. Four years, two months, eighteen days. That's a fake word, *retired*. It is for me. I was booted, plain and simple. Could have gone another ten years. Retired makes it sound like I've got a shiny gold pocket watch. Not me. What I have in my pocket is a rock with the word *watch* scratched into one side and the words *fuck you* scratched into the other.

I was a good cop. I know that even if nobody else does. They all used to know it. I know it was rough going after Marlo. I saw myself, believe me. But even then I kept my head down. Did my work. Cleared my cases. The squad was sympathetic. They let me have my space but they also kept me close. Poker night would come up on the calendar and someone – Deke or Smitty or Marty or Stretch – would always track me down, corner me in the breakroom or the elevator, and ask me if I needed a ride. Poker night and everybody is suddenly big into carpooling with sad-sack Mack. They wouldn't take no for an answer. I tried plenty of times. They wouldn't take no. They were a good bunch, those guys. Still are a good bunch in my book, even if they all hate me. I miss them.

I'd probably hate me too. If I thought what they thought. If I didn't know better. I'd hate me too. A traitor to the cause of justice. A lowlife criminal with a badge. Good riddance you crazy, miserable, sad-sack, no-good criminal. I'd hate me too.

*Crazy.* They all think I'm crazy. Once the report leaked, that was it. It was all right there in the psych eval. Ray Mackey is not only corrupt, he's *Looney Tunes.* I probably am crazy. That's the one bad thing they think of me that's the closest to being true. If the shrinks have a special name for you, then who are you to say you're not crazy?

Depersonalization-Derealization Disorder. That's the special name they have for me. If it was more common, the shrink would use a snappy shortcut. *DepDerDis* or *Triple-D* or *3-D* because we're always in such a hurry to oversimplify what we've worked so hard to overcomplicate.

But *crazy* works too; it's short and just trips off the tongue.

*Triple-D.* Not a bra size. I wish it was. It means I see myself as a separate person. I don't mean I imagine myself abstractly. I mean I see myself sitting on a dining room chair behind an old oak desk petting my dead wife's cat and looking at pretend crime-scene photos. I see it all, including the parts of me that don't show up in the mirror. I see the back of my head. I see the sweat on my neck and the stoop of my shoulders and the roll of dough beneath my shirt that, less and less, divides my lower back from my backside. I see *me*, the guy in the chair, the old hump struggling in the heat to be a crime writer, all at once, as if my brain is tapping a surveillance feed from a camera that floats around me in a circle about five feet off the ground. Sometimes ten, twenty, thirty feet off the ground when I'm outside walking around in the world. There I am getting into my car after a shift at the mall. There I am eating a cheeseburger in the parking lot. There I am waiting in line at Value Liquor.

It's everywhere, all the time. Twenty-four-seven, three-sixty-five.

It's not like I never have a normal perspective. I see what's in front of my face just like anyone else. But my *3-D* vision is always there, playing in the background. All I have to do is stop forcing my conscious brain to see things normally. When I have to work that keypad at the checkout stand, I'm like anyone else. But as soon as that's all done and the card is back in my wallet, *boom*, I'm watching the guy who looks almost exactly like me pick up three bottles of Old Forester, lower them one at a time into one of Marlo's eco-friendly cloth bags, and head for the door.

He's almost exactly like me. *Almost*. Because sometimes, most of the time, there's an aspect to that guy I'm watching walk around below me that doesn't seem like me at all. It's like hearing your own voice on a recording. You know it's your voice. You remember recording it. But the sound you hear coming out of the speaker does not sound like the voice that you've heard coming out of your mouth your entire life. It sounds like someone else's voice. But if it's not your voice, then whose voice is it? Who the hell *is* that? Welcome to my world.

The guy at the desk empties the glass and rubs his eyes and wipes the sweat from his forehead with the back of his hand. He gathers the photos into a stack and pushes them away like a bad habit. He lowers Phil to the floor and stands up with a groan, stretching, hands on his hips. He looks around the room, rotating his head from left to right and back again like the fan behind him has finally taken control.

He looks in defeat at the Smith Corona. He's got a laptop tucked away in the bottom drawer. It works perfectly fine, compared to the Corsair, which is completely missing the *R*. And the *A* and the *Y* barely leave any mark. He doesn't care. Like Marlo always said, never second-guess your instincts or your inspiration. The old Corsair inspires him to write. He likes the percussive sound and feel of it. Like little gunshots.

Not Smith & Wesson gunshots; Smith Corona gunshots. He uses the noisy, antiquated machine to ease himself into a new story. Once he gets going, he pushes it to the back of the desk and switches to the soft clicking sounds of digital sterility. He's a sentimental romantic, this guy. Crazy, sad-sack Mack. He overindulges the past. He holds onto things he shouldn't.

Still. He shakes his head in disappointment. He hasn't written a word all night. He sighs to himself, trying to decide what to do next.

I know *exactly* what he's going to do next.

# TWO

Bucks is a bar tucked away on the corner of Seventy-Third and Warner. Not such a bad area of town if you don't care about where you find yourself after dark. Tattoo joint on one side, a Korean kid who looks about thirteen with a design fetish for dragons and motorcycles and the yin-yang thing. On the other side is a store about ten feet wide by fifty feet long called The Bodega, owned by a guy from Newark named Rocky. He's four-foot nothing, shaped like a fire hydrant under a porkpie hat. Rocky will talk your ears off, but he sells those little sausage and cheese nibs you can't find anywhere else. Phil is crazy for them, so sometimes it's worth the risk of losing an ear, popping in right before Rocky gets out the hook, pulls down the bars and closes up for the night.

Next to The Bodega is Sandwich Heaven, which makes the worst Philly cheesesteak this side of everywhere, including heaven. Sliced tire tread drowning in melted basketball shoe leather, and the bread is usually gummy and wet like it's nervous about the meat.

Down the street is a strip club. Prancers. I've been inside the place once, years ago, looking for a witness and expecting to find reindeer onstage doing the cancan. I found neither.

Bucks is nothing fancy. A long bar that curves in front of a smoky-mirrored wall that gives the pyramid of bottles some illusory depth. Some round tables, every one of them with at least one short leg. A jukebox in the corner that has never worked. Two dart boards. Three booths in the back near a short greenish hallway to the bathrooms. The place is dark and quiet most nights. There's a television up in the corner, but it's never more than a light show. Bucks couldn't care less about the big game. It isn't a sports bar. It's a place to buy a drink and think things over. Remember.

I knew Buck way back. My first time I asked him about the name. Bucks. He asked if I was regular police or the grammar police. Wasn't about him, he said. It was all about the money. He'd pointed to the ceiling, which was papered with bills. Not monopoly bills. Real bills, all signed with a red Sharpie. Mostly American singles, but you can make your way around the world if you really care to. Buck said he'd charge me extra for an apostrophe if I wanted one. Otherwise, five drinks would get one of my dollars on the ceiling.

I've got more of my money above this bar than in my retirement account. My savings plan started when Bucks ran out of ceiling.

# THREE

The sorry hump with writer's block walks in and takes his normal seat at the end. He nods at Doris. She nods back and finishes up with the two pissant headbangers drinking shots and beers to take the hurt out of their arms, freshly bandaged. I can see him steal a glance in their direction. He's trying to guess which one got a motorcycle and which one got a dragon. Then he stops caring.

He closes his eyes and tries to figure out how a resident of the Chandler Belle Vista Apartments – Janice Hinkle, a single woman, mid-thirties, with a crappy but reliable job selling pressboard furniture off a dirty showroom floor out in Naperville – how does Janice become a body broken in two pieces over the spine of a metal fence seven floors below? How does that happen?

He knows how it happened in real life. In real life, it turned out to be suicide. In real life, Janice was Lucy, who had a crappy but reliable job selling boutique greeting cards out of a strip mall in Joliet. Lucy had an abusive boyfriend, a red herring with an airtight alibi. That alibi had closed the homicide file forever. Lucy turned out to be a coked-up jumper who ended her relationship in a swan dive from the third floor of a parking garage. No steel fence to break her fall. It was a lousy municipal bicycle rack that did her in. Lucy would have made for a sad, short, unreadable story. Like most, he supposes.

But Lucy is not entirely dead. She lives on now as Janice. And Janice, he thinks, just might have a page-turner life. He thinks maybe Janice had seen things she shouldn't have seen. Or maybe she was stepping out on the bruiser boyfriend to have an affair with another wrong-sort-of person, someone who had money and was generous with his affection, but, unbeknown to Janice, was unhappily married to the daughter of a mobster. No. Too low-brow. Too predictable. An arms dealer. Something like that. Poor Janice saw something. Knew something. Knew too much. But what?

He has no idea what. No idea. He starts to wonder what poor Lucy would think of her reincarnation as a fictional character. Well. Not so much reincarnation as inspirational recycling. We're all about conscientious recycling these days. It's something we can do to keep our mind off the planet that's dying out from under us. Single-use containers are the enemy. But we're all single-use containers. We're all bags of bones that, if we're lucky and don't eat things that taste good, will last eighty or ninety years or so. If we're not so lucky, like Marlo, maybe it's fifty-two. Poor shit-for-luck Lucy parked herself in the bike rack when she was only thirty-one. So why the hell *shouldn't* someone recycle Lucy's life? Put her tragedy to use as inspiration. Give her a new name and blond hair and a few more years. Put her to work in a pulp-fiction thriller as judgment-challenged Janice who escapes the ignominy of a parking garage death-by-bicycle-rack suicide and who instead lives a life of intrigue before getting bumped off the seventh floor of the Belle Vista by some low-life thug. Thugs, plural. Maybe some very connected thugs. Maybe *government*-connected thugs. Maybe ...

"You here to sleep or drink or keep me company?"

# FOUR

I open my eyes to see Doris pouring a shot of Old Forester. She's a curly, dirty blonde. My age, maybe a year or two younger. Broad shoulders and built like a government building. Married to a memory, just like me. She's as good as they come. She sets the glass on the bar.

"All three," I say. I gesture a toast and throw it back.

"So which one of you is thirsty tonight: the sad ex-cop or the broken widower or the disillusioned writer?"

I smile at that. Doris always cuts right to the bone.

"All three," I say. "Guess we're going to need two more glasses, Doris."

"Damn, Mack." She shakes her head and sends another stream of amber down into the glass. "Not enough Forester on this earth." She sets the bottle down on the bar with a *thunk*. She looks at me with extra purpose. "You ever think that we should hook up? Make it official with tinfoil rings and put the past behind us?"

I roll the shot glass between my hands like she actually means what she said and like I'm actually considering it. I shake my head.

"Buck's ghost would separate my neck from my head like a cherry stem. Buck would do the pulling and Marlo would do the twisting. I'm still quite attached to my neck, Doris."

"Who are they to take a powder so early? To run off with cancer in the night. And, hey," Doris lays the palm of her hand along the side of my face, "maybe they'd want us to be happy."

"Exactly," I tell her. "We'd make each other miserable. They know it even if we don't." I clasp her hand with mine and give her a wincing smile. "Besides, weddings are for saps, Doris. And who'd ever marry a hard-luck couple like us anyway?"

"Rocky maybe," she says, jerking her head toward The Bodega. "He'd do it."

"Rocky'd never make it through the vows. We'd have to listen about the time he took his wife to the beach. I can't hear that story again. One, she should've known better, and two, Rocky thinks they're called *sea enemies.*"

The newly tattooed headbangers want Doris' attention. She rolls her eyes and leaves the bottle. I watch her go, backside moving under that skirt like two cats in a bag, until my eyes skate sideways to the booths in the back. They're all empty except one. A clean white shirt and an ugly blue tie are wrapped around a guy I used to know. We were colleagues, friends of a sort, in another life full of ghosts.

Well. Alive, but dead to me.

I'm about to look away but he looks up just in time. He nods and smiles.

# FIVE

The wannabe-writer nods back to the man in the booth. He finishes the shot, grabs the bottle and pours himself a refill. He gives a brief, *be-right-back* wave to Doris, then saunters across the bar, weaving around empty tables.

"Raymond Mackey," says Smitty, smiling and holding up a hand. "As I live and breathe. Been awhile. Pull up a booth, my friend."

They shake and Ray takes a slow seat, sliding in, trying not to spill.

"You look good. Still working out at Jimmy's?"

"Every day, man. Haven't seen you there in awhile. Retirement schedule?"

Ray can see the instant regret that comes free with stupid questions. He lets it go.

"Too many cops in that gym. I do all my heavy lifting here."

Awkward. Smitty looks uncomfortable. Always too nice, Smitty. Look at him trying to change the channel.

"Hot enough for you, Mack?"

Ray doesn't want to talk about the heat. Only makes it hotter. He ignores the question.

"Drinking alone in Shitsville, Smitty. People are going to start to talk. Take it from me."

"I'm not slumming," he says too quickly. "I'm on the job."

Smitty. The workouts are definitely working out. Bigger in the chest and not as heavy around the middle. But he's still got the short beard to cover his baby face. Always a little too likable to be a good homicide cop. Too many jokes about Brian Smith looking like the department intern, washing his baloney sandwiches down with milk.

So Brian Smith started introducing himself as Smitty, like it was some locker-room name he'd been stuck with and he'd finally given up the fight. He grew a beard and started pumping iron and boozing and swearing every other word. Eating fried chicken for lunch and washing it down with Jack. Turned himself into a bearded, high school sophomore. A steroidal potty-mouth alcoholic kid. He fits in better but he's still too nice for homicide.

"Oh, on the job," says Ray. "Yeah, you sure look like you're working hard there, Smitty."

They both laugh.

"Stripper took a double-tap to the temple last week. Real gangland shit." Smitty points with his drink. "She worked up the street there. Prancers."

"And so you're playing the horndog out-of-town salesman. Killing time between conventions."

"Exactly."

"Where's your partner?"

"I'm breaking in a newbie. Right off the tree. Two days on the job and now he's out sick. So his rotten luck is to be throwing up his dinner and missing out on the girlie show at the same time."

"So then you're going in alone?"

"No need for him tonight. I'm just scoping out the regulars. But things don't get hopping over there for another two hours. Figure I may as well tie one on while I wait."

The hair on Smitty's face parts for a smile of pearly white baby teeth. He raises his glass. Probably alcohol in there someplace, but it still looks like milk.

"It's all for the cover, Mack. Gotta look the part, right? Gotta *feel* the part."

"Of course," says Ray. "But you've got to lose that ring, Smitty."

"I do?" Smitty looks down at the hand that's choking the glass. He married his prom date, this guy. Going strong thirty years. Elaine. Ellen. Something like that. She was the one making him the baloney sandwiches.

"Yes," says Ray. "You do."

"What, married people don't go strip-clubbing? I do. Well. I *have*."

"No. Maybe *you*-you, the *cop*-you, but not the *traveling-salesman*-you. You're from the sticks, see? Someplace in Ohio. Rural Pennsylvania, maybe. A Presbyterian with two kids to show for a thirty-year marriage to a woman on the school board. You love these convention boondoggles so you can get away and stretch your legs a bit. You're not going to go whoring, mind you. Too good a man for that. But you're going to call your wife from the Marriott, tell her about the convention, ask about the kids. Then you're going to tell her about how beat you are and make a kissing sound into the phone as you tuck a few bills and your driver's license into your sock just in case you get mugged and have to hand over your wallet on the mean streets of Chandler. And then you're going to hang up the phone and grab the key to your rental car. You're going to turn up the television, hang the do-not-disturb sign on the hotel room door and head into the night to take in an hour of bump and grind. You'll drive through the city, turning here and there as if at random, but you're really just letting the gravity roll you downhill, all the way to the bottom. Because you may be a traveling salesman from the sticks, Smitty – Ohio or Pennsylvania or wherever – but you've got just enough experience to know exactly how to find the thing you need. So you just let that rental roll and it practically steers itself to that place up the street. Prancers. You'll pick a table in the middle, not in the back; you want a clear line to the front door. And not right up against the stage, either. You need some insulation from temptation. You're not sure what you'll do if you're close enough to touch a naked girl's ankle. And I do mean girl, Smitty. You'll buy yourself a fifteen-dollar boilermaker and a twenty-dollar Chardonnay for some insistent, top-heavy teen wearing a handkerchief and who won't leave you alone to drool by yourself. Eventually, you'll screw up the courage to pay for a lap dance. And what happens from there is between you and the saint of traveling salesmen."

Smitty smiles, enjoying the show.

"But before you do any of that, Smitty, before you even make it out of your hotel room and down the hall to the elevator twirling that rental-car key-fob around your finger, you're going to take off that wedding ring. Because, for you, the traveling salesman, that ring cannot be part of this experience. It goes in the pocket, Smitty, where the top-heavy teen will feel it during that first under-the-table grope, making you – the traveling-salesman you – wish you had thought to put the ring in your sock with the license and the spare cash. Because that ring cannot be part of this experience. Now, the *real* you, Smitty – the you that's an undercover dick scoping out a skeezy strip joint to investigate a double-tap killing – that guy *wants* top-heavy teen in the handkerchief to feel the gold ring in your pocket. You want her to feel your regret. You want that. You do. Because if you really need her to believe, Smitty, that's what's gonna sell it."

Ray takes a sip like he wants it to last all night and sets the glass down.

"Jesus, Mack," says Smitty. "Guess you're still writing that fiction shit."

Ray doesn't take it as a putdown. Smitty doesn't mean it as one. They've discussed his writing – *that fiction shit* – before. Something Ray doesn't do easily.

Writing is a personal thing. A thing no one else can touch. Except Marlo. He'd shared plenty of it with her; dragged her through byzantine plots packed with muddy prose; forced her to sample the torrid, tawdry landscape of his imagination. The blood and grime and the grief of it all. Fictional, but as real as it gets. The humanity curled up inside inhumanity's trunk. The grease and grit beneath the fingernails of the city and the network of backroom handshakes that ran the city. The vengeance and sacrifice and heartbreak, and of course the heroism, not only the extraordinary kind of heroism but also the common kind, insubstantial but critical, like the last dirty pocket change that adds up to just the right amount.

Marlo would nurse a gin and tonic as she read. He would watch the green of her eyes move back and forth in their unfailing rhythm, like a pendulum, or a scythe cutting a path through the wheat. And when he couldn't take the waiting anymore, he'd excuse himself to the kitchen where he would drain another Old Forester and pace nervously in private, not like an expectant father listening for the crying but more like a man on death row walking off that last meal.

She'd always come to find him when she was done. She'd put him out of his misery with a look of satisfaction, returning the pages with an encouraging word or two about what she had read. He never pressed. He knew better. Marlo was the best liar in the business – the best investigators were always the best liars – but he knew she'd keep it up but only so long. If he *really* wanted to know what she thought, well then she would *really* tell him. He didn't want that. When the dealer gives you a king and an eight, or even a king and a seven, you don't push your luck. You stick. He always took the lie. Marlo made that easy.

Not that the guys on the squad didn't know about the writing. They knew. They all knew. There were no secrets in the squad. They knew he was writing detective thrillers just like they eventually all knew that the department's shrink had diagnosed him as *Triple-D* crazy.

He'd once made the mistake of using the department Xerox to copy a chapter. The thing rattled and shook its way through forty-one pages and then took a break, eating page forty-two for lunch. Stretch Martin was the squad expert on all things Xerox. He'd rolled up his sleeves, opened up the beast and fished out the mangled page, read it, and then passed it around before Ray had known what was happening. And that was that. They beat him up about it for a couple of weeks. But then, after the razzing ceased to be entertaining, everyone was full of questions. They all wanted to be characters. They tossed him ideas from their own cases.

That had felt strangely good. Validating. With Marlo gone, that was about all he had for encouragement. There was always Phil. But Phil was not a crime-thriller kind of cat. Her taste ran more toward culinary nonfiction. And yet, Phil was infinitely more encouraging than the typical form-letter condescension he received from literary agents.

> While your novel, *Black Coffee at the Heartbreak Café*, offers a fresh take on the crime thriller genre, it is not suited to our current representational interests.

Translation: We never read it. Stop leaving your flaming bags of pulp at our door. Beat it.

So encouragement was to come either from the boys at CPD homicide or no one. He'd hated the attention and wanted them to stop mentioning his writing.

Until they *did* stop mentioning his writing. Inevitable, because their interest never lasted for long. Real life was always loitering nearby, leaning up against a lamp post, smoking a cigarette and showing some leg, distracting the squad with the curves of real-life concerns, like dead bodies and politics and overtime cutbacks, obliterating any interest they'd once had, ten minutes earlier, in what Raymond Mackey was doing in his spare time in his half-empty house on his Smith Corona.

During such agonizing real-life interregna, Ray, this pathetic, needy hump of a writer, found himself waiting for the subject to come up again, even nudging casual poker-night conversation in the direction of fictional crime. He'd shake his head humorously and rearrange his cards – this one goes here and that one goes there – and then marvel that some mope they had just arrested was so outlandish in some way or another – his hair or his hat or his alibi – that the case report was going to read like, well ... like *fiction*. It was going to read like bad, dime-store *fiction*. He'd keep reordering his cards, just hoping someone would look up from their own hand and take a drink and then pull that dangling thread. *Hey, speaking of fiction ...*

Which, inevitably, they had done. Someone had always pulled that thread, making Ray hate the fact that they were suddenly asking questions again about what he was writing.

That was all before the task force debacle, of course. Before they all decided to hate him. Before they'd all set fire to the brothers-in-arms goodwill and the squad room camaraderie. The poker nights. The sympathy about Marlo, who they had all loved. The concern about his grief. Gone. All burned up. Took about three days.

It was on a Friday word leaked that Ray and Cecil Green had been talking. Cecil was on Big Man's crew and everyone knew it. Street name, Cosmo. Ray's phone and Cosmo's burner, forensics had found, knew each other. Had called each other. Suspiciously short connections; Ray to Cosmo for thirty-five seconds and then Cosmo to Ray for seventeen seconds. That was enough for the squad. That was all it took. News swept through the department, not just homicide but the whole department, like wildfire. Over the space of a single weekend, everything burned down into a pile of ash and hate. By the next Monday, Ray Mackey was dead to them.

Brian "Smitty Smith" had been the only one of them willing to give him the benefit of the doubt. He was the only one for whom friendship had seemed to mean something. During the two-week limbo phase of his suspension, when Ray was still expected to report to work but confined to his desk pending investigation, he and Smitty had gone to lunch a couple of times. Everyone noticed, and Smitty'd noticed them noticing. Heads rotating on their necks like a bunch of owls. Smitty didn't care. They'd gone to lunch anyway.

Talking about work wasn't in the cards. So they had talked about his writing. His *fiction-shit*.

"Yeah," Ray says to him. "Still writing. Got to do something in my retirement."

The lie of that word: *retirement*. It shuts them both up. The uncomfortable silence settles and starts to congeal. Then it starts to stink.

Smitty opens his mouth to say something. Nothing comes.

Ray's cellphone startles the mood. It rings like an old-fashioned telephone, the kind that's always sitting on some fat cat's office desk, big and heavy and black and looking at first glance like it might be an iron or a curly-corded cudgel for braining unwelcome visitors. It's the only ringtone Ray can stand. But the phone has, of late, developed an unfortunate randomness to its volume. Both of them jump.

He lifts the phone out of his shirt pocket and looks at the screen. *Unknown Caller. Number Blocked.* Ray rejects the call with his thumb and lets the phone drop down out of sight, back into his pocket. It was probably the worst thing that could have happened in a conversation with anyone on his old squad: a call to his cellphone that he chooses not to take in mixed company.

The phone ignores his rejection and keeps clamoring for attention.

Smitty is looking down into his drink as Ray is looking down into his shirt pocket.

"Goddamned thing." Ray re-extracts the phone. He glowers and uses more finger force this time. Like the phone needs a more convincing demonstration that he's serious.

Smitty squirms. I can tell Ray feels his discomfort. I can tell he hates him for it. The call could have been from anybody. And for anybody else, that call *would* have been from just anybody. But this is not anybody else; this is Ray Mackey. And Ray Mackey will always have the disease of corruption. Every breath will stink of betrayal. The sound of Ray Mackey's cellphone was like a cough from Typhoid Mary. Tough to ignore.

He almost explains the calls he gets every week, the calls he now always ignores. No idea what cretin is on the other end. Likely some identify-thief scam artist looking to scare out a bank account password or social security number. A robocall offering one last chance to avoid a make-believe debt-collection. But the sleazy horror pitch is always so slow in coming that Ray gets annoyed at the silence and disconnects.

Happens all the time now, these calls. He's almost used to it. The day after he gets elected president, he will change the laws to impose the death penalty on robocallers and hackers and phishers and email scammers and catfishing freaks and everyone else practicing the black arts of the modern tech-villainy that he does not really understand and that make him feel helpless, like drawing a thirty-eight on a bad smell.

He feels the urge to reassure Smitty that it's not Cosmo Green calling from lockup. How likely is it that nearly five years after the department has kicked Ray out on the street for having Cosmo's burner number in his phone, he's still getting calls from that thug? He wants to make it clear that whoever is responsible for making his phone ring is probably a criminal, but it's not *that* criminal.

But then Ray's shoulder muscles relax a little. He takes a breath. He's deciding he doesn't care what Smitty thinks.

"You humps still playing poker?" he asks. Smitty smiles and looks up.

"I'm on a streak, Mack. Can't fucking lose. Weeks now. They all hate me."

"You don't even know hate, Smitty," says Ray. His shoulders are stiff all over again. He can't help himself. He tries to make the self-pity sound like contempt. He wants this to end. He wants to go back and flirt with Doris. Maybe accept her marriage proposal. Maybe make a better proposal of his own.

No. Not that. He just wants to go home. Talk to Phil. He throws back the drink.

"They don't hate you, Smitty. You're too damn nice to hate. Here's what I say. I say you should clean the bastards out. I say push your luck and take them for all they're worth, which should buy you another drink or two, but not much else. It'll buy you half a drink at Prancers. Good luck over there. Eighty-six the ring. And watch your back."

Ray starts to push up from the table, hunching his shoulders for leverage as he grabs his empty glass.

"They're still asking about you," says Smitty.

"Well, then tell them all I said hi and to fuck off."

"Not the guys, Mack."

"Who?"

"IAD."

"IAD." He's no longer rising. "IAD's asking about me."

Smitty nods.

"Asking who?"

"Asking me. Probably everyone."

"Why?"

"Why. How should I know why, Mack? You ever known Internal Affairs to tell anybody anything worth two fucks when they're on the hunt?"

"The hunt for what? For who?"

Smitty shrugs. "Don't know. But they threw me a lot of questions about Cosmo Green. And you. And Big Man, of course. Seemed like they were plowing old ground. Still looking for a mouse in the house. Squeaking out all our secrets. They got fuck-all from me, man. I don't know shit. I'm just trying to clear my cases."

Ray lowers himself again. He looks from Smitty down into the empty glass in his hand, like maybe the answers are somehow in there.

"The mouse. The ghost of CPD. Thought *I* was the fuckin' mouse." He says this to the glass like Smitty isn't there. Smitty answers anyway.

"You were. Probably still are, Ray. Not in my book, you know, but for them probably you still are. If they could've proven it, you'd be a dark stain on the wall of a Cook County cell by now. But IAD is acting like they still have leaky pipes in that task force. Like they're still trying to connect some dots." Smitty leans in. His voice is a raspy whisper pushing a boozy cloud. "You're a fuckin' dot, Ray. You didn't hear this from me, man. I like my job and I want to keep it."

"What can you tell me, Smitty?"

"What can ... Jesus. That's the headline. I just told you. You're still a dot on somebody's fuckin' timeline, okay?"

"What'd they ask you?"

Smitty grimaces and shakes his head.

"Don't put me in that position, Mack. I'm way out of line here. We never had this conversation. Okay? Just ... Look. They asked me about Suri. Okay?"

"Suri."

"Yeah."

"What about her?"

"Had I seen her. Had I talked to her. She's in the wind. They're looking for her."

"What'd you say?"

"The truth. I wouldn't know Suri if she brought me a cup of coffee and a goddamned donut."

"If Suri ever brings you a cup of coffee and a donut, you should watch your wallet. And you can bet that some guy somewhere is wondering where the hell his breakfast went."

They both make sounds mimicking laughter. Ray rolls the glass between his palms.

"Are they coming for me, Smitty?"

"No idea, man. Do you even know where she is now?"

"Different life, Smitty."

"I figured as much. Look," Smitty looks suspiciously at the two headbangers leaving and then at the three other guys who stumble into Bucks, laughing and back-slapping. Smitty refocuses his attention. "They may not be coming for you. Probably not. That crap was a long time ago and you're a civilian now. So I don't know, Mack. I don't know shit. Okay? But I'm done now. Leave me out of this. I'm done."

And he is. Smitty's up on his feet without another word. A pat on the shoulder with a long squeeze, as if he can relate to Ray's situation, and then he's gone. Leaves him in the booth staring down at an empty shot glass with a gut full of fresh acid. His shoulders are hunched beneath the weight of history.

Poor bastard. I can't help but feel for the guy.

Ten minutes pass. Or maybe it's a couple of hours. Doris is standing next to the booth with the bottle of Old Forester. She scoops up Smitty's glass and fills Ray's.

"Want to talk about it?" she asks.

"It's nothing."

"Mack."

Ray throws back the drink and slides the glass forward on the table for another. He looks up at her for the first time, waiting for the sound of more bourbon. Doris gives him a resigned smile and tips the bottle. Ray closes his eyes.

"It's nothing."

# SIX

Marlo. It's a memory more than a dream. A dream-enhanced memory, let's call it.

I keep my eyes closed in bed, if that's where I am, trying to resist floating up through the nether currents of sleep into the painful, swampy muck of consciousness. My neck feels bent like a pipe cleaner. I don't want to feel my neck. My neck wants me to be awake. I try to hang onto the dark where the warm, gold-lit vignette is dropping away, tumbling end over end like a coin losing its light as it sinks to the bottom of a black lake.

It was the time we were parked in the dark outside Victor Roby's place. We were in my shit-show Impala because by then Victor knew Marlo's clean, white Camry from a mile away. I'd waited for her outside her office, then drove her all the way to Near North Side where Victor spent his days playing Monopoly with real money.

We'd tailed him to his home in Glencoe, parking across the street where we could watch the lights come on inside his house, one room at a time. Big, obnoxious thing, Victor's house. A black, three-story concrete shoebox with lots of little square air holes. The place was set well back from the street on the other side of a sparsely landscaped lawn the size of the Pacific. Every time Victor touched a light switch, it was like a bullet of sun punching through the dark side of the moon.

Marlo had me turn the car around and re-park, passenger side to the house, so she could aim her howitzer of a camera at Victor pouring himself a highball in the living room. He lowered himself into a high-backed chair facing the window and talked on the phone, drinking his drink and posing for pictures. Marlo liked to philosophize while she worked.

*People like Victor here don't understand their relationship to the rest of creation.*

*Is that so.*

*Yeah. He's sitting there in a lit room, looking at his own reflection in a window that's up against a midnight-black universe. He doesn't even think about that universe beyond the window. He doesn't think about it because he can't see it. He can't see it because he can't imagine beyond his own reflection. And since he can make that reflection in the window move and mug and shift positions, he gets lost in the idea that the reflection belongs to him.*

I had eased the seat back and said nothing.

*Still with me, Mack?*

*Present.*

*And all that's fair enough, I guess. But eventually Victor makes the mistake of thinking the reflection is him. That he is the reflection. He likes that guy in the window, see, drinking a gin and tonic in his fancy chair. He likes the cut of that man's jib. And why shouldn't he? That man in the window is him, Victor Roby. Not just a reflection of him; it is him.*

The camera was clicking like a happy machine gun. It made a laughing sound.

*And that's the mistake, Mack. Because Victor's forgotten about himself. He's busy watching his own reflection. Meanwhile, the rest of creation is loitering outside in the midnight black universe, busy watching him. Not watching Victor Roby the window-reflection, watching Victor Roby the over-leveraged crook. The Victor Roby who files fraudulent, hundred-million-dollar insurance claims for overvalued discount faux-fur warehouses that he – the real Victor Roby, not the reflection in the window Victor Roby – arranged for someone to burn down. Get what I'm saying?*

*You're saying that Victor here doesn't know he's mugging for a camera owned by Rushmore American Insurance.*

Marlo turned away from the viewfinder and looked at me.

*What I'm saying, honey, is that we live in little bubbles of light. I'm saying we never know who's out in the dark universe looking in. And I'm saying it's always someone.*

She'd pulled a photograph out of her pocket and showed it to me. Victor Roby, Cubs cap pulled low, leaning into the passenger side of a beat-up, run-down Dodge, parked on a beat-up, run-down street in Riverdale.

*It's always someone, Ray,* she'd repeated as she opened the car door.

I'd raised the seat back up and grabbed the camera. I kept one eye on Victor in the window and the other on Marlo as she strode casually across the street, across the ocean of lawn, and up to the front door. If Victor hadn't been blinded by the light, he'd have seen her coming. I'd unholstered and put my piece in my lap, just in case. I didn't have any reason to think Victor was a violent man, but then most people aren't violent people, until they are. I looked through the viewfinder. Marlo slipped the photo into the crack right above the doorknob.

In my memory, Marlo returned to the car. *Time for Victor to get a view from outside the bubble of light.* And then we'd gone out for pizza and beer and then home to pay some attention to Phil and, finally, to go to bed and do what I will never do again.

But in the dream, Marlo pounds on Victor's front door. *One-two-three*, deep and heavy, like she has the strength and moral courage of a hundred men. In his chair in front of the window, Victor Roby jolts at the sound. Only in the viewfinder of Marlo's camera, it's not Victor sitting in that chair. It's me. I'm the one who jolts.

She pounds again. *One-two-three.* I open my eyes.

# SEVEN

Ray convulses awake on the couch, his head bent unnaturally against the armrest and his left arm dangling in space. He jerks his hand down along the floor until it knocks into the empty bottle of Old Forester. The bottle topples and rolls into Phil, who is startled out of the only whisper-patch of sun in the room. She jumps up onto the table and knocks off both the crystal tumbler, which falls and shatters, and the Corey Kluber autographed baseball that rolls off into the kitchen.

Ray is subsumed within the unfolding chain reaction. Like he's just a lever or switch in some elaborate Rube Goldberg contraption, spanning the dream world and the real world, with a purpose too removed from his own pathetic life to comprehend.

Poor Ray. I can't help but feel for the guy. The adrenal rush makes him look a little deranged. He's still too woozy to sit up straight, let alone to get his shit together and answer the door. Which is, what, maybe ten feet from his head.

*One-two-three. Four.*

It takes him another two minutes to get upright. He yanks open the door in an irritated, this-had-better-be-an-emergency sort of way. The noonday sun punches him in the face.

"Raymond Mackey?"

Two men. They'd be less conspicuous in uniform. No one is more conspicuous in plain clothes than cops. The one making noise is a cue ball on top of a fence post. His partner's a muscle-and-bone mailbox in a suit. Ray can barely convince the words to come out and be sociable.

"Who's asking?"

"Sergeant Twill, Chandler Police, Internal Affairs. This is Officer Santiago. Mind if we come in?"

"Do you care if I mind?"

"Not particularly."

They produce identification, but Ray isn't interested. He knows they're the real deal. He closes his eyes hard, squeezing out the excess light so that maybe he'll be able to see more than just shapes. Look at him. His head feels like a thumb under a hammer.

"What's this about?" he asks.

"We need to ask you a few questions."

"Could've called," he says. "Phones are swell for that kind of thing."

"Well these are *in-person* kinds of questions, Mr. Mackey." The sun is splashing off Twill's naked head. It's like talking to a solar corona. "So an interrogation room downtown works for us if it works for you."

Ray runs a hand through his hair. He does this whenever he knows he doesn't have any choice. It's a transparent stall for time just to confirm to himself that he's screwed. Maybe no one else can see the tell, but I can. I'd love to play some high-stakes poker with this hump.

He sighs in irritation, then pulls the door back. He points to the two chairs in the living room across from the couch. Same couch that broke his fall by pretending to be a bed.

Santiago makes a point of stepping around the broken glass before taking a seat.

Twill eases into his first pitch, talking as he walks over to the windows and twists open the Levolors.

"We're conducting an ... *inquiry*," he says. "We'd like to talk to you about Suri."

Light slides down through the slats, scouring the room into a collection of hard lines and sharp corners, irregular planes of metal and glass that send it ricocheting violently in different directions like a match dropped into a dark room full of fireworks.

"What's Suri?" Ray asks. "Is that like a noodle dish, or ..."

Twill turns from the windows, already smiling. Ray closes the door and shuffles his way over to the couch, crossing his arms. Phil wanders in from the kitchen and begins plying Santiago for affection. Santiago scratches her behind the head and gets a meow.

"And who's this?" asks Twill, pretending to smile at his partner. He takes a seat, crossing his long legs. Ray looks down at Phil.

"Suri, this is Sergeant Twill. Sergeant meet my cat, Suri. So. Now that that's done ..."

Twill's smile melts like wax, disappearing over his smooth hairless chin. He gestures for Ray to have a seat on the couch. Ray doesn't budge. Man, he looks like hell.

"Let me be direct, Mr. Mackey. We are aware that when you were on the force, back before you ... *retired*, you frequently used a civil informant who went by the name, Suri, and who you failed to register as a civil informant as required. We, and by *we*, I mean the Chandler Police, are looking for this person. We think she may have information pertinent to an ongoing investigation."

"What investigation?"

Twill's smile is back. Sad this time, like he's about to disappoint a child.

They stare at each other. Ray breaks first. I can see him try not to sound condescending, the way his eyes try to shape his meaning. I can see him give up after the first syllable.

"Look. Sergeant. I don't know you. No offense. You're obviously new. Your rank means you transferred over from halfway up the top of some other shit-heap law enforcement organization. And since no one I've ever known has their aspirations pinned to the Chandler PD, I'm guessing those transfer papers didn't come with a smile, or maybe they did and you were the only one in the room who wasn't smiling. In any case, now, despite your rank, you're out knocking on doors like a regular hump. You want my best guess?"

Twill is not amused, but he's the one who wanted to play ball.

"Let's have it," he says.

"On his way out the door, your predecessor, one Lieutenant Albert Nutsack, stuck you with the investigation that will never close. The search for the mouse in the house. The *drip, drip, drip* from a leaky pipe running through that very expensive shit-for-luck task force that has never been able to find its own ass with both hands. And you don't trust anybody, Twill, not yet, not even your own people, none of whom you really know yet or like. And they don't know or like or trust you either. So you're out doing the work yourself. Probably had to borrow Santiago here. He's along to make sure you don't get yourself shot. How am I doing so far?"

Twill smiles.

"I think you meant Lieutenant Albert *Nosek*."

"Right. Nutsack. So Nutsack's gone now, in the shade with his feet up someplace where he can see the ocean as he sucks down his pension, and you're out in the hot sun looking under all the old rocks, including me."

"Where's Suri?" says Twill.

"Oh, I'm suri, you already asked me that question."

"And you never answered it, Mr. Mackey. So I'm asking again. Politely."

"I haven't seen Suri in years," says Ray. "Alright? I have no idea."

"When's the last you talked to her?"

"Years. What need do I have for a CI when I'm not on the force?"

"You tell me."

"Okay, I will. None. Are we done now?"

"When was the last time you had any contact with Cecil Green?"

"Cosmo? Never."

"Not what I understand, Ray."

"Oh, I'll bet you understand all kinds of things that aren't true."

Twill sighs and looks over at Santiago, who is now lost to Phil's bottomless need for affection. Twill uncrosses his legs and leans forward, supporting his upper weight on his elbows. He talks to the floor.

"Here's what I understand, Mr. Mackey. I understand that the governor of our fair state commissioned a task force to put the hurt on one José Beggamon, aka Big Man. Too much consolidation in the drug, gun, prostitution and human trafficking markets. All the numbers that the people downtown pay attention to are all going in the wrong direction. So they pull out the stops. They make it a multidisciplinary, intercity task force. Chicago. Chandler. Springfield. Every major city in the state. Cooperative arrangements with Milwaukee and Detroit. Even Cleveland."

"Look, Sergeant ..." says Ray. But Twill's got a finger in the air without looking up, like he's busy interrogating the piece of broken tumbler between his size-eleven shoes.

"No, no, hang on. This lumbering beast of a task force pulls talent from all quarters. Homicide. Narcotics. Vice. Computer crimes. Property. What have you. Dedicated officers apply." Twill clears his throat. "Including you, Mr. Mackey. Interviews. Testing. Some are selected. Some are rejected." He pauses long enough to look up from the floor. "Including you."

Santiago looks over briefly until Phil lays down the law and he resumes petting.

"Trying to hurt my feelings, Sergeant?" asks Ray. Twill ignores him.

"And off they go, out into the streets. But, as you say, it doesn't go so well. The single fastest growing criminal enterprise in the midwestern United States is like a vapor cloud. There and then suddenly gone and then back again someplace else. Everywhere and nowhere. Seemingly good information turns up nothing. The undercover operations are blown before any of the good guys get up in the morning. Months of head-scratching and getting yelled at by fat men in suits who want reportable results and don't care about explanations. Don't care about effort. Don't care about good police work."

Twill reclines back into the chair.

"But then ... *then* ... Cosmo Green gets popped. For once, one of Big Man's thugs is where he is supposed to be, doing the thing he's not supposed to be doing, which is handing over a backpack full of heroin to a man with a polished pair of shoes in his closet and a standing invitation to the policeman's ball."

"Look." Ray's out of patience. I can tell by the way he stands there in yesterday's clothes, rubbing his eyes and pretending to be disinterested. The history lesson is spiking his blood pressure. "I really don't need ..."

Twill already has his hand in the air again.

"No, no. Not done just yet, Mr. Mackey. Because it turns out that Cosmo Green has a burner phone on him. Like they all do in this disposable age. So Forensics does their thing. And guess who poor Cosmo's been calling? And guess who's been calling poor Cosmo?"

"I'm not going through this shit again," says Ray.

"Well, we're still going through it, Mr. Mackey. You were our boy. See? You were from the Chandler PD. And now every cop in every department across three states thinks we can't hold our information. They all think we're rotten from the ground up. You say you can't go through it again, but we go through it every goddamned day. All because you and your buddy Cosmo Green were as stupid and careless as you were corrupt. I mean really, Mr. Mackey, if you were going to do it, you could have at least been smart about it."

I can see the blood rising up into Ray's face like a red tide. He's fully awake now. Awake enough to not be stupid. He knows Twill is baiting him. But, knowing Ray like I do, he's also hungry and looking at that bait like it's breakfast.

"I'm nearly five years out. I'm not police anymore. Lieutenant Nutsack took care of that. I'm a goddamned civilian with a crappy part-time job making sure nobody's getting blown in the men's room of the Southside Mall. I don't know anything about anything anymore, Twill, and I don't care to. I've never called Cosmo Green. Cosmo Green's never called me. They'd've locked me up, not asked me to retire early." Ray puts his hands on his hips. "So, Sergeant, other than to ruin a perfectly good hangover and play with my cat, what the fuck do you want from me?"

Twill's hard black eyes condescend for a moment, then look over to Santiago, who pulls a clean square of paper from his suit pocket and hands it over. Twill opens it and reads. Then he hands it out to Ray.

"What do you know about any of these people?"

Ray hesitates, but then steps forward and takes the paper. It takes him all of eight seconds before he's not reading anymore.

"I don't know them," he says. "Who are they? Big Man's lieutenants? I told you I'm out of that game. I don't know anybody." He hands back the paper. "But none of those mooks ever use their Christian names, Sergeant. May as well hand me a list of shoe sizes. Got a piece of paper with any street names on it? That might ring a bell. Photos? You don't have any photos, do you? You have no idea what these skels even look like. You're all still chasing ghosts."

Twill unfolds himself. He's got more of a grimace than a smile now. He pushes himself up onto his feet, handing the paper down to Santiago. He has to flap it in the air to get Santiago's attention. Santiago takes it and stands as Phil leaps up into the warm and newly empty chair, meowing her irritation at Santiago's lack of commitment.

Santiago refolds the page of names back into a tidy square and slips it back into his suit pocket. He follows Twill to the door, pointing to the floor as he goes.

"You know you've got, like, broken glass all over your floor, right?"

"Yeah," says Ray. "I like it that way. Keeps people from taking their shoes off and overstaying their welcome."

The couch rings. I can see Ray's body momentarily seize up. In his head, he's imagining that tiny screen somewhere under the cushions. He knows what it says. We both do.

*Unknown Caller. Number Blocked.*

They all stay where they are and listen to the old telephone sound.

"You want to get that?" asks Twill, frozen in place with his hand on the door.

"Just my golf caddy calling to cancel."

"Do you always make a joke when you lie?"

"You got me, Twill. Sorry. Please tell your mom to stop calling me."

Twill smiles a little and opens the door. He stretches one of his legs out into the blistering white sun.

"See you around, Ray."

"Sure. Let's do this sometime around never, Sarge. Can't wait."

# EIGHT

I do my time at the mall. Four hours from five to closing. Not such a bad gig. Kids being kids mostly, although the job's good for a half-dozen shoplift calls a month and maybe two or three smash-and-grabs in the parking lot. Four assaults and one shots-fired last year. My job is to get the ball rolling and keep tabs on witnesses until the real police arrive and pretend to not know who I am. Those are the bad days. Dealing with the real police.

Normally, I'm just doing three-level laps, alone in a crowd, which is how I like it. The walking keeps me in some kind of shape. Pay is okay for what it is. Worst part of it is the cheesy brown uniform. Looks like a state trooper Halloween costume. Every time I put it on, it feels about as fake as my retirement. It feels like some kind of penance to be mocked by clothing I have to wear through the town square. They assigned me one of those stand-up scooters but I refuse to get on the damn thing. My dignity has its limits. Not that you'd know it.

My boss at Four Corners Security is a big swinging dick half my age. Gary. Thinks he's king of the world with no one to answer to. But there's always someone to answer to. Gary's boss, Danny, looks half Gary's age. If Danny has a boss, then I've never met him; I'm guessing his mommy is putting him to bed by the time I show up for work.

I like the five-to-nine shift. Everyone else in my food chain is off living their lives. It's just me. Tonight's the same. The time passes without me even knowing. I can't stop thinking about Twill. That list of names.

Aaron McQuaid
Timothy R. Pleasant
David A. Wilson
Andrew H. Marx
Louis Knoll

I'd known in the first two seconds that these weren't Big Man lieutenants. You have to look at them as a group. Names that belong together. Too many middle initials. Timothy? Aaron? Come on. The only place these names belong together is in a precinct football pool. These are cops.

Why. It took me another full lap on Level One and a missing toddler in Macy's to figure that one out. Twill was showing me the written equivalent of a lineup. Four of those names were decoys surrounding the name of someone in Twill's gunsights. He's trying to find a connection between that guy and me.

Why. That one's easier. Because rats keep company with other rats, that's why. If Twill's suspect just happens to be an old bowling buddy of the infamous Ray Mackey, the rat cop who was bounced for feeding cheese to one of Big Man's flunkies … well wouldn't that be interesting?

But here's the thing. Why not just ask me if I know the guy? Why go through the trouble of making a list of names and printing it out before pounding on my door? That piece of paper was too perfectly clean and folded, like a brand-new unwashed hanky. Couldn't have been off the printer and in Santiago's pocket for more than an hour. So why go through that whole production just for me?

A missing cellphone at Nordstrom.

Caution cones around the wet cleanup outside Barnes & Noble.

An emergency-exit-only alarm at Starbucks.

Because Twill wants to see if I'm going to lie about it, that's why. He's already decided there's a connection between me and his man. His dirty cop. His mouse in the house. But they want to know more. They've already given this guy the Heimlich and he's coughed up my name. They've tossed his desk and found my note, written in blood, asking if he wants to be pen pals and help Big Man turn the Illinois Penal Code into a knock-knock joke. Twill wants to see if I'm going to lie about what he thinks he already knows.

Which means Twill thinks I'm lying. He thinks I know his suspect on that list of names. His mouse. So he now has two suspects.

And I was lying. Of course I was lying. Never roust a man out of a good dream about his dead wife and think you're going to get the truth.

Because I *do* know his guy on the list. Andrew H. Marx. Old bowling buddy.

Well. More of a friend-of-a-friend kind of thing. Couple times a month at the Joliet Super Bowl. That was back in the day, twenty pounds ago, before Andy had bailed on the dream of driving limos for drunken teenagers on prom night and signed up for cop academy.

And I never called him Andy. We all called him Harpo because he had a dopey smile and fair skin and curly blond hair and because we were lucky to get two words out of the guy all night. That middle initial didn't hurt either. I'm guessing Harold or Howard or Henry. Didn't matter to us. We called him Harpo. The man could hold his liquor and he could bowl like the devil, I'll give him that. Especially for a lefty. That long, rubbery arm unfurling halfway down the lane. The pins saw Harpo coming and dropped away before he even let go of the ball. Just to get it over with.

Harpo's Christian name had stretched its rubbery left arm off the page and slapped me in the face in my own living room. Last I'd heard he was working property crimes down in Peoria. Now, apparently, he's in Chandler sitting quietly on a list in Santiago's pocket. Quiet as a mouse. Who knew.

So, yeah, I lied. Twill already thinks I'm dirty. Let him think it with a little extra gusto. Like Marlo always said, there's no greater advantage than letting people run in the wrong direction.

But why would Harpo throw me to the wolves? Associating himself with me can only make him look worse. Unless maybe they're horse trading. They'll go easy on him if he gives them a name. I've got a name and it's already been broken in. So Harpo thinks what the hell. Gives them the name they really want.

Could be. That might be it.

# NINE

It's a long drive for this time of night, but our man Ray changes out of his uniform and makes it anyway. He'd rather be up in the sewing room banging away on the Smith Corona, solving the murder of poor, swan-diving Janice Hinkle without using the letter *R*. But it's too hot to sit still and make up stories. He's got just enough energy after his shift at the mall to take a sauna and work on figuring out what the hell is going on in the real world. His car is a good place for both.

So he leaves Janice broken into two pieces over the metal fence next to Al's Super Electronics, rolls down the window and aims the Impala for the urban thicket of Chicago proper. He's thinking it's about time to drop in on Ginger. If he can find her.

You can tell he wants a drink. Look at that forefinger on the steering wheel, up and down like it's ringing a dinner bell. The poor lush. This little detour from his life is cutting into his Old Forester time. In two minutes he'll be into the glovebox, rummaging for that pack of Camels. The only time Ray smokes now is when he's in the car which, not coincidentally, is the only place he never drinks.

Here he goes. Right on schedule. I watch him lean over, one eye on the road, stretching and rummaging. Pathetic. Marlo hated his smoking. She did her best. But if Marlo couldn't make that lesson stick, particularly at the end, then there's no hope this lump will ever stop.

Ginger Turner's a Jessica Rabbit redhead who traded her satin and sequins for an abusive father, a speed addiction, and her own float in the Chicago flesh parade. For a while there, Ginger was the hottest ticket on the strip. Worked center stage at a place called Happy's, which – unlike its proprietor, Happy Weintraub, an amputee vet managing his anger with alcohol – lived up to its name most nights.

Every heavy-breathing mook in Chicago lined up for a block just to catch Ginger's bump and grind. The post-show acts were always strictly private, very expensive affairs. Ginger had Lana Turner's body and Kathleen Turner's voice. Ten years later, Ginger had Lana Turner's body after Thanksgiving and Kathleen Turner's voice after catching a cold. Now at thirty-four, Thanksgiving is strictly leftovers and the cold is threatening pneumonia.

But Ginger's still out there. Or she was anyway. The last Ray knew. God bless her. Doing what she can to get by. Happy's is long gone, but there's always a stage somewhere for Ginger. Even if it looks like a street corner.

Her name isn't Ginger, of course. Not any more than it's Suri. Her real name is Courtney Briggs. But when you're living that close to the ground, it's the street that names you. Maybe it likes the color of your hair. Or maybe it knows how popular you are with the Japanese conventioneers, men looking for the exact opposite of the women they're likely to find in a Kabukicho bathhouse. Men who get undressed to find themselves already missing a wallet and discover an open window to an empty bathroom in the Hotel Chump.

And maybe the street knows that *suri* is the Japanese word for pickpocket.

Suri was the name he used. Never her real name and never her show name. When people asked who'd given him the lowdown? The buzz? The skinny? The word? The grease? Then he'd tell them it came from Suri. From Suri? Yeah, Suri. Suri who? Just Suri. Who the fuck is Suri?

She'd always been a good source for Ray. Never played games. Always gave it up for the price of a dinner after her show. She'd never made him shake it out of her. Suri only ever had three conditions.

First. He had to ask nicely. Respectfully. Person-to-person, maybe cop-to-citizen, but never cop-to-criminal. Ray'd never get anywhere with Suri by threatening to lock her up. He could pull that stunt once. She'd do the time and then be lost to him forever.

Second. Reasonable compensation. She wasn't going to ask for the moon, but she wasn't giving it away for free. Self-respect was a precious thing in her business.

Third. She was strictly off the record. She was good for information, not for pointing out mooks in a courtroom or swearing up affidavits. She'd only meet with Ray, not his partner and not some other hump working the case. Just Ray. And she refused to be a CI. If she ever learned that he'd registered her as a civil informant, she'd turn it off in a second. She'd dry up and blow away in the wind.

Suri trusted him. And Ray had always respected her rules. Mostly because Ray had always liked Suri. For a thieving sex worker and needle jockey, Suri was a stand-up gal. She worked for herself, not Happy Weintraub, not a pimp, not a house. Just her. She knew how to survive but she could only do it alone. She had some integrity where it was otherwise impossible to find. An eighth of a snowflake hanging from the heart of July.

Ray fires up another Camel. Cocks his head as he holds in the smoke and then lets the hot wind take it away.

Ray's always been a hunch man. There's a little buzz in the back of his brain. A little upside-down fly on the windowsill that always seems like maybe it's dead until it jolts to life and flips itself over, suddenly full of theories and opinions. Thirty-three years figuring out how a person becomes a body. He's learned to listen.

Which is what he's doing now. Listening to that buzz.

He figures Suri is still a riddle. Figures her full name at the CPD is still *Suri Who*. Otherwise Twill wouldn't have been able to resist asking him about Ginger Turner, or worse, Courtney Briggs. He'd have worked her name into the conversation just to see the *oh-shit* look on Ray's face. Ray figures they've put the word out. They've got every cop and con out beating the streets from Chandler to Chicago for anyone that goes by the name Suri.

And they probably found her. They just don't know it. Five'll get you ten that at some point someone has put those same questions to Ginger Turner: *Hey, who the fuck is Suri? You know a Suri? Where can I find Suri?*

So chances are Suri knows they're looking. Probably no idea why, exactly, or who. But Ray's betting that Suri's instinct for self-preservation has kicked into overdrive. Now she's in the wind, as they say.

But where. Could be anywhere. Could already be dead in some fleabag inn at the corner of Luck and Fate. But Ray's little fly doesn't think so. Obviously. He's not riding a pack of Camels into Garfield Park after midnight just for the fun of it.

South Pulaski is the same as ever. Dirty brick boxes squatting on the side of the road. Churlish, drooping streetlights. Alleys, side streets guarded by wary, broken shopping carts. Chain-link squares every other block with nothing in the middle but dirt and trash and scorched-up, burned-out used-to-be things. No neon. No nightlife. No clubs. No bars except the kind over the doors and windows. Ragged, shuffling shadows here and there that might be people and that might be memories. No carrots for Jessica Rabbit in this place. Not now, not ever.

Ray pulls over and parks across the street from Chicago Sharps, a cut-rate meat market that shares a wall of bricks with Pulaski Spirits. Tonight the liquor store sheds a dull glow like a lantern guttering on a dark beach. The second story is nothing but four windows boarded over with circles of plywood, like wooden coins placed over the eyes of the dead. Except, that is, for the window farthest to the right, directly above the word Sharps. The upper rim of that particular wooden coin is leaking a dim gold glow.

Ray cuts the engine and kills the lights. He sits and smokes and sweats, dividing his attention between the building across the street and the image of South Pulaski stretching away into the cracked oval of his side mirror. He looks for the tail. If Twill is that hot to find Suri, then there's probably a car on him; a couple of suits who've had to follow his retired old ass around Southside Mall for four hours. Poor bastards.

He can't see them, but he can feel them. *Triple-D's* like Ray have a keen sense of what it feels like to be followed and watched. He'd written the feeling off at the mall, just the vibe he gets whenever he sees himself from above. That is, whenever *I* see him. Me.

But now that vibe's stronger than ever. Probably a bad move, coming here.

Ray adjusts the mirror and waits. Traffic is light but ominously slow. Headlight eyes. Angry, bone-rattling, hip-hop hearts. Most of them turn off east or west before they make it as far south as Chicago Sharps, the relentless thumping fading away into darkness like munitions in a neighboring war. But every now and then a car makes it the distance, prowling up alongside the Impala until the open windows line up.

Ray's not up for trouble. Not at his age and stage. He's slow and unarmed. He hasn't touched a gun in years. No need, except maybe to threaten the Smith Corona for more words or to blow that bitchy, rusted, rotary fan to hell. He retired his guns with his badge.

So he knows he won't last long in any kind of midnight fight on Pulaski Road. But he also knows better than to look away from whatever or whoever is gliding up next to him. Never move your eyes away. That's an invitation to finish you.

Reminds him of Marlo: *A man's eyes'll tell you a story, Mack. Maybe a good story. Maybe a real thigh-slapper. But if you want the truth about that man, pay attention to where those eyes are moving. You can bet they're chasing his heart.*

He takes a drag and makes as though he's as game for trouble as they are, looking at whatever that passing window, pumping bass and billowing weed, might have to offer him so late on a Tuesday night.

They're punks mostly, packed shoulder-to-shoulder. White and Black or maybe just varying degrees of shadow. Would-be bangers on the prowl for anything that will prove the men inside. Just below window level is more firepower than Al Capone could ever imagine.

They all get in their hungry, menacing glares. The kids look away as the bass pushes them slowly up the long street of short, sorry lives. Ray watches them go. He snuffs out the last Camel against the door and climbs out.

He crosses the street. Casual. Unconcerned. Just a man looking for a cold bottle of something to cut the heat. He puts one hand on the door of Pulaski Spirits.

His heart makes the sound of an old-timey telephone.

# TEN

I grab angrily at the loud, obnoxious goddamned thing in my pocket. I feel like I'm back on the job, which makes me jumpy. I can't explain it. I was never jumpy on the job. Death around every corner and yet I was never the one who was going to die. Blunt force trauma by asteroid was easier to imagine, and even then I'd find a way to duck. The badge was my shield. Nothing rattled me.

But then Marlo checks out. Then Lieutenant Nutsack retires me to a relatively risk-free life, unless you count cirrhosis and toxic bitterness. Now, ten minutes on South Pulaski and I'm wondering who's going to give Phil her two drops of Old Forester when I don't make it home.

I glance up and down the street for the tail, for the idling sedan that's too clean for this zip code. Then I look at the phone.

*Unknown Caller. Number Blocked.*

I stop the ringing with my thumb and stuff the phone back in my pocket. I yank open the door like maybe it's responsible for the heat and the phone and everything else.

# ELEVEN

Ray steps inside. It's an unforgiving, flickering fluorescence in this place. From above, he looks a little doughy and old. The dark donut of hair on his head is thinner, lighter. The patch of skin, somehow larger and paler than at the mall. He is unremarkably ordinary. The sight of him is not what I'd imagine of the once indomitable Raymond Mackey.

But then, it never is.

The man behind the counter is both older and less ordinary. A pale, featherless parrot in a black, short-sleeve button-down. He looks at Ray with a casual wariness, like maybe Ray's the guy he's been expecting night after night to walk in off South Pulaski with a sawed-off and just end everything. Like maybe the old bird'll reach for the piece under the counter and maybe he won't. Like maybe he doesn't really care anymore.

Ray scratches his bald spot and nods as he steps up to the counter. He checks the mirror in the corner that bends the entire place into a dirty soap bubble. Except for the booze, they're alone.

"Help you?" The man squawks.

"Hello, Carl," says Ray. He lets it go at that.

The man jolts a little. Focuses his attention.

"Jesus," says Carl. The face muscles around that prodigious beak slacken.

"No. It's me, Ray Mackey. Happens all the time with me and Jesus. We're like twins."

Carl's recovery is unconvincing.

"Damn. How you been, Mack? I haven't seen you in … what."

"Don't do the math, Carl. You'll make us both feel old. I get enough of that already. Is she here?"

"Who?"

Ray smiles. "Try again."

Carl swallows. Then he shrugs.

"No, Mack. Sorry. Haven't seen her."

"Always were a shitty liar, Carl. I'll just go on up. I'm slower in my old age so you've got plenty of time to dial that phone and let her know I'm coming."

Ray turns and heads toward the *employees only* door in the back of the store, the one that leads to a dark hallway and a darker staircase. He's about even with the vodka when Carl reaches beneath the counter. Ray talks up to the parabolic mirror in the back corner above the door.

"Think about that, Carl. I'm sure she said *nobody*. But has nobody *ever* included me?"

# TWELVE

There's never been a light switch in the hall. I feel for it anyway and can't find it, just like always. I have to probe my way to the stairs, sliding my hand along the wall until the wood bends away. I take five steps up to a landing where I interrupt either a rat *soirée* or a couple of cats plotting some malicious indifference. Whatever they are, we all scare the shit out of each other. Five more steps and I'm in the second-floor hallway. At the far end, a wash of tired, yellow light seeps beneath a door, pooling up against three large contractor trash bags lined up along the opposite wall.

Then, with a click, it all disappears into blackness.

There's no use sneaking, so I don't. I walk a straight line up the hall to the memory of the light like I'm walking a bottle up the aisle to the checkout counter. At the door, I knock and call out her name but there's no answer. I'm not surprised. That's not how this is going to go.

I fumble until I find the knob and twist. It's unlocked, which means she's been here long enough to relax her guard. With any luck, she's had enough time to snap off the light and hide, but not enough time to lock the door or grab a gun.

Hell, with any luck she'll be relieved to see me.

Luck.

Marlo's in my head. *Luck may be a lady, Ray, but behind those lips is one helluva set of teeth.*

I stand to the side and push the door open with the side of my foot. The room is nothing but different shapes of darkness. The door stops its swinging with a thud.

"I don't want to take your head off, Mack," she says from inside the dark. "But I will."

"I'm just here to talk, Suri."

"Fucking bullshit, Mack."

It's like someone is in the dark, impersonating Suri. It's her voice alright but the tone is something alien. Alien for her, always cool and confident to the core, even in the worst of times. Which makes these times worse than the worst. It's anger and fear I hear in her voice. Mostly fear. Slow-boiling terror. That's the secret ingredient. I try to soften my own voice, leading her back from the edge.

"No. No. It's the absolute truth, Suri. Just here to talk. You don't need to move a muscle. You don't need to come out. And I'm going to stay right out here in the hall. I won't make you shoot me if you don't make me shoot you."

"You're here to cash me in."

"No. I'm here to talk. I'm here to see if you're okay."

"Bullshit. Big Man wants me dead. And you're just the man for the job. You know all my secrets. Should never have come here. Here of all places."

"But you need Carl down there, right? You need a lookout. You need a friend. Someone you can trust. So here you are. Sensible enough choice in my book. They don't know where to find you."

"I think they just did."

"So I'm working for Big Man? That's the word?"

"Don't shit me, Mack. Yeah, that's the word. For years now."

"And you bought that garbage? I'm disappointed, kid."

"Why shouldn't I?"

"Because you're smarter than that, Suri."

She laughs, but it's the kind of sound that disgust makes when it can't believe its ears.

"You disappear like a fucking ghost, Mack. Not a word from you. All I've done for you? All I've done for you and I don't rate a fucking heads-up?"

"I should have. I'm sorry."

"Fuck sorry. Okay? Next thing I'm hearing is you got busted for being in Big Man's pocket. So I figure I had you all wrong; that you'd been conning everyone six ways from Sunday and got yourself locked up, which meant you were good as dead. At least that explained the disappearing act. Few months later and one of Big Man's goons sticks a hundred in my garter. Tells me Ray Mackey sent him."

I thought I was all ears before, but now I'm really paying attention.

"Bullshit, Suri. Who?"

"Who? Like you don't know who. Fat and ugly, that's who. Stinky and heavy, that's fucking who."

"What'd you call him?"

"Sir. He doesn't answer to *please stop hitting me*. His name is Royce."

"Royce. First or last?"

"Last."

"First name?"

"I don't know, Mack. Starts with an S. As in Sluggo."

"Sounds about right. What'd Sluggo Royce want from you?"

"Everything, on and off the menu. And he didn't ask nicely."

"That's all?"

"No. He zipped up, handed me ten more crisp Benjamins, and said I was going to be working for Big Man. I dropped the cash on the floor and told him I don't work for nobody but me."

"How'd he take it?"

"Asked if I wanted to keep breathing. Then he closed both of my eyes for a week."

There's a sound on the stairs. Too heavy for a rat. Carl.

"Ah, hell." I switch to my outside voice. "Carl? I'm not here for trouble. Don't make me air you out in the fucking hall. If you're dead, who's going to work the register?"

Whoever was moving has stopped. I'm not satisfied. Inside voice.

"Suri, listen. Carl's worried. He's just trying to protect you. Don't make him pay the price for no reason. Call him off.

I don't want to shoot him but you better believe I will. I'll empty this fucking thing in his head."

More silence. Just the sound of Suri thinking.

"Suri."

"Carl," she shouts. "It's just Mack. And all his bullshit. I'm fine. Go mind the store. Call me if anyone else comes in. If you hear a gunshot, call the cops. Tell 'em it was Ray Mackey."

A long pause, but then the welcome sound of descent. I wait until I hear the back door to the store open and close.

"Thanks," I tell her, trying to find that soft, reassuring tone again. "Carl gives me the creeps. But he's always been loyal to you. Guess that makes him okay in my book. Sounds like you need all the help you can get."

"Got that right, Mack." All the fear, but half the anger now. "He's the only one I trust."

"No, Suri. Ginger. Courtney. You can trust me."

"Can I?" She's aiming for hostile but misses by a mile. She's pleading. She's desperate to believe. "Can I, Mack?"

"Yes. And you always could. I swear it on the bottle of Old Forester that I'd be home drinking right now if it weren't for you. Now can we stop this hide-and-seek crap and have a real conversation? If Big Man asked me to rub you out, do you think I'd announce myself to Carl? Think Big Man would want to leave that easy trail of breadcrumbs?"

Another fifteen, twenty seconds of thinking. Then a click.

The room skulks into focus beneath a dingy, pallid light.

# THIRTEEN

Ray pivots carefully into the doorframe. The muscles in his neck keep his head rigid. His eyes dart around the squalor. There's one lamp sitting on the floor, plugged into a nearby outlet like it's hooked up to life support. The single bulb inside the dirty shade is a forty-watt smoker's lung about ready to give up. But the lamp shows him around the place anyway.

It's about what you'd expect from a South Pulaski efficiency above a butcher shop and liquor store. One beat-to-hell room, maybe twenty-feet square, plus a bathroom. Two crooked, doorless cabinets over a rusty sink pretend to be a kitchen. A rickety round table is cluttered with fast-food cartons and boxes and grease-stained bags that Carl has no doubt walked up the stairs himself. Beneath the erstwhile window is a neat line of empty and nearly empty bottles. Nothing like cheap rosé and a quart of sloe gin to weather the storm.

In the corner, right next to the lamp, there's a thin mattress underneath a thin woman. She's holding a silver cannon the size of a mailbox. It must weigh as much as she does. Her forearms are braced on the points of her kneecaps. Her hands are shaking.

"Jesus, Suri." Ray holds up both hands. "Put it down. Just …"

"You don't have a fucking gun?" She almost shouts it. "You said you were gonna to empty it! You want me to trust you and you've been lying from the first fucking minute?"

He tries to stay level. Calm.

"Would you have believed me if I told you I was unarmed?"

Suri doesn't answer. Ray answers himself.

"Come on, kid. Of course not. I tell you I'm not carrying and you'd have suspected me more than you already do. You'd have been waiting for me to use the gun I don't actually have. Then you'd decide to beat me to the punch and start squeezing that trigger. That's the part I wanted to skip. You're not the only one that wants to keep breathing, Suri. So yeah, I'll lie to keep living. I'll lie every time."

He lets her think through it. The gun is too heavy to hold for long. Gravity is on his side.

Ten seconds. Twelve. A baker's dozen. She lowers it to the mattress.

# FOURTEEN

It's the sight of her that takes my breath away, almost more than the stink of the room. Not in a good way. Not like the old days when to behold young Ginger Turner on stage, or from across the street, was to feel good and alive in the moment. Not wholesome-good. Good in all the bad ways. Bad-good. The woman on the mattress is a Raggedy Ann doll with a bad dye job rescued from the side of a freeway. She's half the size I remember, swimming in grimy jeans and a blue *I Love My Cubs* jersey that Carl must have brought up with the donuts and pizza. Her hair is dirty and matted and a dull out-of-the-box black. Suri looks up at me with bloodshot eyes that float in their dark, sunken sockets like old tennis balls bobbing in muddy potholes. The right side of her face is the color of rotting eggplant. Jesus.

# FIFTEEN

Ray keeps one hand raised as the other finds the door and closes it. He moves slowly backward until he can feel the door behind him. Then he eases himself down to the floor.

Their eyes are on the same level. Suri leans back into her corner, pulling the gun with her. She holds it in her lap like a kitten. They stare at each other across the room.

"Quite a cannon," says Ray. Suri glances down.

"Carl. He says it's loaded. I don't know one end of the thing from the other."

Ray sighs.

"None of the shit's true, Suri. About me. None of it."

She leans her head back against the wall and closes her eyes.

"I'm listening."

He gives her the history lesson, hitting all the low points. He includes everything he'd never have told a civilian. The task force. The internal investigation. Cosmo Green and his magic burner. Lieutenant Nutsack. Who is he to keep their secrets now? He spills it all.

Almost all. He leaves out the part about the *Triple-D* diagnosis. Smart move. Being crazy's not going to win him any friends. Never has before. Dissociative disorders are only good for disassociating. They're not friendship friendly.

So he tries to leap over the puddle of his dysfunction – that problem he has staying in his own skin – only the puddle is a lake and he catches the outer edge of it with the heel of his shoe.

"I came apart when Marlo died," he says. Ironic. Because he did come apart. Raymond Mackey split into two pieces. He disassociated. And all the king's horses and all the king's men …

Not that Suri has ever known anything about Marlo, alive or dead. Never any reason for Ray to get personal back then. But I can tell he's desperate now. He's looking to earn some trust from the rag doll and her big silver kitten. So he opens up. Marlo waltzes out into the room and does a turn or two around the ruins of his career and the rest of his life.

"Two cops in one marriage," Suri marvels. "Bet that was interesting."

"Wasn't a cop," he says. "Too smart for that. She was an insurance fraud investigator and a PI before that. The best. Taught me everything I know about people. Everything I know about seeing behind all the things that are put in front of us to be seen."

There's a hitch in his voice. Pathetic sap. He has to swallow. Come on, Ray.

"I'm sorry, Mack," she says. "You never let on."

He can't stop there. He can't indulge that pity. He can't take that tone from Suri, looking like she does. He'll never make it. He needs to pull back on the stick, get his nose back in the air.

Ray shakes Marlo free and keeps the story moving, bringing it all current to him waking up thirteen hours ago on the couch. When he gets to Sergeant Twill and the names hiding out in Santiago's suit pocket, Suri interrupts.

"Marx," she says, shaking her head. "That's the guy. Harold fucking Marx."

"Harold?"

"Yeah."

"Andrew Harold Marx."

"Don't know about Andrew."

"Cop?"

She nods.

"How do you know him?"

"Big Man. Look. If you don't already know, then maybe it's better you don't. Stay clear of this, Mack."

"I need to know what's going on, Suri. What the hell happened to your face? Purple's not your color." Ray pans the room. "I don't see any spoons laying down with lighters."

Suri shakes her head and picks at a hole in whoever's jeans she's wearing.

"Kicked that habit. It's still there. Like a hot itch. I could go back to it in a heartbeat. But I'm pretty sure it would be my last heartbeat. So I stay away. Almost a year now."

"Support group? Narconon?"

Suri laughs.

"Kick the junk just to get hooked on Jesus? Not me." She nods to the chorus line of empty wine bottles under the window. "Alcohol's my savior. Booze and cigarettes. And stubbornness. I just did it, Mack. Had to."

Ray shakes his head.

"You amaze me, Ginger. Always have."

"Go home, Mack. If it's like you say, then stay out of this."

"Too late for that. I'm already in deep. I'm here as much for myself as I am for you. Tell me how you know Harold Marx. Tell me why you're hiding out in this ratty shit-hole with Carl's gun in your lap. It can't be for the view."

Suri takes a ragged breath. Ray is expecting words but the sobs make it out first. He knows better than to move. He waits, back against the door, staring at the floor between his legs. She has to fight to pull it together. Eventually Suri climbs up on top of all of whatever she's been trying to hold back. Wipes her nose on her sleeve.

"Fucking Big Man," she sniffs. "Fucking cops."

# SIXTEEN

I'm someplace else as she speaks. Someplace deep in my head where her words fall around me like huge iron beams. They assemble themselves, erecting a city I never knew existed. As I've been plinking away on my Smith Corona, the real world has kept rolling, less like a bright blue marble than a burning tire into a ditch. Ten days after Sluggo Royce blackens her eyes, she gets a call. Harold Marx. He's not one for chatting, Harold. But then Harpo never was either. He tells her to pick up a package at the Best Western on Horner and Third. Don't open it, he says. Hold onto it until someone comes asking.

She does as she's told. The man behind the desk at the Best Western hands her a small, sealed envelope with *Ginger Turner* typed across the front and something round and hard inside about the size of a lipstick. That night, a bruiser she's never met hits her up for a drink.

"He wanted a back table at The Broken Shot. I figure I'm one drink away from him wanting it right there in the booth and that I'm going to have to educate this lunk about what is and is not on my menu. But then he drinks his Jack and looks at me with his dead eyes and says that Marx sent him. And I'm sitting there stunned. Swear to god, Mack, I'm just like looking at the guy. So he has to say it again. *Marx*. So I dig the envelope out of my purse and hand it over. He slides me a pair of Benjamins and then he's up and gone, just like that.

Kept my lipstick on and got a free drink out of the deal. Not bad for seven o'clock."

It happens like that sometimes once a week, sometimes a couple times in a month. Never the same pick-up spot. Never the same would-be john. Suri has no idea what it's all about. She figures she's helping Big Man's left hand communicate with his right hand, like his organization is so fat the hands can't touch each other. She figures they need someone to bridge the gap and that it may as well be her.

She's got no idea who Harold Marx is other than one of Big Man's goons, at least until she asks the clerk at a fleabag on Madison if he saw who dropped off the latest envelope. She'd asked the question before. All she'd get back was a shoulder shrug. The drops were always made on the prior shift so the guy receiving the envelope is not the same guy handing it over to Suri. But the guy on Madison must be working doubles. Same shoulder shrug, but a different follow-through. *Some cop*, he says. *Suit and tie with a badge.*

"I do a lot of things out there in the world, Mack. Things I'll never understand. Things you don't want to know about and that I don't want to remember. This just became another one of those things. When Sluggo first dropped your name, I figured you were in the same boat. Doing Big Man's dirty work. I didn't understand it. Then I stopped trying. Then I learn Marx is a cop. So I just said *fuck it*. Did what I was told to do. Didn't know shit and didn't want to know shit. Two hundred bucks and a free drink for handing over an envelope. And the cherry on top of that shit-sundae is that I don't get my lights punched out. I kept my head down."

But then it turns out that one of those little envelopes didn't have enough glue to keep it completely sealed. Suri couldn't help herself. Ask any cat you know about curiosity.

"That drop was at a punk dive on East Willis. Metal Moon?"

"I know the place."

"I went to the restroom and locked myself in a stall and got a good look inside the envelope. It was a bullet, Mack. Not a bullet. Hollow. What do you call it. An empty."

"A casing?"

"A casing. That's it. 'Bout that big," she says, pinching the air. "Like a lipstick. I tipped the envelope and pushed it up through the hole, out into my hand. I looked inside the thing and I could see a little white piece of paper rolled up in there, way at the bottom. No way of getting it out. You'd need tweezers. I didn't want to get it out. Figured the less I knew, the better. I slipped the bullet thing back inside the envelope and flushed the toilet and went about my life."

"Okay. And?"

"And so that night, this punk in a black GT rolls up next to me on West Palm and whistles. I lean in and wait for him to tell me he's buying himself a treat for his eighteenth birthday. But all he says is the magic name. So I hand over the envelope and hope the thing doesn't fall out in the street. He hands me two bills, light turns green, and the little shit nearly rolls over my foot."

Too much detail on things that don't matter. She's avoiding the end of this story. The thing that's spooked her into hiding. She doesn't want to jump back down into the pain. Can't say I blame her. I know what it's like to look over the edge of that cliff. I give her a nudge.

"Suri. We're both on borrowed time here. I get the set-up. So stop pussy-footing around. What in the hell happened to you? Who did your make-up?"

"Royce," she says.

"No, I mean this time."

"You hard of hearing?"

"Sluggo? Again?"

She nods and sighs, deflating at the shoulders like a blow-up punching bag losing its air.

"Showed up last week in a bad mood. He put me through my paces as usual and then knocked me around like maybe that might make him feel better."

"Did it?"

"Don't know. But he left and that made me feel better. Next time I saw Royce was after that last drop. White Pontiac. Rolls up on Shoreline and Eleventh. Pushes open the door and tells me to get in. Says we need to talk. And there I am, still healing up from the last time. I'm thinking Big Man took one look at that last envelope and thought I was getting snoopy. So I tell Royce the envelope was partly open when I got it. I tell him I didn't see anything. Royce looks at me like I'm trying to sell him a pet rock. He tells me again to get in and he says it like it's the last time he's going to ask. So I do."

I can see her silently reading ahead to the part of this story that's giving her nightmares. She looks at me like she's falling, wounded green eyes clutching for me from across the room. There's a screech of tires down in the street. We both start. We don't have time for this.

# SEVENTEEN

Ray's getting antsy. Looking at his watch. Drumming his fingers on his knee. He's torn between wanting to know every last detail and wanting to get up and run. He's trying to ignore the feeling in his gut. He can't do that. He shouldn't.

I'm watching them like there's no ceiling. No roof. I see them from fifty feet, a hundred feet, three hundred feet, above the building, which is nothing but a filthy stack of bricks dumped on the side of the road. South Pulaski's a dimly lit ant trail stretching out into the early-morning gloom. The ants are few and far between. They have glowing eyes. Most of them keep moving. But not all of them. Some of them are still. Waiting.

Suri takes another breath and dives in.

"He takes me up the block to the empty lot across from my apartment. I figured he was coming up. But as soon as I get out and close the door, Sluggo puts me down with one punch to the head. I try to get up but he keeps at it. I went numb, Mack. I couldn't scream. I couldn't fight back. I just tried … I just tried …" She's not going to make it. "I tried to disappear."

She's crying again. Ray pushes himself up to his feet. He grimaces, trying not to groan at the ache in his knees. He crosses the room and sits down next to her on the mattress.

Suri flinches, gripping the gun, but then she lets him sit. She sobs into his shoulder. Ray looks over her head at his watch. Looks around the room behind her. Looks up at the ceiling, like he can see me. Like he wants me to do something to speed this up. But he knows better. So he waits.

"I woke up in the fucking trunk," she says finally, with a wet sniff. "I bounced around in the dark for quite awhile. Don't know how long. I was in and out. Everything hurt. Especially my eye and my jaw. Something had punctured my leg but I couldn't reach it. My whole face was swelling up. I felt like I couldn't breathe. But I could sure as hell smell. I woke up again when the car stopped. It stunk like death, Mack. Like death was in that trunk with me. I heard Royce open his door. When he got his big ass out of the car, it felt like the whole thing lifted two feet higher off the ground. Felt like I was starting to float."

Suri wipes her eyes and looks up into Ray's face.

"You ever just ... like ... try to climb out of your own body, Mack? Like you're trying to hoist yourself up into a dream because it's better to be watching yourself in a dream, even a bad dream, than actually being you in the real fucking world?"

Ray looks down at her in a kind of frightened stupefaction. We both do. I can tell he wants to say yes. He wants to say he knows exactly what that feels like. He doesn't.

"Suri. What happened?"

She curls up, scrunching the lower half of her body away from him, resting the side of her head in his lap. She snuggles Carl's gun up against her chest.

"It's like ... when I felt Sluggo get out of that car ... listening to him walk back to the trunk ... I knew what came next. I knew what was coming, Mack, and my soul was climbing up into the Big Dream. That's what Delaney would call it."

"Delaney?"

"Oh." She sniffs. "Used to have this regular. Years ago. Went by Delaney. Old friend of Happy Weintraub. Nice enough, but crazier than a squirrel in a nuthouse. Twice as crazy as Happy but not as angry. Delaney never lasted more than thirty, forty seconds in bed. Like, not *ever*. But he liked to lie there in the afterglow and smoke my cigarettes and talk up to the ceiling."

"Suri. Honey."

"This one time, Delaney said he'd started to see himself from up inside the big dream. That's what he called it. The big dream. Said he knew his time was coming because he kept finding himself outside of his own body, looking down. But like I say, Delaney was, like, crazy. You know? Always whacked out on something. So I didn't give it another thought. Month later? I hear Delaney'd caught a bullet. Been dead a few weeks. Which meant, you know, right about that time he was talking up to my ceiling about the big dream. And when I heard that, I figured maybe he really did see it coming. That was years ago. I was still doing my thing at Happy's. Shaking my fruit."

"Suri."

"Hadn't given Delaney any thought since. Delaney and the big dream. Not until I heard Royce walking back toward that trunk."

"Suri." Ray's ready to shake her. He combs through her hair with his fingers. "You're exhausted. You're frightened. You're not making any sense."

"The big dream is what comes next, Mack. You have to die to get into the big dream. Compared to the big dream, our little lives are just, like, nothing. Or, not actually *nothing*, but you know, super small and simple 'cause our puny little brains can't handle anything more complicated. But once you're in the big dream, it's like you can see forever and everything makes sense for a change. And you get to see what's happening back here and check in on the people you left behind that are still trying to slog through one day and into the next. And it's like ... it's like looking down at some puppet show for kids. It's all so simple and silly. Nothing to be scared of or sad about."

"Suri. It's getting late. So late it's early."

"And that's what was happening inside that trunk, Mack. I was in the dark, bleeding, listening to the end coming, and I was already – like right *then* – climbing up into the big dream. And I could see myself. Like I could actually see myself, down there curled up in the trunk of that Pontiac like a little unborn baby. I was watching myself like I was already up there in the dream and looking back down. Already part of history. I was up there in the future, watching the end of my life in an old-timey home movie."

"Suri. What the hell happened?"

She pushes herself up and leans against the wall, wiping her face with her hands.

"I was wrong, is what happened. Wasn't my time for the big dream, I guess. I heard Royce stop and work the key. When the trunk opened, his face came at me like some giant balloon with big dead eyes. He reached in with one hand and pulled me out by the hair. I saw the whole thing from above, Mack. Like a horror movie. Last thing I did before I was all the way out of the trunk was reach for the thing stuck in my leg. I didn't even know what it was. I buried it in his eye. Turned out to be a nail at least two lipsticks long with a head the size of a quarter. Royce dropped me in the dirt and went to work on it with both hands."

Ray's not glancing at his watch now. She's got his full attention. He rubs his own temple like maybe he can feel that nail.

"He had a gun. Can't hold a gun when you're trying to pull a two-lipstick nail out of your eye. Go write that down in a book somewhere, Mack, 'cause it's a fact. The gun landed right on my face. Nearly broke my nose."

"Oh, god."

"I don't remember standing up, Mack. Don't even remember shooting. I just remember looking down at him, watching his body jerk. Like some invisible person was poking him with a stick. I kept at it until his body stopped."

"Jesus, Suri."

"Yeah."

"That's some puppet show."

"Yeah."

"What'd you do?"

"Got the fuck out. Left Royce in the dirt. Got in the car and drove. No idea where I was. Turns out I was behind a landfill out in DeKalb. I didn't know where to go. All I could think of was this place. I knew Carl would hide me. Figured you'd be my biggest risk. I knew you'd know to look for me here eventually if you wanted to find me. But I couldn't think of anywhere else. Big Man would know to check all the fleabags. Like I have the money for more than a couple of nights."

"Where's the gun?"

She closes her eyes and leans back against the wall. She's done. Whatever was left inside of her is now all used up. He shakes her arm.

"Suri. Where's the gun?"

"The trunk." She doesn't open her eyes.

"Where's his car?"

"Target."

"Target. Where? Which Target?"

"Chinatown. Locked the doors and just … walked away. Cleaned myself up inside and then walked to a bus stop. I dropped the keys in a dumpster at the other end of Pulaski. And so here I am." She opens her eyes briefly to look at him, then closes them again. "Waiting for Big Man. Waiting for Big Man to send me up into the big dream." She squeezes his arm, finding new strength from somewhere. "Mack. Oh, Mack."

"What is it, honey?"

"Nothing." She sighs.

"Try again."

"Something I didn't tell you." She squeezes again. "You're not going to like it."

"I don't like any of it, Suri. Let's have it."

"That second-to-last time Royce got rough. I was … I was hurting. And I was really fucking angry. I was doing the work and I was getting paid, yeah, but … the rest of it … I don't know what was up his ass but I'm nobody's punching bag. When he went to piss, I went for his pocket. I found some loose cash. I took it and stuffed it in the pillow."

"Can't help yourself, can you?"

"He had it coming."

"That and more. Can't say I'm broken up about it. You took the man's life, kid. I wouldn't worry much about the money."

"That's not all I took. It was all in one quick grab. I didn't have time to sort it all out. I don't know why I kept the damn thing, but I did."

"What thing?"

She digs in her pocket and hands him a slip of paper.

"It's a dry cleaning ticket. That's how I got his name."

"S. Royce," says Ray. She points.

"The account number's his phone number. I'd had enough, Mack. I was at the end. The booze helped me with the pain, but the problem was it also helped me with the fear."

"Why is that a problem?"

"Because two nights after that, I got shit-faced and called him."

"Not sure I like where this is going. Royce picked up?"

"No. That didn't stop me. I let him have what for. Told him I was done working for Big Man. Jesus, Mack, I don't know what all I said. None of it nice. Except ..."

"Spill it, Suri. How bad can it be?"

"I told him that Ray Mackey knows about everything. Everything Royce did to me. Everything I was doing. I told him you were coming for him, Mack. I said Big Man might think you were on the payroll but that he had another thing coming."

Ray lets out a sigh and rubs his eyes.

"Good Christ, Ginger."

"I know. I'm sorry, Mack. I told him what I wanted to be true."

# EIGHTEEN

I close my eyes, trying to think. Ideas and strategies appear on the horizon like taxis in a downpour. None of them stop to take me where I need to go. I watch them disappear into my rising shit-storm of panic. I try to think of what I have to work with, sifting through available resources. But I can't focus past the sickness I feel in my gut. It's not food poisoning. It's that feeling you get when you wake up in the middle of the night, in a cold sweat wondering if the broken-glass sound in your head is from a dream or if there's someone else in your house. And then you hear it again.

Marlo, suddenly. Sitting out in the car. Looking through the viewfinder at Victor Roby talking on the phone in his fancy chair.

*People only know what they believe, Ray. And they only believe what they see. And they only ever see what they want to see. You want to win the big game? Figure out what the bad guys want to see. Show them that.*

The plan shows up like a slap in the face. I open my eyes. She's staring at me.

"Listen. Me coming here ... that could've been a big mistake, Suri. I had to find you. It was the only way. But ..." I'm already looking around the room for what I need. "Look, you've got to get out of here."

"No shit, Mack. You caught me by a day. Tomorrow's Friday. Carl gets a delivery at eleven. I'm thinking I can ride out in the back of the truck. Like, not even tell Carl, so no one can ..."

"No." I swing the word like it's a club and she jolts at the rejection. "You don't get it. You need to leave right now. Right now, Suri."

"Well fuckin' A, Mack." She's angry and freshly terrified, just like I need her to be. "How? Where? With ... with fucking what?"

I grab Carl's gun before she can yank it away. I open it up. Fully loaded. I snap it closed and push it toward her.

"Keep this close. You might need it."

"What are we doing?"

"Get up. We're going to need this sheet."

"The sheet? What the hell are we doing?"

I grimace an advance apology.

"You're not going to like it, kid."

"Fuck, Mack." She wants to cry. "What."

"I need you to take another ride in a trunk."

# NINETEEN

Neither one of them are in great shape. They're both struggling. Carl at one end of the corpse and Ray at the other. The sheet keeps coming loose and they have to stop and tuck it back in. They kill the lamp on their way out of the room. No one had thought about a flashlight. So they have to find their way in the dark. Out of the room, up the hall, and down two flights of stairs, grunting the whole way. At the bottom, Carl pulls toward the liquor store. Ray pulls the other way.

"Back door," says Ray.

"You're parked out front."

"I'll pull around. Who's going to believe we're hauling her out the front door? She's dead. She's a fucking corpse, Carl. She goes out the back."

# TWENTY

Ray walks through the front door of Pulaski Spirits with a free bottle of Old Forester in a paper bag. He steps out onto the sidewalk and then crosses the road. He keeps his eyes focused on the Impala. Doesn't look left. Doesn't look right. Straight ahead, like there's nothing else to see but his own car. But I can tell that every other sense is working overtime. He's listening. Feeling. Every hair is its own antenna.

Look at that stride. Any sap could tell something's off. Who doesn't look up and down South Pulaski at almost two in the morning? Criminals look both ways. Superman looks both ways on South Pulaski.

He unlocks the door and tosses in the booze. He starts the car and cranks the wheel, pulling away from the curb and rolling north and then east up the alley until he reaches the lot in back of the building. He backs the car up to the rear entrance and the trunk pops open like magic. Ray leaves the engine running and gets out, another thing you never do on South Pulaski after midnight. He raps a knuckle on the back door. It opens and swallows him whole.

Ten seconds. He reappears, ass first, stooped over and walking backward through the door, trying to keep the sheet in place. They pause as Carl makes sure the door won't close and lock him out, then they slowly, carefully – with far too much consideration, frankly, for the comfort of a corpse –

lower the long white bundle down into the trunk. Carl turns in place nervously, then steps away. Ray closes the trunk. There is no bidding farewell.

# TWENTY-ONE

I live in my rearview mirror, waiting for those lights. Nothing but shapes turning to shadow and falling off the back of the world. I point the car south, heading back in the general direction of Chandler. I can't help but wonder whether someone has put together a surprise party for me at home. I hope someone has the decency to feed Phil while they clean their guns.

My phone rings. I fish it out of my pocket. *Unknown Caller. Number Blocked.* I'm ready to reject the call and drop the phone into the seat. I don't.

"Hello?" Nothing. "Who the hell is this? What makes you think it's okay to wake a man up at two in the morning?" Nothing. "Okay, fine. I'm in a buying mood. I'll take a dozen if you tell me what you're selling."

Nothing. As usual. I end the call.

I get off South Pulaski and serpentine my way past the 290. Plenty of steady white lights behind me now. But one-by-one, they eventually turn away or pass. I think maybe I'm home free, at least until I hit a darker stretch of road just south of Lawndale.

That's when a pair of those steady whites behind me puts on a red-and-blue party hat.

# TWENTY-TWO

Ray pulls the Impala over next to a pyramid of corrugated pipes and an old backhoe that looks like a sleeping yellow mantis, construction staging for a ditch he can't see. His flashing tail glides to a stop right behind.

He lets his left arm hang out the window, drumming his fingers against the car door. He can't see much through the halogen spray behind him. They make him sit there for three or four minutes, lights flashing on top of the black, unmarked Caprice. Rubberneckers ride their brakes to get a good look. Eventually the front doors open in unison like some black bird of prey spreading its wings.

One of them is in an open-collar button-down. The other's in a Cubs t-shirt. Badges hanging from their necks. They both have gym memberships.

The one with the crewcut stops just short of Ray's door as Mr. Mustache swings around the passenger side, looking in the windows. Everybody thought to bring a gun except Ray.

"You boys going to go with a broken taillight or speeding?"

"Shut the fuck up, Mack." Officer crewcut readies his piece. "Get out of the car and keep your hands where I can see them. Twitch once. I dare you."

Ray does as he's told. They march him around to the passenger side of the car and get him to lie face down, his head toward the idling Caprice. Mustache fixes him with a pair of bracelets.

It strikes me that Ray's seen this movie dozens of times over the course of his career; looking down on a man kissing the pavement, hands behind his back, cuffs flashing silver in the headlights. Only he's always been the one watching, like I'm watching now, not the one spread-eagled on the road.

He can't see them but he can hear them walking around the back of the car. Ray lifts his head like a turtle. Mustache has got his ear to the trunk.

"How about you read me my rights as I read your warrant?"

They don't respond.

"That sound okay to everybody? I know that's a lot of reading."

Nothing.

"Don't be scared, it's only the law."

Crewcut walks back and buries the point of his boot into Ray's ribs. Ray rolls himself into a handcuffed cocktail shrimp.

"What'd I tell you about twitching?"

Ray coughs and lays his face back down on the road like maybe he's finally learned his lesson. But this is Ray Mackey. He hasn't learned anything.

"You can't search my car without a warrant." He shouts it this time. Like he's trying to raise the dead. "I'm telling you that you cannot open that trunk …"

He gets the boot again, once more in the gut and once in the head. One in the face for good measure. All he can do is cough and spit blood.

"Goddamnit." Mustache points angrily to the driver's door.

Crewcut steps over Ray and moves quickly around the front of the car. He cuts one last look to Mustache, who now seems ready for anything, two fingers on the trunk, gun out. Crewcut reaches down in through the driver's window and pulls the trunk release.

# TWENTY-THREE

Two gunshots, then a third. I feel myself convulse. Takes a second for me to realize I'm not hit. I straighten my body and roll to the Impala, then inch myself underneath like an earthworm moving sideways.

Fresh gunfire has a smell. Like fresh-brewed coffee for some guys. Not me. Always makes me queasy. The scent of hot metal is everywhere. I can taste blood pooling in my mouth.

The car above me is hot. The pavement is hot. Two in the morning and the world is still a goddamned oven. I'm a slab of meat grilling in a panini press. What I wouldn't give for that rickety fan. The quiet of the road is slowly flattened beneath the coming whine of a large, heavy truck.

I lift my sideways head as much as I can and let the blood drool out into a puddle on the pavement. All I can see is two pairs of boots like I'm watching a rodeo from under the bleachers. I imagine them both bent at the waist into the trunk above me. The semi grinds past us in a low roar, bottlenecking a parade of every other mook out in the middle of the night driving a car.

"Motherfucker." The whole car bounces above me in anger.

"Shit. Deno."

"That little mother ..."

"Deno. Deno. Shit."

"What."

"He's gone."

"What?"

Out on the road, a horn sounds off and gets an answer in kind.

The boots scurry away toward the pyramid of corrugated pipes. They're climbing and crawling in and over and around the things like kids on a playground. I think about whether I can inch myself out from under the car, get my hands in front of me and drive. No way. Before I can move, they're already coming back. I want to spit. I don't. I watch, holding my blood and my breath. They angle past the Impala toward the Caprice.

"... at the liquor store."

"Bullshit. She's a memory at the fucking liquor store. She's gone."

"Then we brace the old man."

"Oh, sure. Great idea. I'm sure he's still hanging around."

"Fuck you, Pete."

The cars are still rolling past. I hear the Caprice doors close. Whoever is driving, Dumb-ass Deno or Pissy Pete, pumps the siren once and then once more so they can turn around in the street and head back to Pulaski Spirits. The Caprice rolls up even with the Impala, accelerating, but then skids to a stop as the passenger door opens. One boot hits the pavement. It points under the car, directly at my bloody face.

"What the fuck ... Let's go, man! Pete! Goddamnit!"

"He's under the car, Deno. Has to be. We'd ..."

Deno is not a patient man, apparently, and he does not suffer Pete's second-guessing. The siren is suddenly yowling into the night and the car is moving again, even before Pete's accusing boot is up and gone and the passenger door is closed. I spit another mouthful of blood and try to remember how to breathe.

# TWENTY-FOUR

Not a pretty look for a man Ray's age. Blood on his face, rolling around on his back trying to fit his ass through the opening of his handcuffed arms. Once you start that game, you have to finish it or risk getting your hands stuck between your butt and your knees. Then you can't do anything. Can't use your hands. Can't run. All you can do is sit and wait for whoever cuffed you in the first place to come back and finish you off.

Looks like that's the way it's going to go. A pathetic end for our Ray. Our disgraced cop, wannabe crime writer. Lying on his back in the dirt, spitting blood, legs up, sweating and wheezing from the strain. Cursing up at the moon. Not how a guy likes to see himself. Not at the end. Not with the first chapter only half-written; poor Janice Hinkle in two pieces with government-issue fingerprints all over her back.

What happens to all the unfinished novels? To the brainchildren, born and unborn, of all those writers with a poor sense of timing? What a tour that would be, to wander the purgatory of the unrealized and unfinished, souls like poor Janice Hinkle, with half-expressions on half-faces and bodies bent into question marks. That's a novel right there. Maybe for some enterprising writer that isn't dead or wadded up like a gum wrapper on the side of the road.

Ignominy can be a powerful motivator for some people. Ray finally wedges his right knee outside his elbow. The rest is downhill from there. At least he had the sense to keep the Impala between himself and the road. No one stops. No one has any idea.

He lies there, panting for a minute, cuffed hands on his belly like he's taking a nap. Then, finally, he's up and moving again. He opens the passenger door and then the glovebox. He digs around with both hands until he finds his own spare set of standard issue bracelets. He dumps them out of the leather pouch onto the seat. A set of keys falls out with them.

# TWENTY-FIVE

My head is a burning munitions dump. Two teeth are loose and my mouth feels soupy. I can't stop spitting, even though the bleeding seems to be slowing. I sit in the passenger seat, rubbing my aching wrists.

I pull down the visor. The guy in the mirror is passing out free heart attacks. I look like I crawled out from under an interstate pileup. I head back to the trunk so I can wipe my face with something, like maybe a dirty white sheet that's wrapped around three contractor bags full of garbage. Fortunately, I happen to have one of those.

There are two entrance wounds where the garbage is shaped like a head. There's another in the chest. The bottom half of the victim has been gutted in a rage. Her last meal looks to have been pizza crust and fried chicken bones. Must've been hungry; she ate the greasy paper bucket and the napkins too. I clean my face as best I can, adding blood and road grime to the bullet holes. I close the trunk over the carnage that is not a corpse.

I get in the front and close the door. I find the bag that's been burning in my brain and pull the plug on the Old Forester. It feels like a warm bath on a cold night. Another slug and then I ditch the bottle in the backseat and put the car in gear.

Getting kicked in the face is not how I like to ditch a tail, but now that it's done, I finally feel safe taking care of business. I turn the car around and head north, fighting the impulse to grind the gas pedal into the floor. I've had enough cops for one lifetime so I watch my speed. I grab the phone off the seat and start pushing buttons.

"Mack." Carl sounds uncharacteristically concerned for my well-being. "Starting to worry. Everything okay?"

"Nothing Doc Forester can't heal."

"How many?"

"Two, but it felt like ten. They'd guessed it was a ruse; they just hadn't guessed the right ruse. They seemed upset that I like to wrap my garbage in a sheet. How's our corpse?"

"She wants out of the goddamned trunk. I'm learning some new words."

"I'll bet."

"She's saying you promised she'd be in the trunk for ten minutes, long enough to get to the freeway. But I told her you told me she stays until we get there."

"You're both right. She's in for ten minutes. And then another sixty or so after that. I forgot to tell her that last part."

"Cops."

"First, I'm not a cop. Second, it was the only way she'd ever agree to get in your trunk. She'll be okay. I don't want you to stop till you get where you're going. They're out looking, Carl. Understand? They're not in a good mood. They're lighting up South Pulaski as we speak. You're out of the liquor business, by the way, until this blows over, which might be never. Understand?"

"I figured. Yeah. Fuck."

"I'll call when I can. Meantime, keep the curtains pulled. Trust no one. I don't care who it is. If your mother shows up, shoot her in the head."

"My mother died in 1982."

"Like I said, Carl, if your mother shows up …"

"Where're you going?"

"Chinatown."

I cut the call and mash in seven more numbers. Marigold picks up and croaks out a sleepy greeting on behalf of the Lucky Seven Inn. Not sure what her parents were thinking. Golden perennials are about the last thing that Marigold brings to mind. But then again, Crumpled Cigarette makes for a crappy baby name. It takes her a second to find her memory.

"Mack!" I can hear her fire up a fresh Pall Mall. "Well, I'll be damned."

"What are you doing working the graveyard shift, Goldie? Figured I'd get Frank."

"It's just me now," she says. "Frank found his lost youth inside a lost youth. Said he was in love. Turns out that's not a defense. He's got another nickel to spend in Danville before I can cut his heart out and use it for a pincushion."

"Sorry to hear, Goldie. You're better off. He always seemed bad news to me."

"I heard you went to prison too. They let you out or are you calling me from the Cook County spa?"

"Free as a bird. Always have been. You need to check your sources. Listen, I don't have time to catch up. I'm calling because I've got two people headed your way, looking for a room. Friends of mine. One behind the wheel of a silver Buick and the other having a bad time of it in the trunk. Between them, they have no names, no money and one serious gun. They need one of the back rooms. I'm calling because I'm good for this, Goldie. Give 'em the presidential suite. If anyone comes around asking questions, call me. Don't call the police."

"Jesus, Mack."

"I know. It's a big ask."

I let her smoke.

"Well. I'd be dead if it wasn't for you. But then I guess that's why you called me."

"You're a lot of things, Goldie. Dumb isn't one of them."

"I don't know what you're into, but ..."

"Me neither, but it's up to my armpits."

"Watch yourself, Mack."

"Always do. Thanks, Goldie."

I almost drop the phone back into my pocket. A flashing green dot tells me I've got a new voicemail message from a call I don't remember ever getting. I check the call log. There is no missing call.

I hit the button and listen.

*Hello? Who the hell is this? What makes you think it's okay to wake a man up at two in the morning? Okay, fine. I'm in a buying mood. I'll take a dozen if you tell me what you're selling.*

My ears are ringing with my own voice. I keep pressing the phone to the side of my face like it's a bag of ice. My pulse is stabbing only one icepick-shaped thought into the swollen pink tissue of my brain.

*That is not possible.*

*That is not possible.*

*That. Is Not. Fucking. Possible.*

# TWENTY-SIX

Chinatown at past three in the morning is a cruel tease to a man with an empty stomach. Wentworth Avenue is nothing but an array of signs offering food Ray can't order in a language he can't read. The pagodas are sleeping giants. The karaoke bars are dark and dead.

He settles for an all-night Burger King drive-thru. There're two kids waiting for him at the take-out window, one for each set of chromosomes. They don't seem especially happy to see him. She's tying the guy's apron. Her own apron hangs backward from her neck like a greasy cape. She's missed a button on her blouse.

When they finally get a good look at Ray's face, they cringe. They can't wait to look away again.

Ray drives in slow, square circles, carefully eating his *coitus interruptus* Whopper with the unkicked side of his mouth, craning his neck in all directions. It's been too long. He's got no idea where he's going. It's quarter to four and the Whopper's a memory before he finds the Target.

The lot is empty except for three cars. All three are dark and vacant. All three have big pink Chicago Towing and Impound notices on the windshields. The similarities end there. Only one of them is a white Pontiac. Good bet it's owned by a one-eyed hunk of Swiss cheese rotting in a DeKalb landfill.

# TWENTY-SEVEN

It's good to finally have something to focus my attention. Driving in circles has got me thinking in circles, trying to make sense of modern handheld technology, which is a lot less likely than a pig playing Parcheesi. Put your money on the pig because I can't wring any sense from impossible things that happen anyway. Not on less than one bottle of Forester.

It shouldn't be possible to leave myself a voicemail by answering an incoming call. Maybe if I had a smart phone with a built-in recorder function, I could write the whole thing off as a digital hiccup, something thousands of people are complaining about every day and that some whiz-kid Millennial is busy working overtime, writing code that will fix the problem. But my phone is never going to record my own voice. It doesn't have a recorder. I've got the dumbest phone in the city. *I'm* smarter than my phone. Who can say that these days?

When I'm not puzzling over the voicemail, I ruminate over something less pleasant: Suri's dead friend, Delaney. If seeing yourself from above is a harbinger of doom, then I'm on borrowed time. Somewhere there's a falling piano with my name on it. Not that I make a habit of seeking second-hand wisdom from schizo-junkies. But when you're lying in the dirt kissing the business end of a cowboy boot three hours past your bedtime, your standards for wisdom tend to drop. So I can't help thinking of Delaney, watching himself blow smoke up at Suri's ceiling, days before he died. I can't help thinking of Suri, watching herself coming out of Sluggo's trunk. Climbing up into the big dream that wasn't quite ready for her. Watching. Both of them watching. Just like me.

So either *3-D* is as common as the flu in February or something else is going on.

I make a lazy circle of the Target parking lot, looking for anyone who might be watching me. But I can't stop thinking about the only person I actually know is watching. Me.

# TWENTY-EIGHT

His mind isn't on his work. That'll get him killed.

Ray thumps the steering wheel, kicking himself. He gets it now. He's just paraded his car past a dozen Target parking lot cameras. Eventually some homicide team will get a call about an abandoned car that traces back to a landfill corpse. Someone will think to ask the Target people for the camera footage. Maybe by that time the footage still exists and maybe not. Depends on how soon they find Sluggo Royce and how fast the investigation moves.

Still. It was a rookie mistake. For a cop or a crime writer.

Ray drives off, in no apparent hurry, detouring back toward State Street, and then turns around again before he reaches the freeway. In ten minutes, he's pulling into an empty Wendy's lot. He cuts the engine and sits there, staring at the big red bullseye across the street.

He just sits there.

# TWENTY-NINE

Depersonalization-Derealization Disorder. The big *Triple-D*.

The psych evaluation was Lieutenant Nutsack's idea. I'm as certain of that as I am of anything else. He was convinced he'd found his rat, the mouse in the house taking nuggets of task-force cheese to Big Man's nest. But as the IAD investigation was winding up, Nutsack realized he didn't have the goods. My name in Cosmo Green's cellphone, and Cosmo's name in my cellphone, was damning, but not enough to get me a jumpsuit.

Best Nutsack could do was end my career. He'd have sold his own children to fire me, but someone at City Hall didn't like the idea of buying a lawsuit, let alone a media shit-storm over allegations of organized crime working from inside the Chandler PD. So hush-hush became the plan. Best they would let Nutsack do was force me into early retirement. That went over like month-old chicken salad at a July picnic.

So Nutsack ordered a psych evaluation as part of the investigation. Dr. Lindstrom was the shrink's name. Eric. A little blue-eyed Swede with a cute way of wrinkling his nose when he asked questions that he'd already answered for himself. He'd decided I was crazy before I shook his little hand.

In all my new-found spare time, after it was all over and I was out on my ass, I did a lot of driving around the city. Just me and a gut full of Forester and the Impala and a pack of Camels and a stir-crazy cat that liked the sun coming in above the backseat. As luck would have it, we all regularly ended up a steady half-block behind Dr. Lindstrom's Mercedes. Every day for a while there. Turns out that every couple of weekends Lindstrom and Nutsack like digging up the fairway together out at the Springwell Country Club. They'd make an afternoon of it and then take their little white balls for a drink at the Back Nine Bar and Grille.

Can't say I was surprised. It actually felt good to make sense of it. For a couple of weeks, I was able to convince myself that I wasn't actually crazy. The psych eval was always just a vindictive ruse to keep me from ever working in law enforcement again. A way to twist the knife in my back as I took my retirement. Then Nutsack leaked Lindstrom's evaluation, just to make sure it was a knife I'd never be able to reach.

But here's the thing. Lindstrom wasn't wrong. The crazy is real. At least the *Triple-D* is real. No question I was a sap for being honest. Honest about my grief over Marlo. About my special out-of-body perspective on my bald spot. About all of it. But Lindstrom wasn't wrong.

He'd asked me why I spent so much time imagining myself in the third-person. Following myself around like a suspect. I'd told him I have no idea. Then he'd wrinkled his nose and asked if maybe it was because I felt guilty. Like maybe I considered myself a suspect just like IAD and everybody else did. Like maybe I'd split myself in two so that one of me could follow and accuse the other. One of me was a liar no one could trust and the other of me knew the truth and would always sit in judgment over what I'd done.

Lindstrom had thought the theory worth another nose-wrinkle and a nod as he made some notes.

The report made for a good read. Confirmed what everyone had already been led to believe: Ray Mackey was not just corrupt; he was so corrupt he was crazy. Nutsack had waited for word to get around before closing the investigation and retiring me like a lame racehorse.

The fix was in. No question. They'd cooked this one up one afternoon standing in the dogleg rough three strokes away from the eighteenth hole.

But Lindstrom wasn't wrong. One of me *is* a liar. One of me *will* always sit in judgment. Put me together in one man? I'm as guilty and as crazy as they come.

# THIRTY

Ray pops the trunk and gets out. He unrolls the garbage, tears off two sizable sections of dirty sheet, closes the trunk and heads off across the road. He skirts the perimeter of the Target lot, staying out of likely camera range until he's close to the abandoned Pontiac. He takes one section of sheet and wraps it loosely around his head. Lawrence of Suburbia coming to storm big-box retail. He wraps the other section of sheet around his right hand.

But Lawrence of Suburbia is not here for supplies. He's here to wipe down a car. Like a homeless hard-luck case with a squeegee, hoping for some loose change. He works clockwise, from the trunk, up the driver's side, around the front, down the passenger side and back again, wiping down anything Suri might conceivably have touched. He tries each door handle as he goes. The car is locked tight, just like she said.

# THIRTY-ONE

I have to walk halfway back to Wendy's before I find something that will do the job, a length of pipe in the gutter. Somewhere a metal skeleton is missing a femur. I walk back to the Pontiac, then take a last quiet look at the dim parking lot before I start swinging. I feel the cameras at my back, projecting the company logo between my shoulder blades. I feel like the word on the building. It only takes one swing.

The car alarm comes at me like an angry, shrieking bird. I'm expecting the parking lot to suddenly light up like a prison yard in mid-riot. I'm inside Sluggo's car in two seconds, diving under the dashboard, pulling at wires until the sound finally stops.

I keep moving, resisting the urge to lie there quietly on bits of broken glass, half in and half out, listening for trouble. I wipe down every surface Suri could have reached from the driver's seat and, just in case her memory was spotty, even some places she could have never reached. I find the release and pop the trunk, then head around back for a look inside.

Sluggo's gun is right where she said it'd be. A Model 10 Smith & Wesson thirty-eight. Not a gun for today's criminals. Heavy carbon steel with only six bullets loaded one at a time into a rotating cylinder? Not if you're an ambitious, self-respecting thug. Gang-banging today with a Model 10 isn't much better than showing up with a flintlock and a powder horn.

Also not a gun for cops, for whom keeping ballistic pace with the bad guys is the difference between life and death. Today it's the Austrians and Germans everyone is looking to. The Sigs and the Glocks with more and more Italian Berettas in the mix. High ammo capacity on the inside, lightweight polymer on the outside. Feels like a toy, kills like a plague.

I feel the weight of the thing in my hand as I wipe it down with the sheet.

The Model 10 S&W is as American as apple pie and Type II Diabetes, but it's no longer a tool of the trade. Not anymore. But it sure used to be. Used to be every cop on the street was carrying a Model 10. Yours truly included.

I open it up. It's empty and I know where the bullets are. I snap it closed again. I start to drop it back where I found it, but then I stick it into my belt under my shirt. Dumb move, I know. Taking personal possession of a murder weapon. But my jaw and my gut make out a convincing case about not getting murdered before I can make it to my own gun safe. I figure the ammo is around somewhere. I wipe down the rest of the trunk and move on to the passenger side.

For a lowlife bruiser, Sluggo Royce kept a reasonably clean car. The backseat leather tells me nothing and the passenger seat isn't talking either. But I don't make it easy. I keep at it until the inside of that Pontiac finally begins to sing.

Turns out Royce was big into cheddar popcorn. Reindeer jerky. The dark chaos of Gotham that only Batman can bring to heel. Also photography.

The camera is tucked down between the front seats. Nothing fancy. A flat, silver thing maybe half-again the size of my curiously possessed, unsmart cellphone. I push the top button. It beeps and comes to life, the lens telescoping out like it's glad to see me. I push the button above the back screen. It blazes white with a Sony logo, then resolves to show the front entrance of a building. Wide double doors atop a slope of graciously scalloped concrete steps.

I suppose Royce could've had some fascination for the architecture of municipal police departments. But I'm going out on a limb to think that maybe he was more interested in the guy coming out of those big double doors at the top of the steps.

Swinging those long, rubbery arms.

# THIRTY-TWO

The Pontiac is a pale bubble of light floating in a dark, grey sea of concrete. Ray's down there, half in the bubble and half out, bent inside the passenger door, head wrapped in a sheet, looking at a camera, oblivious to who or what may be headed his way.

His instincts have always served him well. Eyes in the back of his head. The sixth sense that's putting in overtime before the other five senses are through the first cup of coffee. The sense that knows things he doesn't really know. All of that.

But everything decays. Everything atrophies. He used to be in shape. The square, unpadded jaw. Shoulders. Arms. Abs. Back in the day, a punch in the puss by Ray Mackey would put you down and make you think about whether you wanted to get back up again. Maybe you didn't get up. Maybe you just lay there and remembered your mother and said you were sorry.

But now. The only thing this lump has been punching in the past five years are a time clock at the mall and the keys of his Smith Corona. The hair on the top of his head has long since walked off the job and the muscle has gone doughy. His eyes still work a full shift, but the knees and the back are goldbrick whiners always looking for a chair, preferably the reclining kind with a cat on it. He's not the taut, humming guitar string he used to be.

So does Ray see the white Kia with the corporate security logo on the side? Does he notice it rounding the corner and moving slowly along the front of the building?

Sure he does. Just look at the old boy stiffen. Like he's been touched with an electric prod. Look at him climb inside and close the door and smother the Pontiac's overhead light with his sheet until it finally suffocates and dies.

The question is not whether he sees the threat. Any shmuck with two eyes can see a pair of headlights. The question is whether he's seen them in time. Having a sixth sense is all about feeling the threat *before* you can see it. Ray can't do that anymore. Not like he once could.

# THIRTY-THREE

The Kia's a sad little thing. It's shaped like it aspires to be an SUV, but it's never going to make it. It's missing the length, the heft and the attitude. It stops and idles in front of the dark, empty store like a shopping cart separated from the herd. Behind the wheel I can see a fat man in a blue uniform. He's bent down into the glow of a phone and eating a powdered donut.

He's me, this guy. Pretend law enforcement. Guardian of corporate brick-and-mortar retail. Maybe this is the future I'm seeing. Maybe I'm spying on myself with a zoom that can see me five years and eighty-five pounds from now. Royce's Model 10 gouges me in the back, suggesting that I go ahead and end things before my life rolls to the bottom of that hill.

But then who's going to feed Phil?

I power down the camera and tuck it into my pocket. I don't have the luxury of waiting around to see whether this guy's going to turn my way or go for another donut. I keep moving, wiping down everything and looking everywhere I can.

In the glovebox, I find a pair of gloves. Two pair. Three. Not much of a defense against an average January blowing in off the lakes. Each pair is made of powder-blue latex. Either

Sluggo had a strange sense of summer fashion or shy fingerprints.

I keep digging. Screwdriver. Flashlight. Superman. Aquaman. A ziplock bag of Beer Nuts. A ziplock bag with a hairbrush and toothpicks and a small bottle of Tabasco. A complimentary plastic bottle of Chicago Mobile Health hand sanitizer. A pair of tweezers.

A box of ammo for the thirty-eight.

I take the time to open up the Model 10 and feed it until it's full, then snap it closed again. And then I see something else.

In the back of the compartment, my fingers close around a shape I know well. I steal a quick glance at future me, working on donut number two. He's got a cop's yen for fried sugar and dough. I extract my hand.

The thing is fifty calibers of hollow, brass intrigue. About the size of a lipstick. I let it roll around in my palm and then look inside, half-expecting to see a folded-up piece of paper. The car's too dark. If there's anything in there, I can't see it. I try Sluggo's flashlight, but it's as dead as he is. I'm about to stuff the casing in my pocket when I can almost hear Suri's voice.

*You'd need tweezers.*

I sort through the junk in the glovebox again, trying to find the tweezers. I find a second shell casing. Then a third. When I find the tweezers, I insert them into each casing, trying to sense a paper-strength resistance. Nothing.

Movement. I look up.

The guard is out, shuffling for the front doors of the store. I'm fresh out of time.

I shove the casings and tweezers into a pocket and dive back into the glovebox, looking for the one thing that's actually supposed to be in there. I find it and yank, keeping one eye on the guard who's cupping his hands against the glass door of the store. A few seconds and he's going to turn around. Then the only things between us will be the Kia, whatever's left of the donuts, and this windshield.

I have to squint in the dark to read. The Pontiac sleeps at 6912 Wolcott out in East Village. A guy by the name of Anthony J. Rickens keeps it clean and tucks it in every night. Not recently, I'm betting.

Not Royce. Rickens. Either Royce is driving Rickens' car. Or Rickens is picking up Royce's dry cleaning. Where there was one, now there are two. I can relate.

Rent-a-cop is headed back to the Kia. Head down, looking at his phone.

I wipe down the glovebox and punch the overhead light until the plastic housing cracks. I break the bulb inside before pulling the latch on the door.

A cessation of movement. I look.

He's looking directly at me. Over the top of his car. Across maybe eight hundred feet of parking lot. At me. Or, at the very least, at the white Pontiac with the shattered driver's side window. I can't tell what he's thinking. I don't dare push open the door. All I can do is wait.

Soon enough he's back in the Kia. Maybe he's moving on. But I can see he's moving his arms and head with more purpose than before.

It's not bullets that kill the rent-a-cops, it's the boredom. Finding something new and non-routine to investigate on your shift is better than any donut. It's gold. It's finding the map to Jimmy Hoffa's body in a fortune cookie.

No way he's moving on. Not now. He's coming over for a closer look.

# THIRTY-FOUR

The passenger door eases open. Ray backs out slowly in a deep crouch, like an ugly duckling escaping the wing of a swan. He clicks the door closed just as the Kia starts to move, starting a wide arc in his direction. Ray looks behind him. Lots of open space between where he's squatting and the road and the Wendy's beyond. He could run for it. But he knows better. He's old, not stupid.

The headlights sweep through the hot air like a bird of prey on the hunt.

Ray drops to his knees.

# THIRTY-FIVE

My relationship with dirty pavement has become far too intimate. I need to consider other options. A mattress or couch cushions is asking too much. I'll settle for a sunny patch of shag in the winter and cool linoleum in the summer. But doing the dirty twice in one night with concrete is making me feel cheap.

That and my face has a bad case of PTSD. It's waiting for another boot.

I inch myself sideways, just like before, hoping the donut diet will keep this guy from bending over and looking under the car.

Turns out it's *my* diet that's the problem. Even when I pull Sluggo's gun out of my belt and try to flatten myself in all directions like pancake batter on a hot griddle, there is no way I'm fitting under this car. So I'm stuck on the griddle, lying here like a fat roll of bratwurst clutching a Model 10 Smith & Wesson.

The Kia laps my body with a fat tongue of light as it swoops in front of the Pontiac and stops. It backs up. It slowly pulls forward around the driver's side. I can see the tires roll into view, crunching over the broken glass. He's lining up the driver's windows. The Kia's so close to the Pontiac that there's no way for him to open the door.

Only one reason to do it that way. He doesn't plan on opening the door.

I hold my breath and listen to him call it in. He reports it to his dispatch as vandalism of a white Pontiac with a tow warning on the windshield. Broken driver's side window. Nothing inside. They want him to *10-12* while they relay to real police. Future me gives them a confident *10-4* and has himself another donut.

# THIRTY-SIX

He lies there on the ground, battered face on his folded arms, like he's decided to make it a night. He moves only once the Kia is fully out of the parking lot and moving up the access road. He stands slowly and brushes himself off, tucking the evidence that might eventually convict him of murder back into his belt. Using the sheet, he opens the car door and rummages through the glovebox. When he reemerges, he's got the screwdriver and the registration.

He removes both plates. First the back, then the front. Then he goes to work on the VIN tags. He's thinking that if they haven't already made a note of the plate numbers, then maybe it will take them a little longer to connect the Pontiac with whoever's body is rotting in the heat out in DeKalb.

A long shot, sure, but then what isn't? Two inches closer to the sun and the whole planet's a charcoal briquette. Two inches farther away and it's a frozen rock. Life itself has been a miracle on the run from the very first second. We're lucky to be here at all. So he thinks to himself *what the hell* and takes the registration and the plates and then pries off the VIN tags.

The clock is running. Always is. For everyone. He needs all the time he can get.

# THIRTY-SEVEN

I dump the plates and VIN tags in the Wendy's dumpster. I climb into the Impala and take a slug of Old Forester. Second time in one night I've broken my own rule about drinking in the car. Second time I haven't cared. The Model 10 goes under the seat and I head for home.

The pain in my face and jaw is the only thing that's keeping me awake, that and the horn on the bossy blue Dodge that doesn't want to share lanes. I think of home like the whole house is made entirely of pillow. Phil is purring in my head.

Marlo comes to me like a dream.

*Always get to the party first, Ray. And if you can't be first, then be invisible.*

I make a detour to the Chandler airport and park the Impala in the short-term lot. I reach under the seat and return the thirty-eight to where it wants to be. Then I walk to the terminal and wake up a cabbie with a knuckle to the window. He's Indian or Pakistani. Twenty-five, if he's a day. His big brown eyes flutter open like wings, then pulse at me in shock. His mouth is asking about luggage, but those eyes are asking about my face.

It's a short drive. He thinks maybe I want to talk about the heat. I tell him it's too hot to talk about anything and almost too hot to calculate a tip. He takes the hint. He pulls a cigarette from his pocket and lights it up, breaking some rule somewhere but sizing me up as someone who's not going to complain. He reads me like a book. One I wish I was home writing.

"Got another one of those?" I ask.

He looks at me in the rearview mirror and puts his finger to his lips.

"Shhh." He shakes his head sadly. "Too hot for questions."

"Smartass." I dig in my pocket for my wallet and pull out a ten. "I'll trade you a founding father for the rest of the pack and a light."

He smiles and hands me the pack from his shirt pocket, swapping it for the ten.

Luck may be a lady, but right now, in my condition, she looks an awful lot like a Camel. There're five sticks and a lighter inside. I fire one up and pat the cabbie on the shoulder.

"Is it too hot for a name?" I ask. "Mine's Ray. Friends call me Mack."

He extracts a card from his bottomless shirt pocket and hands it back without a word. The kid – Raj Malik – really wants that tip.

I make it easy for him. I lean back and open the window and blow smoke out into the warm morning air. I try to stay awake and keep my mind off the pain in my face by thinking about the boot that put it there.

The foot in the boot belonged to a man with a badge. A cop who didn't know me would have called me *Mr. Mackey* or *Raymond.* Or even *Ray* if he was being cute. But this man with a badge – Crewcut Pete, was it? – had called me Mack. *Shut the fuck up, Mack.* Which means either I know Pete from someplace, and I'm reasonably sure I don't, or Pete knows me. But how? Through whom?

I can't answer that question before it gets a boot to the face from the next question, which is why not take me down at the liquor store? If Sergeant Twill wanted Suri for his investigation, then why not have his boys storm the place before I have a chance to knife her or strangle her to death, wrap her in a sheet and drop her in my trunk? Why hang around outside until I leave, follow me for ten minutes and then hit the lights and siren and pull me over?

These are Wednesday crossword questions, just tough enough to make you feel smart.

Deno and Pete weren't working an investigation, that's why. Deno and Pete were working a coverup. Deno and Pete were Big Man's boys. They want Suri dead and they were expecting me to find her so they could pull her plug. They were planning to wait until I left, but then it turned out I had plans of my own. Just maybe I'd done the dirty work for them and they could arrest me for murder and call it a night. They didn't realize I was just taking out the garbage.

I want to linger on what must have been the looks on their faces after having pumped three rounds of hot lead into a bag of trash. I want to enjoy it. That little movie could last me a whole Camel. But then another question swans into the party and orders a drink: Just how high up does all this go?

That was a Saturday crossword question, hard enough to make you want to set fire to the morning paper and swap the orange juice for something stronger to chase the aspirin.

My Camel runs out of gas just past Chandler High School, home of the Falcons. Raj hands back an empty plastic water bottle for the butt. I unscrew the top and drop it in, pointing at the corner.

"Up here to the left, then right on Maltese. And keep it slow, Raj. I want our time together to last."

Raj cuts his speed and rounds the last corner onto my street. I slump down in the backseat and take inventory. My house is right where I left it. The lights are out and the driveway is empty. It comes and goes, shrinking in the back window like one of those little plastic houses you buy along with a waving paperboy and a few little plastic cows to go along with your model train set, just to give the imaginary passengers on board something to look at again and again.

There's an SUV parked at my neighbor's curb. A black Nissan that comes complete with a kayak rack, running boards, and two greasy lug-nuts smoking cigarettes in the front seat. They've got a spare in the back, just for good measure.

"Which one," asks Raj, coasting on by to the end of the street.

"Can't miss it," I tell him as I reach for another Camel. "Great big place where all the planes land."

# THIRTY-EIGHT

There he sits. Our man. Slumped against the glass in a window booth like a bag of dirty laundry someone left behind as a tip. Daisy Mae's is the only decent coffee shop on West Sixteenth. White speckled linoleum, cranberry vinyl, polished chrome and a bud vase with two daisies on every table. Owner is an old vet named Larson. Larson's in a wheelchair and a long way from being mistaken for anyone named Daisy Mae. Ray figures there's some in-country ghost with that name that Larson carries around in his wallet.

He likes the place as much for Alice and the pie as he does the coffee. They all come as a package. He never has to order any more. Alice knows. She's not Daisy Mae either, but she could be if she wanted to.

The Title One America building looms across the street, a sleek, black glass obelisk that reflects the sun climbing out of bed and stretching its arms as it starts looking under rocks for hangovers and concussions. Alice breezes by and freshens up his cup, taking the empty plate.

"Aspirin kicked in yet?" She asks.

She's an easy blond breeze, this kid. Young and naïve and full of light. She's the wildflower growing on the side of the interstate. The comic strip stuck between the crime blotter and the obituaries.

"Don't say *kicked*, Alice. It's my new least favorite word."

"Well, you should report whoever did this to the police."

"They didn't do it to the police. They did it to me. The police are just fine. And that happens to be my second least favorite word, by the way. You're on a hot streak, kid. Let's go to a casino, just you and me."

Alice smiles with a beautiful kind of sadness, a passing, wistful cloud in a summer sky. She sets down the plate and lifts his chin with two fingers for a better look at the damage.

"Well, I hope you got a picture of them at least," she says, nodding at the camera in his hands. "And if you stayed away from bars, Mack, you wouldn't get into bar fights."

"Ahhh. So that's why they call 'em that? How'd you get to be so smart?"

Her fingers drop his chin and push his shoulder.

"Advice is on the house, tough guy. I'll bring you something for your headache. Anything else?"

"Three eggs, scrambled. And a raw steak for my face."

Alice laughs and shakes her head as she picks up the empty plate.

"Only one I know that orders pie before breakfast."

"Here's a little wisdom from an old man that you can tuck into your apron for later. Life's uncertain, Alice. Eat dessert first."

# THIRTY-NINE

By the time the eggs arrive, the sun has climbed up to the second story of the Title One America building and I'm on my third trip through the photos on Tony Rickens' Sony. There are forty-three photos. Some landscapes. A house here and there. But mostly Tony was a portrait guy. Loved capturing people. Loved it so much that sometimes he put the people he captured in the trunk of his car for a trip out to the landfill.

I don't know all the people in the photos. Most of them I don't. But four of them poke me in the eyes. Number 43 is Andrew Harold "Harpo" Marx, coming out of the Chandler Police Department. Harpo again in Number 38, swinging a workout bag, crossing the parking lot to Jimmy's Gym. Numbers 21 through 33 are devoted to Suri. On the street. Getting in and out of cars. One of her coming out of her apartment. All of them early last summer, according to the date stamp.

Numbers 13 and 18 are of yours truly. One from across the street, me holding a bag of groceries as I unlock my front door. Another of me coming out of Bucks, taken from the lot across from The Bodega. Both show snow on the ground. Five years ago.

But Number 6 is the one I can't stop staring at. It is the reason I don't pick up a fork and start in on the scrambled eggs when Alice brings them to the table and refills my cup. Number 6 takes my breath and doesn't give it back.

Veronica Lodge is wearing a kelly-green blouse, standing in a second-story bedroom window, pulling the curtains. Behind her in the glow of the room is the dark shape of a man's shoulder. March. Five years ago.

"You okay, Mack?" Alice touches my shoulder. It makes me jolt and I turn off the camera. The lens retracts like it's scared or offended and the whole thing goes dark.

"Old photos," I say, slipping it back into my pocket. "Like looking at ghosts sometimes."

Alice moves on as I reach for the Tabasco and shake it too vigorously over the eggs. My aim is off. It takes a napkin dipped in my water glass to get up all the red spatter.

Not that it really does any good. Still feels like I've got blood on my hands.

# FORTY

He's like a sleeping child. Curled up in the backseat, dead to the world. Waiting for his mother to come back, put the shopping bags in the trunk and take him home. But Ray's are not the dreams of a child. He's climbing for the big dream now. Hand over hand over hand, out of the dark trunk of this life and up into the bright effusion of cloud, looking back down over his shoulder at the world pulling on his ankle. Look at his legs, twitching against the seat. This is the big escape.

Sad, silly Ray. Can't see what's coming. Can't see what's on the other side of the glass.

# FORTY-ONE

I rocket awake in the backseat. A man in cop costume is knocking on the window. I rub my eyes and shake my head and then wish I hadn't. The air is hot and stale. My watch and my internal clock accuse each other of lying about the time. He knocks again. It's not a costume. I shut my eyes in a quiet panic as I rummage my brain for some recall of Sluggo's thirty-eight. And the booze.

He's got me out on the sidewalk next to the expired meter before I find my memory tucked away in the trunk with the gun and the Old Forester. He asks about my face like he needs a good story to pass the time as he looks over my license and registration. So I tell him I'm all feet in a life full of rakes. He smirks and tells me I can't sleep on the curb, even if I'm in a car. I want to argue with him. I want to tell him that I can do whatever I goddamn want in the backseat of my own car as long as it's legal and I keep the meter plugged.

But the red flag on the meter is waving its hand to get in a word and the dead man's gun wants out of the trunk, so I decide to keep it short. I apologize and tell the man in blue that he's right. I give him my best impersonation of contrition. He gives me a parking ticket and a free *next time will be different* look over the top of his sunglasses.

I point the Impala north, in the direction of Bricktown. My head and face are swollen and throbbing. Alice's little white pill must be the kind that provides moral support and encouragement, the kind that thinks acetaminophen is a crutch and that wants me to heal my pain without drugs. I'd like to argue the point but my head hurts. I light up a Camel instead and let the nicotine do the talking. Ten-thirty in the morning and the air whipping in through the window is already too hot. Like I'm blowing smoke into the gullet of a dragon.

It's a serious risk that I'm wasting my time. People move on. They change jobs and choose to live in different places. They cut their hair and get married and have kids and become different than they used to be. Not everyone lives in an eddy as I do.

But it's a risk I need to take.

I pull out my phone to check in on Suri and Carl. But then I think better of it. Suri needs to sleep for a week. I call my neighbor instead.

Judy Kravitz is in her early seventies. She moved in just after Marlo passed. Nice enough over the back fence, but Judy's the nervous sort. She's got a healthy case of hypochondriasis with a double side of paranoia. No doubt she has her suspicions about me. I've played up the retired cop angle for all it's worth, but that will take me only so far. What self-respecting paranoid trusts cops, even the retired kind? Fortunately, Judy's a cat person. She'll do anything for Phil, including give the benefit of the doubt to the lump who pays the vet bills.

Judy answers on the first ring. I tell her that the boys downtown are warning people to be on the lookout for unfamiliar cars parked in the neighborhood. Idling, smoke-filled, black SUVs in particular. I tell her to call the police if she sees something suspicious. I can hear her on the move, making a beeline to the nearest window. I tell her I'm out of town on an errand and ask if she'll go over this afternoon and open a can of food for Phil. She's done it before. She's got her own key.

Judy makes a gasping sound that tells me the motley crew is still parked on her curb. I can feel her thumb make a panicked leap for the number nine. The call disconnects. But my cellphone decides it's not done. It jangles up at me like an old-timey telephone.

*Unknown Caller. Number Blocked.*

All I can do is stare at the damned thing in my hand. Three jangles, extra loud. I've tried not answering because I'm busy. I've tried not answering out of irritation and anger. Then I've tried answering and ended up leaving myself a message. This time I think I'll try something new and not answer out of a sense of confusion and foreboding.

When the sound stops, I call Marigold and ask about the others.

"Wasn't happy coming out of that trunk, Mack. Well, I'm pretty sure she was happy to be out but not so happy about having been in. Holy crap. Thought she was going to shoot us both with that thing. It's bigger than she is. The guy, what's his name, he calmed her down soon enough. I dropped by an hour later with some bagels and candy bars. You know, the presidential suite breakfast here at the Lucky Seven. She was sleeping like a baby. I'm guessing she'll be out till early afternoon. You coming out?"

"Later. Some things to take care of first."

"Busy, are we?"

"I have to show an ugly face to a beautiful woman."

"Show her yours instead, Mack."

"Keep your eyes open, Goldie. Call me if you need me."

# FORTY-TWO

He gets lost twice, road construction forcing detours into corners of Bricktown and West Lakeview that he doesn't care to explore and that obstruct his memory. Back in the day, Veronica Lodge lived a couple blocks off North Leavitt, south of Clybourn Avenue, where a good arm could send a small rock into the Chicago River. Takes him awhile, but he eventually finds the neighborhood, then the street and then the house. It's a cute little number, with a tidy front porch and concrete pavers like gray lily pads across a small green lawn to the sidewalk. The house was always cuter than Veronica Lodge, but only in the way that a ladybug is cuter than Lady Godiva.

He parks up the street and watches.

I know what he's thinking. The lie he's trying to sell. He's telling himself that he's just getting the lay of the land; looking for anything out of the ordinary; making sure he's got the right place and that she still lives here. But the only thing out of the ordinary is the strange guy in an Impala, smoking a Camel at the curb, checking his swollen mug in the rearview mirror and trying to scrape together some nerve. If you didn't know any better, you'd expect a corsage next to him in the front seat.

Come on, Ray. Pull yourself together.

# FORTY-THREE

I cross the street easily enough but climbing those four little steps to the porch is like marching up the down escalator. There may be other things in the world that I want to do less than this, but I can't think of them. Even Crewcut Pete's boot is looking pretty good. I take a breath and ring the bell.

I can feel eyes at my back as I wait and listen for movement inside. I could teach Judy Kravitz a thing or two about paranoia. I do my best to ignore the sensation. I poke the house again.

I feel better when she doesn't answer. My confidence returns, all sheepish and shy and full of excuses, just as I'm turning to leave. I look up and down the street. If someone is watching me, they're not interested in me returning the favor. I take the first step down to the yard but the door behind me has other plans.

"Hello, Mack."

"Hello, Ronni." I say it to the street and to the guys with the coffee breath and the donut-dusted, two-day beards and the binoculars that I can't see.

I turn around to find the past leaning up against the doorframe in bare feet, blue jeans and a butter-yellow cotton blouse that knows how to fit in all the right places. Veronica's got a face for old magazines and classic movies, the kind that makes a man wish hats hadn't gone the way of the pocket watch. She's cuddling a large mug of coffee like it's a puppy.

Ronni. She hasn't aged. She hasn't moved on. She hasn't swapped addresses or cut her dark mahogany hair. It's Ronni. And it's me looking at Ronni. Just like always.

Then I see myself in her expression.

"Jesus, Mack. I hope the other guy looks as bad as you do."

"Trust me, the other guy's never going to get that blood off his boot. Thought maybe you weren't home."

"You know my shift. And my number." She looks down into her coffee. "Not that you ever use it."

"It's not like you've been calling me, either."

"You told me not to. You know that."

"I don't know anything anymore, Ronni. I don't know the time of day. All my clocks have gone cuckoo. I take it you're still punching a clock at the asylum."

"The asylum." She laughs a little. "We're not all crazy, Mack."

"No," I say. "Just me. I thought there was a chance you'd quit that place."

"Once a cop ..." She shrugs and takes a sip.

"Not me, Ronni. I was once a cop. Now I'm not anymore."

"And how's it taste?"

"Like a shit sandwich with pickles and a side of lonely. But I sleep at night."

Ronni smiles in that way she does, half-mocking, half-secret.

"Sleeping with a clean conscience, are we?"

"I sleep alone. I can't speak for you, but my conscience hasn't slept or taken a bath since the last time I stood on this porch."

She drinks her coffee and sizes me up like she's deciding whether to respond.

"And you're putting that weight on me?"

"No. That's my anvil to drag around."

"Lie much, Mack?"

"Only when I'm awake."

"So why should I get a pass? Takes two to tango. Right?"

"I had left-feet enough for both of us, Ronni. Maybe you let me make the mistake but I was the one who made it. Every day a new excuse kicks open my door and sashays in with a sales pitch. And every night I drown the bastard in a glass. Because I don't get an excuse. I carry this one to the bitter end."

"Jesus." She shakes her head in soft amazement. "I'd kind of forgotten your anti-self-righteousness. No one beats up on you like you. You always beat them to the punch, don't you? Maybe you should check your own boots for that blood."

"And, not for nothin' but I should have called. I should have explained. The earth swallowed me up, Ronni. The job saved me from myself for a while. Me and my perfect pink pancreas. But I didn't have room left for anything or anyone."

"Especially not me."

"Yeah. Yeah, that's right. And I'm sorry for it."

"Why are you here, Mack? To apologize? You could have called. I'm in your phone. Right there with Cosmo Green."

Classic Ronni. Icy cool on the outside, molten on the inside. It's a hard slap and it stings. I let it go, shrugging it off like that kind of remark can't hurt me anymore.

"That's not why I'm here. And this isn't a phone-call-kind of conversation. Yeah, you're still in my phone. You'll always be in my phone, Ronni, and maybe that should concern both of us. But forget about whose phone you're in. You should be more concerned that you're in a dead man's camera."

I finally have her attention. Ronni takes me in slowly from head to toe. Then she turns and walks off into the house.

She leaves the door open.

# FORTY-FOUR

She puts him at the kitchen table. The room is orderly and clean, sunlight buffing squares of deep-blue tile, splashing off the glass and stainless steel. A wicker ceiling fan stirs the air like three spoons in a bowl of hot coffee. It tries to turn the page of the *Trib* that sits open on the table to "Lifestyle" but keeps dropping the corner.

"Still into the horoscopes, I see," he says.

"Wouldn't miss it."

"Did it say something about an unexpected visitor? Maybe someone looking like the after-picture in a drive-safely ad?"

She doesn't answer, scooping the paper away. She slides a mug in front of him and fills it with coffee. Ray sits up straight in the chair, self-conscious about his posture. Trying to suck in his gut. He watches her walk the pot slowly back to the counter like someone who doesn't mind the supervision.

"So. Are you … *with* someone?" he asks.

She turns, lifting an amused eyebrow. Bad banter, Ray. Come on, you putz.

"Next question," she says. But then she sighs indulgently. "No."

"How is that even possible, Ronni?"

"Trying to quit," she says. "I joined assholes anonymous. You?"

"Come on. It's me and my cat and a half-empty bottle. That's about as much as I can handle. You still working up in Records?"

She nods and pulls out a chair.

"They moved the whole department under HR."

"Well, that sounds about as fun as making origami in the rain. Guess you don't get ..."

She cuts him off, waving the back of her hand.

"Enough, Mack. This isn't how I want to spend my day off."

"Okay." Ray squares himself to the table. "I'm not here to waste your time. I'll keep it short. You know a man named Anthony Rickens?"

"No. Should I?"

"I don't know. That's why I'm sitting here."

"What's he into?"

"He's big into recycling right now."

"He's the dead guy?"

Ray nods. "Pretty sure, anyway." He fishes for the camera.

"So?"

"So he knew you."

He turns on the camera and queues up photo six of forty-three. The woman in the window, pulling the curtains. Behind her, the dark shape of a man's shoulder. He turns it around and hands it to her. He watches her face. Her eyes take it in like two sponges dropped in a puddle.

"That's you," he says.

"Yes. It is."

"And that's me."

"Yes, it is."

"Five years ago. The Westmark."

"Yes."

"Why, Ronni? How?"

She looks up at him for the first time. Then back down at the camera.

"I don't know. What's his name? Riggins?"

"Rickens. Anthony J. Lives out in East Village. On Wolcott."

They stare at each other as she holds the camera with one hand and tips her mug with the other. Ray watches her throat take the coffee.

"How'd he go?" she asks.

"Not quietly."

She looks at him hard, understanding what she shouldn't yet. No slouch, Ronni.

"Jesus, Mack."

"What."

"You want me to look him up. Five years and here you are. Always helpful to have an ex-mistress working in Records with access to a police database."

"That's not what this is, Ronni. You're in the photo. I'm here out of concern."

"Sweet. So you don't need me to risk my pension for a little extracurricular research."

Ray doesn't respond. Because he can't.

"And I'm supposed to do this for *you* of all people. Maybe if the Pope needed a solid, Mack. But *you*? They'd tar-and-feather me and then they'd fire me alright. Out of a goddamned cannon."

She leans in against the table, like the thing she needs to tell him next is top secret. Like she needs to whisper. Her face is young and flush and naked. Ronni needs cosmetics like Popeye needs a can opener. Look at him. The lump. The sap. Look at his nostrils flare, taking her in again. She smells like lipstick on a cocktail napkin. Whether she needs to whisper or not, she does it anyway.

"Don't know if you're aware ... *Mack* ... but you're not real popular over there."

He doesn't back away. Their faces could squeeze a balloon.

"Come on, Ronni. You're telling me you're not just a little curious?"

She seems to replay the question in her head a couple of times. Then she leans back and hands over the camera.

"It's in the past, Ray. It's done. We're done. He's just some guy with a camera getting his jollies. Can't begrudge a man for looking. I've been looked at before. Plenty. Haven't I?"

The flirtation is hard for him to ignore. She waits for him to pick it up like a fifty-cent piece glinting in the gutter. Certainly counterfeit. She's testing him. He resists.

"You're not seeing the big picture here, Ronni. Rickens is rapidly becoming one with a landfill. He bought the farm working for Big Man. These aren't opinions. And I don't want to hear any cheap-shot bullshit about me and Cosmo Green. You're not the only person in this camera. You're not the only *cop* in this camera. Or the only woman. One of the others recently took a long ride in a small trunk. I put in thirty years at CPD. I know other people with access to a police database. But I came to you."

She's not buying it. Doesn't even blink.

"Yeah? Any of those other people with access not want to cut out your tongue?"

"That what you want to do, Ronni? Cut out my tongue?"

"Wrong body part, Mack. You weren't the only one in a relationship."

Ray blinks. He even swallows. Worlds are colliding in his head. He doesn't want this conversation. I can tell he wants to stand up and walk out. He wants to run. Outside, a chopper throttles up and past. He waits until it fades.

"Yeah, well I was *married*, Ronni. Your ... *relationship*, as you call it, was all but dead. You said so."

"Yeah, well, not dead enough. I paid a price. We both paid."

"What are you saying? What price?"

She looks down at the mug and takes a breath. Then she swallows.

"I'm saying my *relationship* found out ... about *us* ... just like your *marriage* found out."

Ray's face retracts, like it needs some greater distance from the words she's speaking. Words he doesn't understand. Like she's inexplicably slipped into Farsi.

"My wife never found out, Ronni. My wife knew everything else. Everything in the world about anything, she knew it." He holds up the camera. "But she died never knowing ... *this*. And I thank the god I don't believe in every single day."

Ronni studies him from across the table. Quiet. Almost sad. Like he's a three-legged puppy trying to climb up onto a sofa.

"No. Mack. Listen to me. She *did* find out. He told her."

"No. You don't under ..."

"Goddamnit, Mack." She smacks the table with her hand. His entire body tenses. "Shut up for two seconds. Listen."

"I am listening. Ronni. I am. I'm just not understanding."

"My stupid shit-head of a boyfriend told her. He found us out, Mack."

"How?"

"Fuck if I know how. Maybe your dead friend there showed him a picture. Point is, he tracked her down in a rage and he told her."

"My wife. He told ..."

"*Marlo*. Ray. He tracked Marlo down and he told her. I figured ... I figured ..." She breaks off and shakes her head in disbelief. Her flawless forehead is perplexed. "You mean she never ... *told* you? She never told you that she knew? Ah, Jesus, Mack."

Poor Ray. I can see the blood draining from his face. He doesn't care anymore about his posture or his gut. Doesn't care about how he looks to Veronica Lodge, Destroyer of Worlds. He sags in the chair like he's been knifed. He's forgotten about the coffee in his hand. He swallows bitter air instead. Black, no sugar.

"How do you know this? Ronni, how ..."

"Because my asshole-for-a-boyfriend told me. Maybe ten days after you gave me your big speech and turned invisible. He knew I was ready to kick him to the curb. And you were salt in the wound. So he wanted to make it hurt. He knocked me around and he wanted me to know that he'd knocked you around too. Not face-to-face, but worse. He'd done some research. He'd tracked down Marlo."

Ray closes his eyes. His head pivots back and forth in slow rejection, like it's trying to sweep away her words. He speaks without looking.

"I can't believe what you're telling me. I can't. My brain won't allow it."

Ronni lowers her hand on top of his. She gives it an empathetic squeeze. Ray opens his eyes. They look at each other for a beat.

"Sorry, Mack. I can sure pick 'em. I was giving him every signal in the book. A smarter man would have read the writing on the wall. A better man would have just walked away. Quit me in a heartbeat. Like you did. Found someone else." Ronni shakes her head at something impossible. "But then again, Pete's never been the smarter, better man. Not once in his rotten life."

# FORTY-FIVE

The day rolls beneath me in a hot, bottomless stench. I am numb and blind, like maybe Ronni serves her coffee with two lumps of nerve toxin. Someone else drives my car because it cannot be me. I am not present. I am off rotting in the landfill of the past.

The people that I suddenly care nothing about are piled up into a fetid heap in the backseat, like so many bags of garbage wrapped in a sheet. Suri and Carl and poor, dead Delaney. Sluggo Rickens-Royce. Sergeant Twill. Deno and Pete. Veronica Lodge. Janice Hinkle has leapt from the ledge and landed on top of the whole rotting pile.

Dr. Lindstrom's back there too, legs crossed, wrinkling his nose.

*Do you think it's possible, Detective Mackey, that you follow yourself because you feel guilty? That, psychologically speaking, you have a need to judge yourself for what you've done?*

With me in the front seat, smoking a cigarette, looking out at the burning blur of the world, is my wife. Marlo. Phil is in her lap, purring, fine white fur in the hot breeze. Marlo strokes her and lets out the smoke in a tight stream for the wind to savage. Phil turns into a camera with a lens that looks like a sawed-off shotgun. Marlo looks at me.

*What I'm saying, honey, is that we live in little bubbles of light. I'm saying we never know who's out in the dark universe looking in. And I'm saying it's always someone.*

I drive without direction until I'm almost out of gas. I fill up and drive some more.

I end up on Elmore, in the lot across from The Bodega and Sandwich Heaven. Rocky's inside The Bodega, holding court with three guys now paying the extra price for some beef jerky. Rocky keeps talking and they keep nodding as they inch for the door. They don't know the rule about The Bodega: Never get within ten feet of Rocky inside the two o'clock donut hole. He's hungry for company and he's got nothing else to do.

Up the street, Prancers sits quietly on the corner, waiting for the sun to stop caring and for darkness to transform what the daylight finds depraved and demeaning into something mostly harmless. I decide that Prancers is probably exactly where I belong. That's the kind of man I am. That's my level.

Then I hear my name. Muffled and distressed. It's coming from the trunk. Old Forester needs some air.

# FORTY-SIX

He sits slumped in a back booth for the second time today. It's starting to mold the shape of his spine. Doris is on the other side of the table, watching him torture an empty shot glass. She's already cut him off. Only four-thirty, sure, but Doris could see the half-bottle head-start when he knocked on the front door.

It's too early for Bucks to be anything but dead. It's just the two of them and the sound of the traffic. The dying sun mashes itself against the tinted windows; even the heat wants a cold drink. Doris is trying her best.

"So she knew. So she found out. She loved you, Mack. To her dying breath. That's the only thing that matters. We all make mistakes. You have to live with yours and I have to live with mine. And Buck and Marlo? Well, they don't have to live with anything, Mack. Not anymore. They made their mistakes and we forgive them and the world keeps turning."

"Not Marlo, Doris. Marlo didn't make mistakes. Only one."

"Don't say it."

"Trusting me. That was her one mistake."

"Mack."

He's not listening. May as well be alone in that booth.

"Her pancreas was a rocket ship. Six weeks from diagnosis to dead. She kept it to herself for the first three of those weeks. Tired, sure. Weak. I thought it was the flu. Kept working her cases. Putting the screw to Victor Roby. And that whole time she knew everything, Doris. She knew the kind of man I was. Gave me the chance to come clean. And I never did."

"Mack ..."

"Then about three weeks in, she let me in on her little secret, no doubt curious as to whether that would change things. Like maybe she could expect that death would rattle my tree and shake loose the truth. But not me. Tight as a clam. That time just ticked away. I never told her."

"Mack. What would have been the point of you telling her? Or her telling you that she already knew? On her deathbed? None of it mattered. If Marlo knew anything, Mack, then she knew that much. It didn't matter. A stupid fling? Lasted, what, two weeks?"

"One."

"Right. Okay. One goddamned week. Buck's affair lasted a year-and-a-half, Mack. And, yeah, I wanted him dead six ways from Sunday for awhile. But then, it just didn't matter. He learned from it. We both did. And then it just didn't matter. And if I'd found out about it, knowing that I only had a few weeks left to look at his beautiful black face ... Come on, Mack."

Doris wants to know more about Ronni, so he tells her. She wants Ronni to shoulder at least some of the blame but Ray won't have it. His fault. His decision.

"Sounds to me like she knew what she was doing, Mack. You work with someone and you get to know them. You think about them. You watch them. Curiosity builds. Attraction builds. That St. Patty's Day party was a long time coming, if you ask me. She made it happen as much as you did. She saw Marlo's ring. You better believe that."

"I was the one who took it off, Doris."

"Okay. Why? Why did you take it off?"

He lays his head on the table. Doris leans in and cups a hand over the back of his neck. He talks sideways, out at the empty bar.

"I don't know. Because I was a major league ass who wanted to feel ..."

"What, honey."

"Better. Superior. Marlo was ... she was a fucking genius, Doris. So much smarter than me, it's scary. My badge? My years as a homicide dick? None of that impressed her. She made more money than me. She kept better company than I did. I stood out in her world like a kangaroo smoking a Camel at the bar, holding her coat and nursing a bourbon. She included me, don't get me wrong. But in that world, I was just a bag of muscle with a badge, tipping a glass to look at my watch. She was the best goddamned investigator to walk the earth, Doris. She ran circles around me. The academy taught me nothing. Experience has taught me some. But Marlo. Jesus. She taught me everything. She dumbed it down every day so I could keep up."

"Doesn't matter, Mack. She loved you. She married you. She stayed with you."

Ray's not listening. It's just pretty noise coming from Doris' face. He sits up and rubs his own face, forgetting how much it hurts and then not caring. Rubbing it harder. Wanting it to hurt. He keeps going.

"And then there was Ronni Lodge. Younger. Gorgeous. Less experienced. No dummy, mind you. But, unlike Marlo, Ronni was the one working to keep up with me in the smarts department. She was locked away on the third floor in the Records office, looking at homicide detectives come and go like we were gods. And yeah, St. Patty's was just a party. I get that, Doris. But I was the one who saw it coming, and I saw it coming in slow motion. All I had to do was step out of the way. She'd have ended up with someone else. But I *didn't* step out of the way. I chose not to. Marlo was in New York testifying in court. Putting away the bad guys. And I'm taking off my tie in the goddamned Westmark ... *Shit*. Took a whole week for me to pull my head out of my ass."

"But you did, Mack. Look at me." He doesn't. Doris has to reach out and work his face manually. "Look at me. You *did* pull your head out. You ended it. That counts. It has to."

"Not enough, Doris. Yeah, I ended it. But I never came clean. And Marlo died knowing. She knew all along. Woman knew everything. She never told me."

"Because it was irrelevant. At that point, it meant nothing."

"Or maybe it meant everything, Doris. Maybe she left this world disappointed. Maybe she left *because* she was disappointed. Maybe she found out this terrible thing about the man she married and she tucked that little ugly secret into her pancreas for safekeeping."

Doris, bless her. She keeps at it. It's a hopeless case to make. To a guy like Ray? Hopeless. And he doesn't make it any easier. People start showing up in ones and twos, looking for someone to pop up from behind the bar. The cash on the ceiling keeps them occupied but that won't last long. Doris leans over and plants one on Ray's forehead.

"Got to go to work, Mack. Billy's got the crud and Kyle won't be in for another two hours, so it's all me right now. But you listen to me. Are you listening?"

"I'm all ears and asshole, Doris."

"I want you to think about something. What if it wasn't me sitting here. What if it was Marlo. What if she were to come down from off her barstool cloud, no doubt smoking and drinking and laughing up a storm with Buck, to listen to you talk this way? What if she's been paying attention this whole time? What do you think she'd tell you?" Doris wipes the lipstick off his forehead with her thumb. "You think about that."

# FORTY-SEVEN

Doris is a blur of conviviality, making up for lost time. First-timers. They want to know about the ceiling made of money. She hams it up about Buck, glancing my way every now and then. She fires up the box under the bar, deputizes Ella and Billie and Sarah, sending them out to sing me some company. In fifteen minutes, Doris is back at the booth with a full shot on a fresh napkin.

"Last one," she says. "On the house. And don't leave me a tip. But here's one for you."

She taps the napkin. It's a colorful rendering of a Bloody Mary; a stalk of celery in the glass like a leafy green straw. Standing in the background like a hero to save the day is a bottle of Tabasco. "Bloody Hot!" it says in a flaming font. Doris doesn't care about any of that. She's pointing to the phone number written in cool blue ink.

"You need me, you call me."

Then she's back across the bar. I don't see how she gets from here to there. My brain is skipping like a needle over scratched vinyl. Marlo pops in and out. Smiling here. Laughing there. Looking through her camera. Across a dark street and a green lawn slipping a *fuck you* photo in the crack of Victor Roby's front door.

But, as much as I try, I can't keep the others out of the frame. Ronni leaning up against her doorway. Ronni in her St. Patty's Day green. Ronni in that goddamned photograph. Pete, swinging his shit-kickers into my face. That makes me the shit.

But it also makes Pete the link between past and present.

If Ronni had hoped to get rid of me, her little revelation made that impossible. I needed answers and I needed help. Ronni didn't want me sleeping in her kitchen so she ended up good for both.

Turns out Ronni pulled Pete Phelps out of a rookie lineup in a cop bar out on West Monroe. They were both with friends and the friends found new rides home. It was doomed from the beginning, according to Ronni. Too much hard-charging cop machismo for her. But it stuck for the better part of a year. He was ready to carve her name into his forehead after six days. She was never ready. They used his place to take the edge off three or four times a week. Ronni reserved her cute little house in Bricktown for *me-time*. Knowing Ronni, she's got a problem shitting where she sleeps.

Back then, Pete was in his first year working patrol for the Chicago Police Department. There'd been some talk about him transferring to the Chandler PD, just to be closer to her. Then there'd been a signed application. But that fell through. The budget cuts were a good cover but the truth was that Ronni nixed his application with a word to her sergeant. She hasn't seen him for years. As far as Ronni knows, he's still over there. Last she checked he'd traded in his uniform to work the narco squad.

In the air above me, Billie's on about her body and soul, singing like her glass is empty. The question in my head is about the boot wrapped around Pete's foot and just how it ended up planted in my face.

My best guess is that Pete and Tony Rickens go way back. Rickens snaps a photo featuring Pete's girl making time in the Westmark with a Chandler homicide detective. Pete does some snooping. Talks to a few people. Finds the detective's wife and her ticking pancreas. Tells her a story. Shows her a picture or two.

What I can't figure is why Rickens and his trusty camera were down in that Westmark parking lot in the first place. If Rickens is on Big Man's payroll, then what does Big Man care two flying figs about Ronni Lodge scratching an itch?

It takes the full shot of bourbon in front of me to jar it loose. I slap the empty glass down on the table just as Billie passes the torch to Ella and "Someone to Watch Over Me."

The photo's not about Ronni. It's about me. I'm in that camera too. It's all about me.

I head for the door, stopping mid-bar to go back for the napkin and Doris' number just so I don't look like an ingrate. On the way out, I wave it at her like a hanky.

"Watch yourself, Mack."

"Always do, Doris."

# FORTY-EIGHT

Work, such as it is, is saving him again. Pulling him out of the muck of despair. He sits in the car for a long time. Staring into space. Watching Rocky make his rent. Watching the blue neon lick at the dark air above Prancers. Thinking. Putting things together.

The trunk pops. The door to the Impala swings open and out he comes, carrying the empty bottle of Old Forester like the head of a vanquished enemy. Ray looks in all directions, then bends himself inside the trunk, trading the bottle for Sluggo's gun. He closes the trunk and climbs back into the front seat. The door swings closed with a click. He wants to go home.

# FORTY-NINE

I want to go home.

I want to feel Phil's purring in my bones.

I want to put my head in the freezer and think about things.

Trouble is, I don't know who or what's waiting for me. Maybe no one. Maybe that lottery check I'm due. Maybe a bullet with my name on it. Which reminds me.

I tuck the gun under the seat and dig around in my pocket for the shell casings I took from Rickens' car. Doris' napkin and Sluggo's tweezers come out with them. I toss the napkin on the dash and open the glovebox. I find my penlight and shine it inside the shell. The first two are empty. The third casing shows a white roll of paper jammed inside. It takes some work but I finally get the thing out. I unroll it and open it.

The slip of paper is ripped down both sides. The letters are at the top, in green type.

"IWEATHER CO"

Beneath that are three words in small black print.

"SHIP NOT SAFE"

It's either a warning to sailors or it's a message from a mole. It's about a load of drugs or girls or guns. Whatever it is that Big Man is shipping, the task force is onto it and Harpo Marx is the man to send up the flare. So Harpo scribbles out a missive, rolls it up, sticks it in a bullet shell and delivers it someplace for Suri to pick up. Then Suri takes possession, hands it over to whoever is asking, some low-level mope working for Big Man, who then turns it over to Tony Rickens, idling up the street in his Pontiac, reading Superman comics and eating Beer Nuts. And taking pictures. Which reminds me.

I pull the camera out of my pocket and power it up. It glows in my face like a square moon. I scroll through the photos until I get to the one of yours truly trying to unlock his own front door holding a bag of groceries.

January. Five years ago. In the photo, the street between me and Rickens' lens is covered in snow. I could fry an egg on that street right now. I squint my eyes. The coat I'm wearing is black and trim, it fits me twenty pounds ago. Now it fits some guy who shops at St. Vincent DePaul's. I don't remember the gray triangle between the shoulders. I squint at the image.

It's not a photo of me.

It's a video of me.

I poke myself in the triangle.

Me watching me watching me. I can feel my *Triple-D* light up inside my head like Times Square as the ball drops.

It's an odd thing, watching yourself. The guy in the video does not look like how I feel when I move. I want to believe it's someone else. Someone for whom I have no responsibility.

Except that it *is* me. The schmuck in the video, that lump, that moral coward, is me.

He finally manages the key. The door opens to a figure in motion, emerging from the dim interior to greet the guy with the bag of groceries.

Marlo.

My god. *Marlo.*

She flings her arms around the guy's neck and kisses him, placing her bare feet on the toes of his shoes. He keeps stepping forward into the house, lifting her as he goes. He's strong and fit and so sure of himself, this guy, this strapping, confident guy, kissing Marlo on the mouth like she was essential for breathing.

Because she was. She was essential for breathing.

The guy closes the door with an elbow and suddenly they are gone.

Marlo is gone. Again.

I'm breathing as if through a pillow. I cannot pull enough oxygen into my lungs. My heart beats its fists against its cage. *Marlo.*

The moving image un-zooms. I am looking for a fleeting instant at a shaky, jarring image of the passenger seat of Rickens' Pontiac. The image bounces off the edge of someone's knee, then down at the dirty floor mat. My thumb spasms a pause.

It's blurry. But I'd recognize those boots anywhere.

# FIFTY

The Impala cruises by the house three times over twenty minutes before pulling up alongside the curb at the end of Maltese Road. Ray cuts the lights and engine and watches the place he wants to be. Staking out his own house. He can see every window on both levels. Nothing stirs. If someone's waiting for him, then they parked on another block and walked over. They didn't mind the exercise. And they're patient. And not afraid of the dark.

He can't keep his hands off the camera. He replays the video a dozen times. Five dozen. The inside of the car flickers ghostly white. I can see him in there a block away. Stupid.

# FIFTY-ONE

Marlo's moving image is like a drug. I can't get enough of it. I'm too permeable. She flows through me like water through a sieve. And every time that front door closes, I realize that I have kept nothing of her. That I'm empty again. Emptier than before. So I play it again.

Every so often, I force myself to look up and study the familiar shape of my house. Unlit. Unchanging. Then I return to the camera and watch the video again.

I have the thought to check all the other photos, just to see if I missed other videos. But photo six of forty-four is the only photo that moves.

Wait. *Forty-four?*

I have no reason to trust my memory. Too much to drink. No sleep. Too emotional. Probably nursing a concussion. But I could have sworn ...

I scroll through the photos for the what has to be the tenth time, whispering the count to myself as I go. *Thirty-eight. Thirty-nine. Forty.* All of them are as they ever were. Until I get to the last one. Photo forty-four. How have I missed it?

It's a terrible photo. Underexposed and overexposed at the same time. Nothing is clear. It's a Rorschach blur. No one would think it anything but a grab bag of light and shadow. Except me, for whom light and shadow seem to arrange themselves into something like ... this can't be right. My head throbs like a foot under a tire.

I stare at the square of light until my vision blurs. Ten different people would come away with twenty different impressions. Some of those people would take the time to rattle on about having seen Jesus in a ketchup stain or in the trunk of a tree. I know how to play the cloud game, too. But this time, my soggy brain keeps coming back to the same impression: a darkish blob, let's call it a man, bending toward a large whitish blob the shape of a car, let's call it a Pontiac. He's a mess of a shadow, sure, but the very top of the shadow is much lighter, like maybe it's wrapped in a sheet. The shadow would seem to have an arm. Two arms. The tip of one arm is whitish, like the head. The tip of the other seems to glow.

Lawrence of Suburbia. Me. Camera in my hand. This camera.

I stare, dimly remembering a sound that registers in my brain on a ten-second delay. That sound is me gasping.

I hit the detail button on the Sony. The photo was taken at three forty-three this morning.

That's not fucking poss ...

My phone finishes the thought. The old-timey ring delivers an old-timey heart attack. I clutch my chest, feeling the outlines of the thing in my pocket. I want to look. I want to confirm. But I don't. I know what it says. I grab for it through my shirt like I'm trying to suffocate something alive and upset. I close my eyes until the clanging and vibrating stops. In my other hand, the camera screen goes black from inactivity, then the thing shuts itself off with a bright little chirping sound.

All I can do is breathe in the dark and stare up the street at my house, silence ringing in my ears. Phil is inside that house. She is on top of the television or in the chair by the window or under the sofa. She is waiting for me. She misses her ritual fingertip drop of Old Forester.

She's the only thing that is real. The only creature on the earth I pretend to understand. She is the only thing left in the world that grounds me in my life. I reject everything and everyone else. There is only Phil.

I put the camera in the glovebox with the shells and the tweezers, then grab Sluggo's gun from under the driver's seat and tuck it into my belt. I take a breath and reach for the door handle.

But then I stop.

I know I must do the thing I do not want to do. I try not to think about it. I just do it.

I reach into my pocket and extract the phone. I navigate quickly to the screen devoted to recent calls. It's right there at the top. *Unknown Caller. Number Blocked.* Easily ninety percent of the most recent calls say the exact same thing.

I highlight the call and push the corresponding number to return the favor, to ring the phone of the person calling me. I close my eyes.

The phone rings in my hand. Louder than ever.

# FIFTY-TWO

Ray does not cross the street until he's even with Judith Kravitz' house. He looks at his watch. I can see him thinking. Judith would skip breathing before she missed canasta night at The Kennedy Club. She's gone for at least another hour.

He moves quickly and quietly, through Judith's side yard, through her side gate and into her backyard. He walks the fence line, fingers brushing the wood, all the way to the very back.

In his heyday, Ray could have cleared that wooden fence like it was a crack in the sidewalk. It takes more effort now. A *lot* more effort. But he does it without grunting or falling or getting stuck like a kitten up a tree. Not bad for a lump. He lands clean and quiet in his own backyard, standing still for a full minute to allow any *what-was-that-noise* check to come and go at the window.

He unfreezes, pulling the Model 10 out of his belt. He holds it stiffly at his side as he moves for the back door. He presses the side of his head against the wood, listening, stretching his left hand down into his pocket. When the hand reemerges, Ray's fingers are already sorting the keys.

# FIFTY-THREE

Phil's head is the first thing I see. She meows and brushes her body against the slowly opening door. I return the keys to my pocket and scratch her behind the ears as her tail hooks my leg.

I close the door one millimeter at a time, then stand as still as I can. I breathe in and out. I listen to molecules. I hear nothing but my ancient, heroic air-conditioner fighting the good fight and losing.

Five minutes. Six. Seven. Phil meows for attention. The house is still.

Two options present themselves up the dark hall ahead of me: the kitchen on the left or the living room on the right. If I was a smart, self-respecting killer, would I be reclining on a love seat or making myself a sandwich in the dark?

The empty football under my ribs has an opinion. Phil agrees.

The hall is the opposite of the nightmare kind, short and stiff, not long and stretchy. Phil pads up ahead of me and disappears around the corner into the kitchen. I hold up near the doorway, listening in both directions, both hands clutching Sluggo's thirty-eight at my waist like it's a driver on the eighteenth tee at Pebble Beach. I take a breath and pivot quickly into the doorway, rotating at my hips like they teach you for long drives, swinging my arms up and into the kitchen.

The room is empty of killers. Phil is up on the counter next to the refrigerator. She's unhappy with my progress. I'm ready to check the living room when I spot the door on the far side of the kitchen. My cellar's a small concrete room that comes with a single pull-string lightbulb. It's where I keep things I don't really want, like old boxes of back tax returns and people who want to shoot me. No reason for that door to be cracked. But it is.

I cross the kitchen in three steps and nudge the cellar door with the toe of my shoe. It swings open. I aim down into the dark.

Phil meows. Angry. Insistent. I turn to say something with my eyes about patience and virtue. I never get the chance.

# FIFTY-FOUR

The doorframe above Ray's head explodes into splinters. Phil is instantly airborne and out of the room before the man moving across the hall into the kitchen can cross the threshold. Ray, too, is in motion, ducking and swinging the thirty-eight around in the direction of the sound. His hand rams hard backward against the doorframe to the cellar. There is no shot because there is no longer any gun, which clatters down the concrete stairs behind him.

The man is a shadow in the kitchen doorway, dressed in black with a black cloth mask over his face. But he's tall with long rubbery arms, one of them a gun-length longer than the other.

# FIFTY-FIVE

I barely get a sense of him. His height. His limbs. The size of his head. No way I can see his face. My brain superimposes Harpo Marx's face and it fits just fine. I lunge sideways behind the island, taking down the block of knives as I go. They crash to the tile, spinning and skittering in all directions.

So I have my choice. The tendency is to go big. Thanksgiving dinner, twenty-pound turkey big. But a knife doesn't work in a gun fight. Not unless you can throw it so that the pointy end sticks. I snap up the boning knife.

"Harpo!" I hear my own voice like it belongs to someone else. I'm hoping his old nickname will slow him down. I don't hear him moving. "Let's talk about this! I'll take you to Suri. I'm not interested in dying to protect a woman that doesn't have common sense enough to protect herself." Silence. "My cop days are done, Harpo. I'm too old to have any kind of beef with Big Man. You want her, you can have her."

Silence. Then a step. Toward the island. He's being careful. Too careful for anyone who thinks I'm armed with a knife made for salmon. Which maybe means he thinks I'm loaded, ready to pop up on him like a jack-in-the-box and put six bullets in his chest. I inch forward, keeping the island between us. We're like two hands in a slow-motion chase around the same square clock. My nine to his three. My ten to his four.

"Talk to me, Harpo. We can work this out. Like old times."

My eleven to his five.

"Let's go throw the ball at some pins. What say, Harpo? Come on, pal."

When the island clock strikes twelve-thirty, I throw the knife. I throw it hard and I throw it blind. Not at Harpo. I throw it to the right of Harpo, so that it hits my toaster oven. Harpo might have expected a flying knife. They're all over the floor. But anger at the toaster oven is going to catch him off guard.

That, and no one ever expects a rolling island.

# FIFTY-SIX

Ray puts his back into it, heaving against the island for all he's worth. Big Man's tall man is worried about the short, little oven. It's all too fast and unexpected. He doesn't get what's happening until the island's ramming into his legs. He takes a step backward to get out of the way, but the thing keeps coming.

The next half-step back saves him from the island but it comes with a dramatic change in elevation.

# FIFTY-SEVEN

I can hear Harpo disappear from the room. Like he's falling down a well. Ass over teakettle, pitching backward down a long flight of hard, narrow concrete stairs. There's only one thought in my head, trying to push its way through the sounds of a large man falling a long way: When Harpo and gravity resolve their differences, he'll be down in my cellar with two guns at his disposal.

I pull myself up off the floor and yank the island out of the doorframe. I plunge myself down the stairs into the blackness. I can't see him but soon enough I'm on top of him at the bottom, swinging before he can get up. I'm sure he can't see anything either. Stars maybe.

He swings at me like a man that doesn't know up from down. I'm connecting on every punch. He lands nothing. His lanky arms are suddenly a disadvantage for close combat.

I can feel him change strategies beneath me. He's stopped trying to hit me. He's grappling around in the dark for his own gun. But it's my left knee that finds the hard shape he wants. My knee has never been good with guns. My right hand stops with the punching and takes over.

I push the barrel with a lot of force into Harpo's forehead. That gets his attention. Suddenly he's not interested in tussling. The gun barrel burrows harder into the cloth mask. I imagine the little angry red circle it's making at the top of his face, like a tiny third eye. I roll him over and straddle him, now pushing the gun hard against the spot where the skull and the neck go their separate ways.

I stand carefully, one foot between his shoulders so I can react at the first movement. I swing my arm in the dark above my head until I find the string. I pull it.

Light.

# FIFTY-EIGHT

They both see it at the same time. Sluggo's gun, that old Model 10, glinting silver in the burst of tired incandescence. Those long arms put it within reach. Both of them know it.

Harpo stretches. Ray puts all his weight on the foot between Harpo's shoulders, then brings the other foot down hard on his straining hand.

Howling pain. Retraction. Ray picks up the gun and stabs it into his belt. Harpo writhes, one hand clutching the other. A tangle of black hair has partly escaped from beneath his head wrap. Three little blue beads quiver in the light like prisoners emerging from a hole on the other side of a prison fence.

Black curls. Black. This man ...

# FIFTY-NINE

This man is not Harpo Marx.

Behind me is a stack of boxes sealed with duct tape. On top of the boxes are three rolls of man's best friend. I stretch over, using the Smith & Wesson to give my reach the extra few inches I need. I tip the nearest roll of tape upright and insert the barrel. The tape hops on board and I bring it to me.

We tussle again as I sit him up. Calming him down takes a sharp knock on the head with his own Sig Sauer and a promise to get the bullets involved. I use two full rolls of duct tape to pin his arms to his side and his ankles and legs together. I drag him backward by the armpits until he's propped up against the concrete pillar in the center of the room. Most of the third roll of tape makes him one with that pillar, from his neck to his waist.

I step back, panting and sweating, taking in the gray, leathery cocoon. He looks relaxed, legs stretched out, head through the top end, like the caterpillar decided to watch some television before finishing the job. I reach over and try to pull the mask over the back of his head. The neck tape won't let go. I have to grab it by the eye-holes and rip.

Inside is a sweaty, bloody mess of a face. This guy looks about as much like Harpo Marx as I do. South or Central American. Mexico. Bolivia. Guatemala. Large, dark eyes.

Olive skin. The kids in school teased him about the acne. That's when he turned to a life of crime.

"Talk," I say.

"*Jódete.*" He spits blood.

"Who sent you?"

"*Jódete, gilipollas.*"

The blood vessels in his right eye are swelling into red bolts of lightning.

"Why did Carmen Miranda wear fruit on her head?"

"*Jódete!*"

No hesitation. He shouts it at me this time, writhing in his sticky gray sleeping bag.

I know *fuck you* in every language. This guy doesn't speak a word of English.

So I leave him there. I plunge him into darkness with the pull of a string and climb the stairs back up to the kitchen. I close the door to the cellar and turn on the kitchen light.

Phil is sitting on the counter next to the refrigerator. She meows.

# SIXTY

Ray is moving slowly, his body remembering its age. He babies his right hand. Been a long time since those knuckles have felt any bone.

He takes care of Phil, then puts the kitchen back together, pushing the island back to its proper place in the sea of white tile. Returns the knives. Apologizes to the toaster oven. Then he moves on.

He leaves the lights off in the living room, collapsing backward onto the sofa with a groan and lays both guns on the floor. Phil finishes her food and relocates to his torso. She rises and falls with his breathing, like she's floating on a raft, purring contentedly. The sound of it closes his eyes. God knows what he's thinking.

And so do I.

*Marlo.*

# SIXTY-ONE

I keep seeing her. The way she glides out of the dark, from about where I'm lying right now into the light of the opening door. I keep seeing that face as her arms open, encircling the shoulders of the young, strapping, confident man in the video. The man in the slim black coat who doesn't yet seem to understand the vile person he is on the inside. The man who does not deserve the encircling arms. I keep playing it over and over in my head. Cutting it off as the door closes and then starting again.

In my dream, I'm the one answering the door. And it's Marlo on the stoop. Across the street behind her, Victor Roby is in a car taking pictures with a rifle. Marlo places a hand against the side of my face. The other hand gives me a photograph. A man wrapped in a sheet is bent into the passenger side of a Pontiac. He's digging in the glovebox. Marlo closes the door.

I jolt awake. I look at my watch. One-fifteen. Phil is looking at me like I woke her for a reason. I scratch her head until she stretches and settles again. My brain reaches for the video. It plays again. Again. Once, I let the memory run all the way to the end. All the way to the leg in the passenger seat emptying down into the boot.

Pete was in that car.

Pete was in Sluggo's car outside my home, watching me. Watching Marlo. January, five years ago. Two full months before St. Patrick drove a couple of snakes out of the green punch bowl at an office party and up to the Westmark hotel.

Which means Pete knew about me all along. Knew about Marlo all along.

Which means …

My phone rings. It's coming from the kitchen. By the time I relocate Phil and get there, the ringing has stopped. The man in my cellar is yelling rude things in Spanish. I can barely hear him. It takes a minute but I find the phone on the floor under the sink counter. I look at the screen, bracing for another existential blow to the head.

I'm wrong. Marigold.

I hit the button to call her back. Goldie answers in less than a full ring. She's crying.

"Mack … oh my god, Mack. You're there. You're there."

"I'm here, Goldie. What's wrong? What happened?"

"You told me not to call the police. I didn't, Mack. I swear I didn't. But they're sure as hell here now. I lost count at fifteen. Jesus, Mack. We're even. We're so goddamned even."

I can hear her light a cigarette. I can hear her shaking.

"Goldie. Listen to me. Breathe. Focus. What happened?"

I let her smoke. All I can do is wait.

"Shooting, Mack. Lots of fucking shooting. That's about all I know. The guy … what's his … the guy …"

"Carl?"

"Carl. He's in bits and pieces all over the wall. Three other guys I've never seen before are … are … they're out in the hallway just … just … Jesus, Mack. I'll never get this place clean."

"Suri." I nearly spit it at her. "Where's Suri? Where's the woman?"

"The Buick she climbed out of squealed out of here like a comet. I'm assuming she was inside. And not in the trunk this time."

"Shit. Goldie, I'm sorry. What's happening now?"

Another long, agonizing drag and exhale.

"I'm upstairs. In my bathroom. I've been answering questions for an hour."

"What have you told them?"

"What I heard. What I saw. That I don't know anything about the people I rent to and that I've never had any reason to care much until today."

"What about the payment records, Goldie? Hotels don't let people stay for free."

"I told them they seemed desperate and didn't have a credit card. Told them Carl paid me twice the room rate in cash and promised they'd be gone after one day. I told them business has been slow and so I took it. I never mentioned your name, Mack. Not once."

"Thanks, Goldie. You're a good egg. But listen. They're going to run your phones. That'll lead them to me. Twice, including now. So that jig is up. I don't want you to be an accessory to some obstruction rap or to whatever in the hell happened out there. You need to come clean. Go tell them everything. Do it now while they're still taking pictures. Don't leave anything out."

"Are you sure? Tell them about this call? I'm hiding under a toilet to make this call."

"Everything, Goldie. Tell them everything. Tell them I told you to say hello."

# SIXTY-TWO

Phil is back up on the counter. Ray slides the phone into his pocket and brings his face right up to hers, nose to nose, scratching her behind the ears.

"Got to get moving, Phil. Busy day ahead. You guard the prisoner. And finish my novel."

Ray collects both guns and jabs them behind his back. He makes a beeline for the garage where he pulls Marlo's green ten-speed bike off the ceiling hooks and brings it to the floor. Both tires are flat. He doesn't care. He could stand to lose a few, but it's not the exercise he's after. It's the four-foot, pink plastic-coated cable with the combination lock. He hunches over the bike, twisting dials and arranging numbers.

Marlo's birthday. Wrong. Their wedding anniversary. The lock opens. He uncoils the cable from beneath the seat like a pink snake.

Phil is waiting for him at the garage door when he comes back. She follows him up the hall and back through the kitchen. She has no interest in going down into the cellar. She watches him open the door and go down alone.

He doesn't need to pull the string. Enough of the kitchen light has followed him down the stairs for him to see. The tall guy who's not Harpo can see, too.

"*Jódete! Jódete!*"

"I know. I love you too, pal." Ray loops the lock around the man's neck and the concrete pillar. A perfect fit as long as Not-Harpo stops pulling. Ray inserts the lock and scrambles the numbers. "Just in case you're ready to turn into a butterfly before I get back."

"*Jódete!*"

"You're welcome."

# SIXTY-THREE

I force myself to keep the camera in the glovebox. I have to stop it. The thing is kryptonite. It's going to get me killed.

It's a long drive out to East Village, but the air has cooled all the way down to ninety-one and I like the way it feels around my aching head. I roll all the windows down and let it blow. Doris' phone number gets airborne off the dash but I catch the napkin and stuff it down into the cupholder, suddenly wanting that Bloody Mary. The windy, low-vibe solitude gives me and the Camels a chance to catch up and think about certain things, all those shy details and wallflower connections that don't like to be looked at or thought about.

I finish one and fire up another. I'm weighing the advantages of becoming nocturnal.

The two-story number at 6912 Wolcott is not the place I'd imagined Tony Rickens laying his head at night. Pale yellow, for one thing, tucked neatly into the keyhole of a well kept cul-de-sac. White provincial trim around multi-paned windows for another. Then there's the blue plastic swimming pool on the front lawn. I had imagined something more ... what ... evil and lair-ish. A squat, dark shack built for one. Something that might invite me to break a side window so I could climb in and look around while Rickens was off feeding the worms in DeKalb. I was wrong and not just a little bit.

I drive away slowly and circle the neighborhood to kill a few minutes. When I come back, I'm coasting with the lights off. I roll the Impala up to the curb and cut the engine. Then I sit in the dark and wait. I think about heading back home. I'm not breaking in anywhere tonight.

# SIXTY-FOUR

There are at least twenty windows watching him. Four dark, square, glassy eyes for every sleeping house. Plus me.

Ray climbs out, leaving the front car door ajar and walks up the street like an insomniac out for a stroll. He strides up the driveway of 6912 like he's on the mortgage, then slips along the side wall of the garage. A tricycle is sitting beneath a small, high window. Ray reaches up and grips the sill, then he makes himself taller.

It takes him only maybe fifteen, twenty seconds and he's walking back down the driveway. He starts for the car but then thinks better of it.

Today's trash day on Wolcott. The Rickens' home does not put off for tomorrow what can be done the night before. Ray changes course. He lifts the lid on the plastic can and rips open the plastic bag on top. Checking on the neighbors will do him no good. He keeps his head down, ripping and sorting and reading.

A light comes on in one of the dark, square eyes across the cul-de-sac. Ray doesn't look. He drops the garbage, closes the lid and moseys away, hands in his pockets.

# SIXTY-FIVE

I'm halfway back to Chandler and the horizon is already starting to burn white when my phone rings. I hate that I can't throw the thing out the window. I venture a wincing look at the screen. I answer in relief.

"You mistake me for a morning person. What if I'd been sleeping?"

"I knew better." Veronica Lodge needs to register that whisper as a weapon. "I came in to work early. I did some looking into Anthony Rickens like you asked. We need to talk, Mack."

"Oh? Let me take a wild guess. He's a cop with the Chicago PD, moonlighting for Big Man on the side. Three dependents: a wife, Elaine, who sells for Mary Kay, and two boys, Anthony Junior, mid-teens, on the honor roll at Whitney Young High, and Jack, a toddler with a bee allergy and a thing for dolphins. Tony and Elaine are switching to no-load mutuals and swapping out their investment managers because what good is the racketeering racket if your pockets are so full of hands. Junior gets his dad's hand-me-down comics. Little Jack isn't much for reading but he's big into swimming. And when dad's away on business at the landfill, the gang likes Chef's Mistake pizza, thick crust, extra sausage. How'd I do?"

I've taken her breath away. I miss the whisper.

"Ronni?"

"Jesus, Mack. What the hell did you need me for? I said I'd help."

"Yeah, but you never said when. I found some spare time between my seat cushions. Anything on Deno?"

"Yeah. Dean Porter. Chicago homicide. Look, we need to meet."

"Why?"

"Documents, Mack. The kind that connect a lot of dots."

"Okay. Where and when?"

"Not now. I've got to make a living."

"Lunch."

"Can't. Tonight. After my shift."

"Seven."

"Eleven. I'm roped into birthday drinks."

"Happy birthday."

"Not mine, dummy. And I don't want you coming by my house again, Mack. You're too hot. Your name's bouncing around here like a pinball. Some kind of massacre up in a no-tell hotel outside Bloomington. I don't know what happened and I don't want to know so don't tell me. I'm just saying they're looking hard for you."

"Thanks for the tip. And just for the record, you called me too hot. That's never happened before. Eleven o'clock where?"

"You know where. Watch yourself, Mack."

"Always."

# SIXTY-SIX

Chandler is sunny and bright and starting to bubble in the pan when Ray gets back. All his windows are up. He's driving with one wrist on the wheel, head tipped back against the seat, eyes half-open. He looks like hell. You'd think, given the risks of going home to rearrange his kitchen and take a nap, he'd have taken eighteen seconds to change his clothes. That he'd pick out a shirt that isn't made of cotton and parking lot, streaked with grime and blood. That maybe he'd even tuck it in and wash the boot prints off his face and run a comb through the donut on his head.

You'd think that. But it's Ray we're dealing with here. This hump's just putting one foot in front of the other. He's lucky to be doing that much.

He pulls the Impala into a Walmart lot and parks. Not in the back of the lot where there are still rows of empty spaces. He finds a space in the front-middle of the lot with only a few empty spaces on either side. It'll be full in less than an hour.

Ray walks across the street to a car rental. In fifteen minutes, he's driving a blue Taurus back across the street. He parks the Taurus next to the Impala like he wants them to get to know each other. Sluggo's Smith & Wesson goes in the trunk of the Impala, under the trash bag corpse. *Jódete*'s Sig Sauer gets tucked beneath the seat of the Taurus. Doris' phone number goes in his pocket. Ray opens the glovebox and holds the camera in his hand like he's trying to guess the weight.

Man, just look at this guy. This sap. He wants to turn it on, bring it to life. He wants to watch the video. He wants to marvel all over again at photo forty-four of forty-four. I can see him thinking. He wants to spend the whole day curled up with the thing, parsing light and shadow. Looking at those clouds..

But something is still working inside that overripe melon. He straightens his back and looks around. He sighs and puts the camera back in the glovebox. He closes the little door, then the big one.

He locks up the Impala and mounts the little blue bull, threading his way out of the lot to the main road. It rolls forward for all of a hundred feet before pulling off the road and up alongside a long silver trailer that looks like the wingless fuselage of a plane. Two men are on ladders trying to hang a sign above a sliding drive-up window. Hill o' Beans, it says. The gal inside the window is trying to look open for business.

But the problems of three little people don't amount to much. Not to Ray. Not when he's thirsty and he needs the caffeine.

# SIXTY-SEVEN

If everybody's out looking for me, the last place they'll think to check is the Chandler Police Department. I pull the Taurus into a good spot across the street, with a clear line of sight to the front door and the entrance to the Police-Only parking lot. I watch people come and go in and out of the building through those big double doors. People who in a different life, I'd probably know. People I'd greet and for whom I'd hold the door. I'd hold it for as long as it took. Wait for them to make it all the way up the steps. Slap them on the shoulders. In a different life, I'd be one of those people.

All I can do is drink my coffee and wait. Turns out I don't have to wait long.

# SIXTY-EIGHT

Ray climbs out of the Taurus, bends back in to grab a large cup of coffee, then closes the door with his hip. He has to let a garbage truck pass, but then he's across the street and striding through the police parking lot like a man late for a meeting. He's standing on the passenger side of Andy Marx's Stingray convertible before Andy's pulled the key out of the ignition.

"Hey, Harpo. How're you doing, buddy? Got you some coffee." Ray hands over the cup with a smile. Harpo takes it, completing the handoff while his brain is scrambling to reconcile the friendly tone and the vaguely familiar face. Ray reaches down and unlocks the door and opens it. He climbs in, pushing a nylon workout bag from the seat to the floor. "Let's go for a drive."

Harpo stares. He doesn't understand. He keeps holding the cup in the air like maybe he wants to return the coffee because it's not what he ordered. Too much foam. Or not enough.

"It's a latte. You like lattes, Harpo? I figured you might. I like it black, myself. Sig, here, is the same. Black as night. No sugar."

Harpo sees the Sig Sauer twitch in Ray's lap. A bit slow out of the gate, but Harpo's catching up now. He looks back up at Ray, takes in the condition of his face. His clothes.

"Mack ..." he says.

"Yeah, I know. Let's go take in a movie."

# SIXTY-NINE

He heads north like I tell him. The hot wind has a better time blowing around Harpo's car than anything I've been driving. More hair to play with. Harpo doesn't seem to be sharing in the fun.

Never was much of a talker, Harpo. The not-talking and the hair got together and bought him the nickname. Although now he looks a little more like Art Garfunkel, circa 1970-something, after a barber lured him into the chair with a lollipop. Fair skin. Watery blue eyes. Best looking mole Big Man could ever hope for. And he bowls like Satan, to boot.

Today he's got two parallel scratches, angry and swollen, stretching like tire tracks from his right ear down the side of his neck.

"Tattoo's infected," I tell him, nodding. He doesn't look at me.

"Stray," he says. "Should never have picked her up."

"Trick with cats is to know your place. If you don't, you'll learn soon enough."

Harpo almost laughs. I settle for almost. I don't tell him where we're going. We do twenty-five minutes of the left, right, straight-ahead thing until there's only one place we could be going.

"You weren't kidding about the movie," he says.

"Kidding takes a good sense of humor. I don't have one of those anymore. Pull in up there. Aim for the shadow."

The McClatchy Drive-In was big in its day. Double features every night. Cars full of beer and popcorn and a lot of half-dressed teenaged hormones. Eventually, surround-sound multiplexes connected to shopping mall food courts took away the business. McClatchy changed the business model to adult films, packing the place with cars full of drugs and popcorn and a lot of half-dressed hookers. Then trouble decided to take in the late show. Four shootings in three months and the city flexed its muscle. Now McClatchy's a big bumpy parking lot behind a shuttered building in an amphitheater of trees. The speaker posts are still cemented in place, like a stumpy forest of dirty, yellow stubble. There is no screen.

I direct Harpo around the far side of the boarded-up building that once upon a time smelled like butter and money.

"Right here's good. Turn it off and hand me the keys."

Harpo hesitates. I can see the worry.

"Come on. Think about this. You think I can't pull the trigger if the car's running? You want to test that theory?"

The car goes quiet. He holds his keys up on a finger. I lift his coffee out of the cupholder and we swap.

"Cellphone too. On the dash."

Harpo does as he's told. Then he takes a drink and makes a face, returning the cup.

"Well, it was piping hot when I bought it. First order of business is for me to know where the gun is. Because I know it's here, Harpo." I pat him down at the waist. "Lift your pant legs. Where's your service weapon?"

"I don't have it."

"Bullshit."

"I'm on suspension. LT's got me riding a desk. Pending investigation."

He says this last bit like it hurts. But I'm an old, retired ex-cop. Cops don't get to be old or retire standing up by trusting others. I conduct a quick search of the front seat, starting with the workout bag under my feet. I unzip and start to rummage.

"Like to stay in shape, do you? Good for you, Harpo. Obesity's a killer."

It's what you'd expect. Gym shoes, size 200-wide. Shorts. Socks folded up into a ball. Muscle-tee. A plastic Target bag with a new deodorant, a Gatorade, a hairbrush and a bottle of wintergreen mouthwash. No gun. I stuff the Target bag back into the gym bag, zip it up and toss it in the backseat.

I open up the glovebox. Sunglasses. A smiley-face "I Donated Today" sticker. Peppermint gum. A box of mints. Cinnamon mouth spray. I want to ask Harpo about his bad-breath complex but I stop caring when I see the gun tucked away in the back. I keep the Sig steady. I pull the gun out carefully.

"Harpo." It's a three-fifty-seven magnum Derringer. Tiny little silver thing. Four separate barrels, like one of those old pepperboxes. It's not the bullet chambers that rotate in these things; it's the striker, hitting one of four separate, dedicated firing pins before it moves on to the next. I break it open like you would a shotgun and take a look inside. It's a full house. I snap it closed and look at him. "And to think I bought you a coffee."

"You asked for a service weapon. That's not a service weapon."

"Got me there, counselor. Bet this baby tucks away nicely in a purse."

"I like guns. So sue me. It's a collector."

"Some people collect gloves in these gloveboxes."

"What do you want with me, Mack? You're the last person, literally the last person, I want to be seen with right now."

"I'm hurt. Tell me about this investigation."

"Why?"

"Because I'm holding two guns and asking nicely."

"IAD's up my ass."

"How long?"

"Ten days."

"Twill?"

"Yeah. Twill. Self-righteous prick. The new guy wants a big bust so they'll like him downtown."

"What's it about?"

"Task force leaks. Twill's adding two and two and getting thirty-seven."

"Bad at math, is he?"

"And faces."

"How so?"

"He thinks I'm you. The next you, anyway. Only you're the one that got away. And on Nosek's watch. Twill's convinced I'm getting the loose change in Big Man's pocket. Just like you, Mack. Only he's hell-bent on making my story end differently. He's not handing me a gold watch when this is over. He wants my head on a spike to pay for your sins."

"No one can afford my sins, Harpo. You all lawyered up?"

"Yeah. Nothing to do but wait for Twill to finish."

"What's he got on you?"

"Think he's going to tell me that? Your reputation is for being crooked, Mack, not dumb."

There's a compliment in there someplace, making love to the insult. I let it go and keep the pressure on.

"Then let's play detective, Harpo. What's he asking about?"

"Your old snitch. Suri."

"What about her?"

"Where is she. When did I last see her. Last time I talked to her."

"Well?"

"I don't know, never, and never. Only thing I know about Suri is that she stinks to high heaven like you and Big Man. Twill says he's got me as her handler. I'm the task force leak, and Suri's the conduit, and Bob's your uncle, and the fucking world's in the crapper." Harpo pounds the steering wheel once with both fists. Then he sighs and looks at me holding the Sig. "That's me being darkly ironic in case you're wearing a wire."

"You've never had any contact with Suri at all. You expect me to believe that, Harpo? Such a short conversation and you're already on lie number three."

"You asked for my service weapon."

"You knew what I meant. And I have a cat, Harpo. You may have been picking up stray pussy but those aren't cat scratches. When was the last time you had contact with Suri?"

"Never. I'm getting a lot of questions about the last time I spoke with you, too, Mack. Twill seems to think we're in contact. Guess now I've got something new to report. Not that it will help my case any."

"Let's put a pin in that. What else is Twill asking about?"

Harpo rubs his face with both hands like he's in the shower and mumbles something I can't catch.

"Again."

He drops his big, bowling-ball-grabber hands into his lap.

"Ginger Turner."

"Who's that?"

"Burlesque queen turned pole jockey turned junkie hooker. I busted her right before I showed up. I got reassigned to Chandler from Chicago PD when the task force accepted my application. They wanted someone from Chicago vice and I was ready to get out of that place. When I transferred, the ink was still wet on this one bust. Twill likes to slap the arrest report down on the table like it should mean something special. It doesn't. Not to me."

"What's the story?"

"Caught her dead to rights testing the springs in the backseat of a car."

"Who's the john?"

"Some punk in his daddy's caddy. It was a small deal. As small as they come."

"And?"

"And nothing. I write it up, file it away. Then Nosek tells me to kick the case."

"Nutsack? Chandler IAD? Why does he care about a Chicago collar?"

"How should I know? I was brand new, trying to get along. I shit-canned it. I didn't care."

"He didn't explain?"

"No. Personal favor kind of thing. I figured the john was the nephew of a friend or something. I called the Chicago DA and told him the bust was bad. Told him I skipped the Miranda. The DA was just as happy to let it go."

"And so this Ginger person ... Ginger who?"

"Turner. She flew away. Never saw her again until Twill shows me her mugshot and my own arrest report. I told Twill that kicking her loose was Nosek's idea but he doesn't seem to believe a word I tell him. It's not like I can prove it."

"Has he reached out to Nosek?"

"Twill doesn't copy me on the investigation plan. And come on, Mack. Nosek's on the City Council now. And he's not stopping there. So he's sure as hell not copping to cutting hookers a break."

"Okay. What else?"

"Last time we met, Twill put a shell casing on the table. Said he found it in my desk. Lots of questions about that."

"What's the answer?"

"Not sure how an empty casing is in with the paperclips unless someone wanted it to be there."

"Is it yours?"

Harpo shrugs.

"Could be. Like I said. I like guns. A buddy and me target shoot with fifty-caliber Nighthawks. Could be mine, yeah."

"What buddy?"

"I don't want him involved."

"He's already involved. What buddy?"

"Guy named Argus. He owns the gun shop on West Baker. We go way back. I'm godfather to his son, Blake. Target shooting is our thing. Once or twice a month."

"Do you know a guy named Tony Rickens?"

"Rickens. Sounds familiar. Who is he?"

"An aspiring photographer. Portraits. He wanted to make you a star. What about a guy named Pete Phelps?"

"Him I know. Chicago PD. Narcotics. Hardcore asshole."

"Any contact with him recently?"

"No. Not since I left. Should I have?"

"Just curious."

"No you're not."

I can't help but smile.

"Boy. No fooling you, is there, Harpo? What about a guy named Dean Porter? Goes by Deno."

"Chicago Homicide. Don't really know him. Rumor mill makes him as bad news. A player. Powders his nose after hours. I never hung with homicide over there. Most of them are a bunch of freaks. Chandler Homicide's different. Your old crew. All those guys are pretty chill. Now they're all pretty chilly. Most of them look at the floor when they see me coming. Word gets around."

"Like a fart in church. Next. What's the latest on the task force?"

The question is heavier than the others and Harpo's got the expression to prove it. Sharing task force intel with none other than Raymond Mackey, the rat that got away. The very thing Harpo's accused of doing. The very thing for which Twill wants to send him away. I sit quietly and watch him work on it. But then I can tell he's going to balk. I make it easier.

"I don't want the whole article, Harpo. I'm just looking for the headline. How's it doing?

Harpo blinks. I've loosened the jar.

"Task force is sucking air," he says. "Hasn't had a decent bust in fourteen months. Fifteen. Big Man is running circles around us. *Them*, I should say. I'm not part of the *us* anymore. I'm off the team. And it's not just Chandler PD sucking air; all the other networked departments too. Chicago. Detroit.

Milwaukee. Shit. Cleveland. Everybody's getting skunked. Blown covers. Guns, girls, drugs. Across the board. The suits and ties are upset and so the brass is upset. They're whipping everybody for results and they're whipping all the IADs for some answers. Especially Twill. Because of you, Mack, Chandler PD's the department with a rap for leaks. Twill's trying to save his own ass with my head."

"There's a trick. Speaking of heads, what the hell happened to your face, Harpo?"

"I told ..."

"Right. The stray cat. Cats have nine lives. You've only got one."

"Really?" Harpo snorts. "You going to shoot me, Mack? Am I supposed to believe that?"

"Of course I'm not going to shoot you. Who do you think I am? I'm going to take your cute little gun and your phone and your car. If you level with me, I'm going to call a cab to come pick you up. If not, you get to walk back to town on a triple-digit day. Bullets are not your problem. Not today anyway. I'd be worried about dying of dehydration or being really late for work. So let's have the truth this time. Who's the woman with the nails and what'd you do to her?"

"I don't know."

Harpo talks to the hands in his lap like they're the ones that asked the question.

"Confession's good for the soul, Andy."

"I don't know who she was. Okay? Shit. Five days ago I'm in a bar ..."

"What bar?"

"The Laredo. On Fifth."

"That's not a bar. That's a pit around a stage around a pole."

"Whatever. So you know the place. I'm three sheets and looking for distraction. Twill's making it real clear he's not going away. Word is out that I'm a rat for Big Man. Everyone's looking at me sideways. Almost no one will talk to me. I live at the goddamned gym or at the target range just to blow out the stress. I can see my whole career circling the drain and a lot of orange onesies in my future. So, yeah, I'm stressed out and letting my standards drop."

"You let anything else drop at The Laredo, Harpo?"

"No. I left at closing time. Some woman comes up ..."

"Dancer?"

"No. I mean, maybe, but no one I'd seen working that night. She makes like she wants a date and I push her off and I'm not so nice about it. She comes at me with her claws. I'm in no position to arrest her for assaulting a police officer. So I gave her a stiff push and a mean look. She ran off. That was that."

"Would you recognize her if you saw her again?"

"Please. I was lucky to find my car. She had hair and tits and lips. And fingernails."

"Did you get handsy with her before she combed your face?"

"No. And fuck you for asking."

"Have I offended your sense of decency?"

"What the hell are you doing, Mack? What's this all about? I mean, maybe you're pumping me on Big Man's dime, but from what I understand this is not exactly how Big Man usually goes about things. And I don't think Big Man cares anything about these scratches, even I did deserve them, which I don't. So I guess I'm a little confused here. You're one to talk about my face. One look at your face and I'm thinking you're into something deep and ugly. That's not any kind of retirement I'd want." Harpo's expression softens, dropping out of confusion and into a pillow of empathy. Now he's the one working the lid on my jar. "What's going on, pal?"

"First, as to my face, I'm just working out the kinks with my exterior decorator. Second, you can call me pal next time we go bowling. And, third, if you want to ask me questions, you have to buy me coffee and put a gun in my face. We're not taking turns here, Harpo."

We look at each other across the car for a couple of beats. He's not done. So I wait.

"Okay. Just one then. One question, Mack. One."

"Cosmo Green."

"Yeah. Cosmo fucking Green."

"Never met the guy. Never talked to him on the phone. It was a set-up, Andy. And a good one. Nutsack got his fall guy and the gutter ball kept rolling. You're going to want to know if I think Nutsack was dirty. I don't know if he was dirty. Maybe. Maybe not. Just like I don't know if Twill's dirty. But they're both cogs in a dirty machine. A machine that needs a goddamned firehose. Or maybe it just needs a fire. All that and a second mortgage'll buy you another latte. Okay?"

"Who set you up? How?"

"Nope. Here's how this is going to work, Harpo." I reach in the back and bring up the gym bag. I unzip it and dig for the Gatorade. I hand it to him. "Have another drink on me. You might need it. When the cab gets here, take it back to the station. Your car will be in the lot. Your phone and the keys will be under the seat. Once I wipe it down, your cute little Derringer here'll be back where I found it."

"And you?"

"Long gone. You're going to get your things and go inside the building and start hearing my name in every other sentence. Something about Bloomington. Believe what you want. I'll see you in the funny papers, Andy."

"What should I say about this little chat?"

"You mean to Twill? Does it matter what I think?"

"No. But I'm curious."

"You're curious alright, Harpo. You and a lot of dead cats. Go kick Twill's door in, is what I say. Tell him the truth. I bought you coffee and took you to the movies. Sig and I took you prisoner and threatened to kill you for a fly-on-the-wall view of his investigation. I suspect that'll make you look a little better. Co-conspiring friends don't take each other hostage."

"Too convenient. He'll think I made it all up."

"Tell him the truth is putting fiction writers out of business. If that doesn't work, tell him I told you to keep Santiago away from my cat. He'll believe you then. Better yet, tell him to go to my place and feed my cat and while he's at it, he can feed some tuna to the Big Man goon tied up in the cellar. Can't miss him. Looks just like you except for everything."

"You're kidding."

"See for yourself. Lady next door has a key unless you want to look around for the broken window. Tuna's in the left cupboard above the sink. You're going to need a knife and some bolt-cutters and I don't mean for the tuna."

Harpo shakes his head in disbelief.

"This mean we're friends?"

I ooze dubiousness.

"I don't have cop friends anymore. And I was always a Groucho guy anyway."

"But I can tell you believe me. Don't you?" Art Garfunkel's gone. He's left a blue-eyed Golden Retriever puppy to keep his seat warm. "You believe I'm being set up just like you were set up. You believe I'm clean of this. I believe you too, Mack. I do."

"I couldn't care less what you believe. I believe in Ella Fitzgerald. Can you sing a verse of 'Summertime'?"

He doesn't answer.

"Right. Then the only thing I believe, Harpo, is that it's time for me and Sig to go. And I believe that very strongly." I drop the gym bag on the floor and give the gun a twitch. "Out."

# SEVENTY

He's a man of his word, our boy. Got to give him that. The taxi. The Stingray back in the lot. The keys and the phone under the seat. The Derringer cleaned and tucked away. Biggest risk is that someone with a badge sees him climbing out of Harpo's car.

But he manages without anyone the wiser. He's back in the little blue Taurus, blasting the A/C and easing away from the curb. He has to stop to allow two uniforms to cross the street in front of him. They wave to thank him. Ray smiles. Waves back.

He's into a new pack of Camels, burning his way south on I-57, halfway to Danville when his phone rings.

"Mr. Malik. What's the word, Raj?"

"Just like you said, Mack. I'm parked outside your place. He used my phone to call someone for the address. He's showing a badge to the lady next door. She doesn't look happy."

"Judith? That just her disguise. She's never happier than when she's suspicious. You should be very suspicious if Judith ever actually looks happy. Did Harpo ask you to wait?"

"Yeah. He said he may need to use my phone again."

"Keep your phone out of it. Let him ask for Judith's phone next time. That'll be a fun conversation. Listen, Raj. My house'll be crawling in twenty minutes and that thing in your hand's got my number on it. More than okay by me but more than a little interesting to the guys who wear bracelets on their belt loops. How fond are you of answering the same questions over and over?"

"Not very."

"Smart kid. Go ahead and split. Don't tell Harpo. Just go. I'm good for the fare and an embarrassing tip. In the meantime, Raj?"

"Yeah?"

"Take a tip that's not so embarrassing. Don't trust anyone in this town. Especially the cops."

# SEVENTY-ONE

Been awhile since I've been buzzed into the visitor wing of Danville Correctional. There was once a time when I was out here four days a week for a solid month, working a triple-homicide trail that led back to an old-home-week powwow out in the yard. I don't know the staff out here anymore. But they know me. And not in a good way.

I go around and around with the intake, a guard, and a supervisor about me not being on Cecil Green's approved visitor list. No exceptions for former law-enforcement. I have to promise that I'll shut up and go away if they'll go ask Cosmo if he's willing to have a short conversation.

So they do. He does. I'm on his list.

They don't like it but a deal's a deal and rules are rules. I pay extra with a fifteen-minute time limit and a body search that leaves me wanting a shower. The guy looking for a hand grenade in my crotch wants to know about my face. I tell him he needs to buy me dinner first and he offers to even-up my bruises. We agree to skip the dinner and try fucking ourselves instead.

They make me wait at a table in the visitor room for an hour before Cecil Green shows his face, one I've never seen without a paperclip to hold it still. They march him in and sit him down on the metal stool. He's a skinny black man with a lazy brown eye and a fat red lip. His shoulders have a permanent hunch, bending his body into a question mark. But the question of Cecil Cosmo Green is as easy as they come, ready-made for the Monday crossword.

Six letters, begins with S. Rhymes with pimple.

"Ten minutes," says the guard.

"The deal was fifteen," I say, stupidly.

"Nine."

"I can't afford this conversation. Do you mind?"

The guard shuffles away, taking his time. Cecil and I stare quietly at each other until the guard's out of earshot.

"Scarce believe my ears," Cecil says softly. "Raymond Mackey to see me. That you? Raymond."

"In the flesh," I tell him.

"Damn." Cecil eyes me up and down like I'm an exotic bug he wants to flatten under his shoe. He's not sure whether I can fly. "What you want, Raymond Mackey? You want in? Feel left out of the fun? How about I take retirement and you wear the jumper?"

"Bitter, are we? Attitude is everything, Cosmo. You know that."

"Fuck you, man. Here's what I ..."

"Keep your voice down."

He responds to the stern tone and looks around. The same guard is walking another inmate into the room and sits him down two tables away. Cecil's un-lazy eye tracks the newcomer. Then he's back on me with a menacing whisper.

"Here's what I know, you old, white mother-fuck. I know two phone calls sent me to the shit house and I know the same two phone calls sent your corrupt cop-ass to a fuckin' Barcalounger. That's some shit right there, Raymond Mackey. Some *shit*. I need me some friends like the ones you got."

I hold up a finger and wag it. Only one of his eyes cares enough to watch.

"I got one friend, Cosmo. Just one. But he's got friends everywhere, see. Eyes everywhere. Ears everywhere. *Your* Barcalounger is all about being alive. Got that? My one friend can yank you out of that chair right quick. And I mean before the sun drops behind the walls of this place."

I can see Cecil swallow the lie. It doesn't sit well. He's popped off and said his piece but now he's not so sure that was such a good idea. He takes a look at the guy two tables over, still alone. We both do. He's white and bald with the ugly opposite of the Sistine Chapel on his scalp. He's got arms and fingers to match. He's waiting for someone who's never coming and never was coming.

Cecil looks back at me and hisses like a snake with a boot on its rattle.

"What you want with me, man?"

"Me? I don't want anything, Cosmo. But that one good friend of mine? He wants some information. Only reason you're alive is that he trusts you. You've got what? Eight months left?"

"Seven. I'd be out already, but ..."

Cecil looks around, sullenly. I pick up where he left off.

"Not your first fat lip, is it? Got to play nice if you want to go home, Cosmo."

"Got to stay alive first. If you got to do the extra, then you do the extra but you got to stay alive, man."

"My friend knows you'll be looking for work. He needs to know who he can trust. Who he can't. Understand?"

Cecil's offended.

"I'm a fucking *soldier*, man. He knows I'm going to lay it down."

"Like I say, Cosmo, you're in the joint and you're still breathing. That's no accident."

"All a brother got to do is ask, man. All Big …"

I cut him off with a sharp flick of a finger and a glare to match.

"Ah, ah. No names. This conversation is being recorded for purposes of customer satisfaction."

Cecil takes a breath. He picks at a sore on his hand with a dirty thumbnail. Then he looks back at me and leans in like he's giving me a stock tip.

"All a brother. Got to do. Is mother. Fucking. Ask."

"Good."

"Your friend has him lots of friends. That's the truth. But not all them friends know each other. Understand? Hard to know who's who is all I'm saying. Who's still in and who ain't. I don't mean no offense."

"None taken. This time."

"What you need, man?"

"My friend got hold of a certain... device. It's been tucked away in a sealed bag for as long as you've been gripping these bars. And the sealed bag's been tucked away in a little locker in a big concrete room. But he's got it now, see. And he's had a look inside. And you know what's been tucked away in that device all this time, Cosmo?"

"Tell me."

"An extra chip. And not the potato kind or the poker kind or anything like the one you've got on your shoulder."

He's confused. His good eye actually slides to his shoulder and back.

"Huh?"

"Someone knew where you were every step of the way, Cosmo. You were a flashing red blip on a screen. And so my friend is ... what's the word ... *concerned* ... he's concerned that one of his friends isn't really a friend. Understand?"

"Look. Here's the history, Raymond Mackey. You call me, man. Tell me when and where. I say okay. Next night, same time, you hit my ass up again. I call you back. You change the when and where. I say okay. Three days later I show up to make a deal at a surprise party. They take the shit and pay for it with bracelets and a free lawyer. And here I fucking am, man."

"Who gave you the burner?"

"Slappy G. Same as always."

"Slappy."

"Yeah. Slappy Gin changed them burners out every week. Clockwork."

"Okay. Who'd Slappy get it from?"

"The Russian. Far as I know. Like always. Could be Slappy switched up the supply. But listen, man, none of that shit is me. Understand? Slappy hand me a burner. Say Raymond Mackey going to hit me up with the deets. I say *who the fuck, Slappy*? Slappy say *mind you own business, Cos*. And I do. Then I *am* the business and my shit's in jail."

"The Russian."

"Yeah, man."

I look at the guy two tables over. He's twiddling his tattoos. Cecil looks too. I lean in close enough to smell Cecil's lunch.

"You didn't hear this from me, but my friend has lost that loving feeling for Russia. Understand? He's out in a big way. My friend is all about cleaning house."

I sit back and watch Cecil go to work on that. Just enough to question everything he thought he knew. I wait until I think it's safe to stick the shovel in again.

"So let me ask you this, Cosmo. You know anything about Slappy taking some Russian lessons on the side?"

Too much. Even Cecil's lazy eye struggles out of bed at this one.

Crime fighters have an instinct for bullshit. Crime writers do too. They know when they've written a character off the edge of the cliff of plausibility, so that he just kind of hangs there, Wile E. Coyote style, grabbing at thin air as the reader rolls their eyes. I can tell by the look in Cecil's eyes that I've just handed my story an anvil.

Cecil's face implodes into suspicion. He looks briefly at the other jumpsuit in the room, then comes back with a whisper.

"Slappy's fucking dead, man."

I give him my best look of irritation.

"Of course, Slappy's fucking dead. Slappy got sloppy, Cosmo. Try to keep up, will you? I've only got two minutes left. When Slappy was alive, you know, back when he was handing you Russian burners, you ever hear Slappy and the Russian talk about ..."

But Cecil's spooked now. He doesn't know what to believe or who rattles him the most, me or the illustrated con two tables over, either of whom could be Big Man's eyes and ears.

"Don't know shit. Okay? I look like the kind of guy who's ever been in a room with the Russian? We don't breathe the same fucking air. I got the burner from Slappy. Like always. And then you took it from there. Raymond Mackey. Go on back to your Barcalounger. Have you a cold beer and leave me be."

I give him a doubtful squint and shake my head.

"Beer gives me gas, Cosmo. More of a bottom-shelf hooch guy. Old Forester, neat."

"Okay, Old Hooch. Well, you tell your one friend I'm good for it. Like fucking always, man. I'm good for it."

Cecil stands abruptly. Meeting over.

The skinhead masterpiece at the other table looks our way for the very first time. First at Cecil, then at me. He shrugs.

*Meeting over, Hooch.*

# SEVENTY-TWO

A hole in the sky is on fire. A round, flaming island in a pale, blue sea. Ominous white warships tower on the eastern horizon as Earth's airy skin bubbles and blisters.

Ray's back in the little blue bull, buzzing back up I-57. Smoking and thinking. Sluicing Cecil's bullshit, looking for a glint of gold. Mile after mile, he's lost in the puzzle.

But then I can see his eyes soften, losing that hard focus. So I can tell she's in there with him. Marlo. Has to be. He can feel her sealed inside the glovebox of the Impala, surrounded by Walmart shoppers. Locked away in a dead man's camera.

In his head, he's crawling inside to be with her. Inside the Impala, the glovebox, the camera. He wants to watch her – again – coming out of the darkness toward that opening door. Flinging her arms wide. Those flying eyes. That smile. The ghostly smell of her. He wants to stay in there with her, inside Sluggo's camera, for a digitized eternity. Thirty-one squares of light away from the impossible clouds of shadow in photo forty-four.

Ray pulls the phone from his pocket and opens the screen of recents. If the memory of an image in a camera is a poor substitute for Marlo, then an incomprehensible call log is even worse. He can't afford this. Not now. Mooning over the dead is desperate, distracting and dangerous. He's already got one *Triple-D* weighing him down. He doesn't need a spare. The first *Triple-D* makes you crazy. The second gets you killed.

Ray sighs. His thumb hovers over the button.

# SEVENTY-THREE

Three calls while I was chatting with Cosmo. *Unknown Caller. Number Blocked.* I'm crazy to think it's her. It can't be. It isn't. It has to be. It is. And back again.

In my head, the darkness splits into a crack of light, like a door slowly opening. Like a trunk slowly opening. Suri stretches out a hand and grabs the lowest rung of a ladder. She starts to climb up into the big dream. Delaney had known his time was coming. Once you start watching yourself ...

The empty cupholder wants my attention. My head can feel the blue loops of Doris' phone number on the cocktail napkin in my pocket. I jam my hand inside and pull it out. The Bloody Mary. The stick of green celery is like a straw in a glass of burning lava. The bottle of Tabasco in the background says it all. *Bloody Hot!*

# SEVENTY-FOUR

Ray's thumb makes a dive for the *back* button. It hopscotches across the keypad like there's no rhyme or reason to it except maybe to keep from making his own phone ring and hearing his own voice. The thumb finally stops. Ray stuffs the napkin back in his pocket and presses the thing to his ear.

"It's me. Yeah. As well as can be expected. I suppose so. But it feels like the walls are closing in. Yeah. Just like you said. I have a favor to ask. It's way out of line, so I shouldn't ask but I am anyway. It takes a man to admit he needs help and I need yours. I need your help almost as much as I need a drink. Yeah. In an hour at Bucks? Thanks, Smitty."

# SEVENTY-FIVE

Feels good to be out of the wind and the sun. I tell Doris to hold me to two shots of Old Forester, no matter what I say or do. I don't trust myself but I trust Doris. Both shots are a memory by the time Smitty shows. I order a third and she brings it to me. This is why I trust her.

"Jesus, Mack," he says. "You look like shit. What happened to your face?"

"New workout program. I'm keeping people's arms and legs in shape."

It's awkward. Smitty's picked up some second thoughts on the way over and the booth's too small for all of us. We talk about the goddamned heat, waiting for Doris to bring him a drink before I can get down to business and not be interrupted. He tells me rain is coming. Like that's going to bring some relief. I tell him the only thing worse than this kind of heat is the soggy kind of heat.

It looks like he wants to debate that proposition so I change the channel and ask him about his dead, double-tap dancer. Smitty can tell I miss the action. Finding all the pieces that don't want to be found. Putting them together. You can take the cop out of the puzzle but you can never take the puzzle out of the cop. He laughs at me wanting an update but not unkindly.

"Been, what, forty-eight hours since our last drink? I can't solve them that fast, Mack. Witnesses don't talk to me like they talked to you. You had a gift."

"Guess time's passing differently for me, Smitty. Seems like a lifetime ago. A lot's happened in forty-eight hours."

"It looks like it."

Doris shows up and sets an icy white glass down on a napkin. Smitty thanks her. He waits until she's gone. His face is wincing, like he's expecting a tour of open wounds.

"Okay. I don't know what this is about, Mack. I was thinking about your call on the way over. And I just ... this is not something ..."

I recognize rejection when it's clearing its throat to sing. I don't give him the chance.

"You were right, Smitty. Twill's horny as hell and humping my leg. He thinks Andy Marx is dirty and that I got him that way. He thinks ..."

Smitty waves me off.

"Stop. Mack. Please. Hold on. I told you last time. I can't be a part of this. You know how many people are out looking for you right now? I shouldn't have told you that people are looking but I figure you already know that. I shouldn't be here. But hell, now that I am, I should be giving you a ride downtown in the back of my car. Jesus Christ, Mack. What went down in Bloomington?"

"I wasn't in Bloomington. Nice this time of year but I can do without the bullets. I do have a theory about Bloomington though."

"No. Don't tell me. I don't ... I can't do this."

He starts to stand but the drink in his hand just got here and doesn't want to leave the table. He sits down again. Then he gives me the finger; the one with a ring on it.

"I got a wife, Mack. I know you don't have a wife anymore and I'm sorry as hell about that, I really am, but I've still got one. She's a professional volunteer. She'll work for anyone that can't afford to pay her any money. Okay? You get the picture? It's all on me. It's all on my paycheck. And I've got a kid, too. I wasn't smart enough to have a kid who's stupid, Mack. I was dumb enough to have a kid who's smart. The Ivy Leagues are going to eat me for lunch. So I can't lose my job. I can't set fire to a career just because Twill's looking for another head on his charm bracelet."

"Smitty ..."

"No. I'm sympathetic, Mack. I am. I feel like you got a bad rap before and it feels like you're warming up for the same nightmare again. But I can't get involved in this. I can't give you information because that makes *me* a mole. And I don't want *you* to give *me* information because I'll only have to cough it up on the first question and that makes me a shitty friend."

I hold up both hands. Surrendering.

"I'm not asking for information, Smitty. And I won't give you any. I don't even have any information in my pocket to give you in the first place. Although I suspect my pockets'll be full in about," I look at my watch, "six hours and change."

"I don't want it, Mack. I don't know what you're into but either find somebody else or keep it to yourself."

"Smitty, listen. All I'm asking for is good police. Someone on the inside who knows what it means to protect and serve. I don't trust Twill farther than I can throw him. I don't want another Bloomington. If you're good police, then you don't want another Bloomington either."

That did it. Now he's listening.

"Hold on. Wait. What are we talking about here, Mack?"

"I've got a meeting tonight. A source. You don't want to know and I don't blame you so I won't tell you who. But this source has the goods. From the inside."

"The goods on who?"

"Don't know yet. I'm guessing I'll get a bead on whoever's after Suri and why. Maybe I'll get the Chandler PD mole. The keys to the kingdom. Or maybe none of that. Maybe I'll get a discount coupon for the next Chandler PD bake sale. But I've been promised documents. Okay? And my source is now officially scared shitless." I let it soak into the soil, then I keep pouring. "It's already raining, Smitty. It's raining bodies. I count five. Four down in Bloomington and another out in DeKalb. I don't want to be number six. I don't. I've got a cat to feed and a book to write and the bourbon isn't going to drink itself. But, brother, if someone on the inside has got the guts to get the information out of CPD, then someone's got to have the guts to do something about it. It's either that or Big Man can just write his own ticket. And only one of us at this table still has a badge."

Smitty looks at me hard. The gears are turning.

"What are you asking, Mack?"

"I just ... Hard for me to admit this. I'm old and off my game. Retirement has a way of dulling the senses. I'm a mall cop now, Smitty. Okay? I knock teenagers around for sticking merch in their pants. I'm not up for this level of play anymore. Not alone, I'm not. Not by any stretch. It has to be me that does it but I need real police on-site. Someone sitting in an unmarked out in the parking lot that can spot trouble headed in the front door and call it in. Or at least someone that can stop trouble on the way back out. Someone who knows enough to step in if I walk out of that hotel arm-in-arm with a good buddy or two, or three. I don't have any good buddies, Smitty. Understand?"

I let him think. He's teetering. I give him another push.

"Look. If nothing happens, which is most likely, then you were never there. If something happens and you have to call it in, then you were only there because I called and asked you to meet me for reasons unknown. There's no downside for you here."

"Really, Mack? No downside? Three of those dead raindrops are cops. Tell me again about how there's no downside."

"Not asking you to mix it up. Just look for trouble. Ring my phone. Call the cavalry."

"And the upside?"

"Protect and serve, brother. Maybe this handoff tonight gets Twill and IAD what they need to move on. Yanks Big Man out of CPD root and branch. It's a real-police upside."

Smitty's face arranges itself like it can see the future.

"Shit. Goddamnit, Mack. When and where?"

# SEVENTY-SIX

Ray leaves before Smitty can change his mind, swinging by the bar on the way out. Doris is drying a glass. Ray jerks his head back toward the booth.

"Whatever he wants, Doris. Run a tab. I'm good for it."

"My goodness, big spender. What's it take to be your friend?"

"Nine lives. Otherwise, it takes a death wish or poor judgment. I'll take either."

"Right. You watch yourself, Mack."

"Always do, Doris."

Ray gives her a wink and knocks the wood just once. He turns and heads for the door.

Outside the bar is the inside of a sauna. The air has turned heavy and wet and the sun is not going peacefully into that good night. She's being buried alive as the thunderheads watch.

Ray stops on the corner to fire up a Camel. He blows a long, tight stream at the rooftops. Toward me.

Ray can walk and smoke at the same time. I've seen him do it. But he doesn't. He stands there on the corner and takes another drag. Like he can feel the eyes on him and doesn't care. Like he's waiting for everyone to catch up.

When he moves again, it's in a saunter to the corner before crossing the street, smoke trailing behind like he's a slow-rolling train. Rocky's leaning in the doorway of The Bodega, waving his porkpie like a paper fan.

"Hey! Macaroon! What's the word, buddy?"

But Rocky's missed the train and Ray keeps moving. Ray raises his cigarette hand as he goes so the Camel can say hello and goodbye.

The other hand is busy working the phone.

# SEVENTY-SEVEN

Chicago Towing and Impound is a tired ball of light imprisoned by a chainlink fence. Inside the ball are rows of dusty, dented and dingy automotive inmates, waiting for someone to care.

Well, I care. So does the gleam in my eye and the fifty in my pocket.

I'm counting on the stringy-haired Led Zeppelin fan sitting in the trailer and looking at phone porn to care less than I do.

The kid wants me to prove that I'm Anthony J. Rickens of 6912 Wolcott. I tell him I'd sure like to do that but my driver's license is in the car with the medicine I need to stay alive long enough to pull together the money I need to bail out my white, vandalized Pontiac. He wants me to come back with cash, credit or a cashier's check. I'd tell the kid I'd like to do exactly that because until that cash, credit, cashier's check thing happens, I'm stuck driving my sister's crappy blue Taurus. I point to the curb in a humiliated accusation and ask how long he'd be able to drive that thing and still call himself a man. The kid actually considers the question.

"Couple of hours, maybe. I need payment, man. Sorry."

I reach into my pocket and invite Ulysses into the discussion.

"This is all I've got right now. I don't need a receipt. And you get to keep the Pontiac in jail. I just want my driver's license and my hydrochlorothiazide pills."

The kid's phone rings like maybe the porn is tired of waiting. He shrugs and sticks Ulysses in his pocket so he can answer the marimba. He points over my head, then closes the trailer door.

Doesn't take me long to find Sluggo's ride, quiet and brooding between a red F-150 with a white hood and a black Monte Carlo with no rear axle. I pull Doris' cocktail napkin out of my pocket and use it to grip the passenger door. It's locked. Fortunately, the pipe I laid into the driver's window thirty-six hours ago is still paying dividends. I climb in behind the wheel and use the napkin to open the glovebox.

The plastic Baggie is right where I left it, hairbrush and the small bottle of Tabasco tucked neatly inside like shaving cream and ketchup, or nose clippers and nondairy creamer, or any number of other things that don't belong together in a glovebox.

I'm curious, sure. I'd like to test my theory right here and now for the Ford and the Monte Carlo to witness. But I'm not curious enough to go another round with Led Zeppelin. I roll up the bag and wedge it down beneath my waistband. I close the glovebox door with the napkin and close the driver's door with my hip.

I'm back through the chain-link gate and climbing into the Taurus before the kid is off the phone. I tuck the Baggie under the driver's seat and swap it for the Sig Sauer, which I put in the passenger seat next to me. I start the car and look at my watch. It reminds me with a slap just how quickly time can move when you're not paying attention.

Marlo's in my head as I pull away from the curb. Her memory comes with a voice and a smell and a touch. She quickens my old and desperate heart.

*Never be late for your own surprise party, Ray. If you can't be early, better not to go.*

# SEVENTY-EIGHT

Business is down. The Westmark parking lot lays in a flat empty sprawl like the space inside the chalk outline after the body's gone. The Taurus approaches the drive, hesitates, then commits. Ray finds a space in front and pulls in just like he's any ordinary guy on any ordinary night.

He's not any ordinary guy, of course. He's Raymond Mackey. There's only one of those. Maybe two. And there's nothing ordinary about tonight. Numbers on a wheel are seemingly ordinary numbers until the little white ball stops bouncing around and picks one. Then *a* number becomes *the* number and the ordinary becomes special and the world will never be the same. Everything we do in life is the last thing we will ever do until the precise moment that we do something else. And then *that's* the last thing. Every time we see someone, whether we love them or hate them, is the last time we will ever see them, for the end of time and beyond, until the precise moment we actually see them again. And then *that's* the last time.

At some point, that last thing we do really is the last thing. At some point, that last time we see someone really is the last time. Then there is no more bouncing around the wheel of numbers. Then it's done. Nothing in life is ordinary. Not ever.

Ray puts the Taurus in Park. He cuts the engine and kills the lights and stabs the smoldering Camel into the cupholder. All for the last time.

\

# SEVENTY-NINE

I stuff the Sig into my belt and pull my shirt over it. The guy in the rearview mirror looks like he wants to report a hit-and-run. I promise him a stiff drink and a good night's sleep when I get back. He's not buying it. I can tell he's lost his trust in everything and everyone. Even me. He turns away as I open the door.

The sky behind the hotel lights up in the pulse of a silent white flare of heat lightning. I pause on my way to the entrance, looking around a parking lot dotted with sleeping cars. In the back shadows of a hedge border, Smitty's car is only pretending to sleep. He flashes his lights. I don't acknowledge the signal. I turn and continue on my way, looking at my watch. The sky booms with thunder. The whole earth feels the sound in its chest.

Corruption has its paperwork and routines. Perfidy has its process. First one there gets the room and texts the other. That's how it always worked before and that's how it will work tonight. I was usually late. I hate texting. Tonight I'm thirty minutes early. That puts it all on me.

I'm feeling sickly nostalgic to be standing at this counter again. It's basically the same as before. They've tweaked the color scheme and put some potted plants in the corner and they've propped a clerk up front with a name tag suggesting that it's okay to call her Sandy. Other than that, everything is exactly the same. I ask if room 305 is available. Sandy smiles with an understated incredulity. She thinks I'm adorable to be so optimistic in my condition at ten-thirty in the evening. I want to tell Sandy that she's mistaking morbid curiosity for optimism and that real optimism would be expecting I'm going to make it to eleven. But that's a conversation for tomorrow's newspaper.

She hands over the card key to room 407 and points me to the elevator.

The room is the same, too. It's not room 305, and yet it's exactly the same. Every mirror remembers my stinking, cheating face. I keep the lights off and look through the peephole at the room across the hall. Then I pull out my phone and sit on the corner of the bed.

I never text. With my lowbrow phone, texting is technically possible but discouraged, like shaving with a steak knife or cutting prime rib with a razor. Each button corresponds to a number and three letters. To get a letter you want, you've got to push the button either twice, three times or four times in quick succession and then wait two seconds and move on to the next letter. God help you if your fat fingers make a mistake or if someone's holding a gun to your head. It's faster and easier to train your cat to send a telegram.

So I don't text. Last time I texted anyone, it was in this very building. Even then, I never had to worry about the letters. All I needed to text was a number: 305. It's no different this time. Just the number. Off it goes, into the ether.

I stuff the phone in my pocket and lie back on the bed. The light fixture is a single giant eye. Watching me. I can't help but think of crazy Delaney, sprawled on a hotel bed. Suri handing over her cigarette. Delaney sending a cloud up to the popcorn ceiling, blowing smoke in his own face as he looks down on the bed from up in the big dream. Suri said she thought he was crazier than a nuthouse squirrel.

*Until I heard Royce walking back toward that trunk.*

The knock comes at ten past eleven. I sit up on the bed and pull the Sig from my belt. I step quietly across the room and push my eye to the peephole.

They each have a gun. Deno's got both hands on the grip, pointing at the floor. Pete holds his with one hand up near his face, barrel pointed to the ceiling. They stand across the hall with their backs pressed against the wall, one on each side of the door to room 406. They're both tense and ready to go. I stare at them. We all breathe together. They have no idea I'm watching.

Marlo, like an aroma. *We never know who's out in the dark universe looking in. And I'm saying, it's always someone.*

Pete does the knocking. Soft. One knuckle. Like a woman. He puts his thumb over the peephole.

The door to 406 opens with some enthusiasm. Judging from his face and the bottle of bubbly in his hand, the man on the other side is expecting company. He's a science teacher, this guy. A professor-type with the round, clean glasses, and the mustache, and the plague of pattern deforestation on top of his head that he can't do anything about. His wife travels for work. That's when the professor here travels across town to the Westmark, where there's more room and less risk than under his desk. The white hotel robe doesn't flatter him but I'm guessing it's an improvement over whatever's underneath. Whoever he's expecting, he looks about as surprised to see strangers with guns as Pete and Deno are to see terrycloth slippers.

Badges are the only way to explain the guns, so out they come, swinging from lanyards as Pete and Deno push the poor professor aside and barge into 406 for a look around. They clear the room and burst back out into the hall, stuffing guns angrily into holsters, all in under eight seconds. Pete wants the professor to close the door and stay in his room until he is advised that the area is safe. Pete says this to the number 406, which is now all that is left of the professor.

"Fuck," mutters Deno off camera. Then they're both gone.

I pull out my phone and dial.

"Smitty."

"Mack. You okay?"

"Yeah. I'm learning a lot about who to trust. Still got your eyes on?"

"Right where you left me."

"You're going to see two hard cases come out. Both cops. Chicago PD."

"Jesus, Mack. What've you gotten me into?"

"They're both locked and loaded and pissed off for being played. Keep your distance."

Smitty makes a sound at the unnecessary tip.

"Will do. Thanks for that, chief."

"Ten bucks says they're headed for a black Caprice. But whatever they climb into, Smitty, follow it and let me know where they go."

"Thought we were clear on this, Mack. I'm not engaging these guys. I don't know which end is up in this thing."

"Not asking you to engage. Just follow."

"What about your source?"

"No-show. I'll cool my heels for another fifteen because there's no sense in being half a chump. I don't like to waste my time unless I can waste all of it. Call me when you're on the road. I'll meet up with you."

"Where?"

"Wherever they end up."

"Then what?"

"Then you go home to your not-for-profit wife and your tuition-bait kid with a slap on the back from yours truly."

"I can call for backup."

"That gets you involved."

"I can be anonymous."

"More people with guns who hate me? Pass. I'll go it alone."

"Don't be an idiot."

"I'm just watching and learning. Like I said, that's about all I'm capable of these days."

"Hope you know what the hell you're doing, Mack."

"Pretty long odds, Smitty. I'd stick to poker if I were you."

I kill the call and return to the corner of the bed, setting down the phone and the Sig next to each other like I'm putting a couple of kids down for a nap. I snag a look at my watch and flex my right hand, which is swollen and sore as hell from showing *Señor Jódete* around my basement. That makes me wonder what he looks like as a butterfly, and then about just how many police were crawling through my home, and then about how Phil is making out without her drop of Forester.

But then, I know exactly how Phil is making out without her drop of Forester.

Another knock – soft, feminine – pulls me and Sig quietly off the bed to the peephole. A woman. Not a woman. A girl itching to be a woman. Bangles on slender wrists and hair to slender shoulders. She's dressed for height and heat. I can only see the back of her. She gives 406 another soft knuckle.

The professor opens his door and I do the same. He's still in the robe. I seem to surprise both of them.

"How old are you?" I ask.

"Me?" The kid splays her fingers over her barely covered chest.

"No. Him. Your age I'm pretty clear on. He's the one pretending to be a teenager. All my years undercover and it's still the statutory rape investigations that confuse me the most."

The power of speech has fled the scene. They can't take their eyes off Sig hanging from the end of my arm. I point at the girl.

"Now, how about you go home and sneak back in your bedroom window. The officer down in the lobby will take your name and address."

The girl turns and speed-walks up the hall, disappearing around the corner. I turn to the professor, who's started breathing through his eyes. He's developed a stutter.

"I ... I ... I ..."

"And how about *you* get back in that room and stay there like my partner told you to. Open that door again before an officer comes by to take your statement and we will come to your home and arrest you on your driveway. Do you understand?" We stare at each other. "Do you un ..."

"Yes. Yes."

His door closes with a thud. I'm in the hall, one foot still propping my door open, alone. Alone, but not alone. I'm being watched. Maybe it's just the peeping professor. Maybe. I point to 406 with an accusing finger.

"I can see you," I lie. "Go sit on the bed. Go call your wife. Then call a lawyer."

The feeling is now a pair of eyes lighter, but still there. Inside, my phone wants my attention.

# EIGHTY

Ray steps back inside and lets the door slam. He scoops the phone off the bed.

"Smitty. Yeah. Not yet. Where are you? Which direction? Okay. Don't get made. Keep your distance. Yep. I always do. Thanks, man."

He disconnects and crosses the room, stuffing the phone in his pocket and the gun back in its hiding place under his shirt. He turns the knob slowly and eases out through the door, closing it without a sound until that loud, unavoidable click at the end. He turns and waits a few seconds for the professor's curiosity to screw up its nerve. Then he points at the peephole again.

"What did I say? You think this is a game? Sit your ass down on that bed."

He waits another second or two, then heads up the hall to the elevator.

On the ground floor, the elevator doors slide open and Ray steps off with his fingertips brushing the handle of the Sig. To anybody else, it looks like maybe the antacids aren't working.

He absorbs in all directions. To his right, there's an older couple at the front counter. Sandy's explaining the rules and pointing at things with two fingers. He can't see the lobby or the adjoining bar. To his left is the tiled hallway that leads to the back exit.

Decisions. Right gets him a shot of Old Forester and a route to the Taurus without having to walk around the building. Left gets him outside unseen.

Left it is.

Blackjack is either a game of mathematical odds, blind luck, or instinct. Depends on who you are, although less on your abilities than how you choose to justify your choices. Life is no different. And when you bust, you bust. Doesn't matter whether you forgot to carry the one in your head or your luck dried up or your instinct got locked out in the rain. There you stand, looking like a chump with an empty glass while the croupier with the secret smile reclaims his cards and all your chips. Doesn't matter, at that point, what went wrong. It just doesn't.

Take a good look at the cards in your hand. Life's got its own croupier. All those cards belong to him. Not a smiler, this guy. Black robe. Sharp blade on a long pole. Can't miss him.

# EIGHTY-ONE

Three steps outside and I see the idling Caprice. Deno's behind the wheel. He hits the party lights just as Pete materializes out of the dark behind me and jams a gun barrel into my kidney. I make a move for Sig but Pete's too fast. The gun is gone and I'm spinning face-first into the wall of the hotel.

The Westmark folks have spared no expense in making the concrete look like broken river stones. The building takes sides, cutting my face open on the first hit. Pete bangs my head again and then once more just to make sure I get my money's worth. He holds the hotel up with my face as Deno pulls my hands behind me and ratchets on the cuffs. The world is alternating red and blue. I'm spitting blood and wearing bracelets. Only forty-eight hours and life's repeating itself.

"You have the right to remain silent," says Deno, just in case someone's watching. He pats me down and finds the phone in my pocket. "Anything you say can and will ..."

# EIGHTY-TWO

It can and it will. So Ray doesn't say a word.

He bows his head under the force of Deno's palm as he gets stuffed into the backseat. I can see him in there through the back window, half in, half out, head down, shoulders slumped. Like a man accused. Like a criminal.

Pete climbs in the other side, closing the door behind him and pulling Ray fully inside. Deno closes up the driver's side, climbs behind the wheel and pumps the siren twice for the full show. The Caprice lurches forward, circles around the back of the building to the closest exit and speeds away.

It's a short drive. The top lights go dark within two blocks and in two more blocks, the headlights do the same as the car pulls into the shadows behind the Chandler Carpet Barn warehouse. Deno keeps the Caprice running. He pops the trunk and opens up the backseat and yanks Ray by the neck out onto the parking lot. Pete's already out and coming around the back.

It's not pretty. Not for an old hump like Ray. Not for anybody. They both go at him pretty good. His hands are still in the bracelets. Nothing he can do but take it and bleed. When they're done, they try to stand him up but it doesn't take because now his legs don't work and all the oxygen he needs is still down there on the parking lot. Pete has to drag him back to the open trunk by the armpits and then stand him up again.

Gravity takes it from there. Like it's on the payroll.

# EIGHTY-THREE

I am alone in the dark. We all are. You and me and the rest of the planet. We don't know where we're going and every moment is our last. We're all in the trunk. All any of us really want is that crack of light every now and then to keep us oriented. A touch of something soft and warm. A whiff of the familiar. A taste we know. A voice we trust.

I come and go in the hot blackness of my rolling oven. Ninety degrees. Maybe more. Blood is clotting in my nose. Breathing is difficult. My left ankle feels like it's been run over. Both of my arms are asleep and I join them off and on, dreaming of banded lobsters in the boiling pot. The road beneath me is paved in Braille. It keeps me conscious with a single, endlessly repeating word that I can read with my whole body.

*Pain. Pain. Pain.*

All trunks these days come with a latch. Sensible, well meaning, big-government regulation intended to give abduction victims one last shot at some fresh air. And I know exactly where that latch is in a Caprice, assuming it hasn't been disabled. But you can't legislate your way out of unconsciousness or handcuffs. All I can do is ride and hurt and think of Suri in her trunk. Smelling death and decay. Listening to those footsteps. Climbing that ladder up into the big dream. Reaching down out of the clouds for her own hand as the light and the stink poured in and pushed the lid open.

Marlo. Suddenly. Cleaning her camera like it's a rifle.

*Three types of people in the world, Ray. Those who believe in what they know. Those who know what they believe. And real detectives, who believe in knowing nothing except what the littlest hairs on their neck tell them is true. And that, no matter how outlandish or impossible, they take for gospel.*

The car around me slows and makes a lot of sharp turns over a lot of sharp bumps. They wake me up. Help me to focus. The pain comes in pairs of pairs.

*Bump-bump, bump-bump. Bump-bump, bump-bump.*

Railroad tracks.

I'm not so far gone that I can't do the math. I'm guessing we're somewhere in the neighborhood of Bedford Park, home of the Belt Railway of Chicago.

The car slows to a stop and the engine goes quiet. The air smells hot with blood and diesel. Light rain spatters against the trunk lid above me. In the distance, the rolling stock booms like thunder. I can feel Deno and Pete get out. The car lifts. Like I'm starting to float. They close their doors. No one's talking.

The trunk does not open. Each second is a black hole stretching to minutes that stretch to years out from the event horizon, which is the long metal groove in front of me. The groove capable of splitting along the middle and moving like a mouth.

I close my eyes. In my head, I can see the car. The Caprice. Not from inside the trunk. From the outside. From above. The metal above me is transparent.

And there I am, curled up, down there like a criminal fetus in handcuffs.

Look at him in there. Me. Ray. Good old Ray Mackey. Me. The washed-up lump, waiting to be born all over again. Waiting to take my hand. His hand. My hand. His hand. Waiting to climb up out of that trunk and up into the big dream. Look at him in there. Poor Ray. Little criminal. What'd you do that was so bad, Ray?

Marlo. In her hospital bed. Tubes. Beeping. Her hand.

*Not much time, Ray, I know. Suppose I could have told you sooner. But what good would that have done? I'm not so big on long goodbyes. I've had it better than most. I'm satisfied as long as you take good care of Phil. Don't make my cat an alcoholic, Ray. Look at me, honey. Watch after yourself.*

The metal groove splits in half. The big mouth opens, flooding blackness with something less than blackness. White lightning behind a dark anvil of cloud gives instant, blinding shape to a row of boxcars looming above the blur of a head.

The head tilts one way, then the other. Finally my eyes can focus enough to make out a sad kind of smile.

I spit blood. At least it's not a surprise.

"Hey, Smitty."

# EIGHTY-FOUR

Deno and Pete pull him out of the trunk, like a bag of flour, and let him drop at Smitty's feet. The rain falls against the sky in tiny streaks of silver. Smitty squats.

"What'd I tell you about the rain, Mack? I've got a nose for weather. Always have."

Ray groans and coughs into the ground.

"Jesus, guys. Sit him up. Sit him up. Get his face out of the dirt. Have some respect for a fellow officer. This guy was one of the best. He really was. Sit him up, for chrissake."

Pete grabs Ray by the shoulders and props him up against the bumper. Ray's eyes are closed. The rain slides down his face in dirty, bloody rivulets. The ragged bellows of his chest move a mouth that hangs open like it's on a broken hinge.

"What'd we learn tonight, Mack? Huh? We learn anything? You have any fun? Or was all this a waste of time?"

Ray swallows hard, like whatever's in his throat is too big to make it the rest of the way. He spits red, making Pete take a step back. He flutter-opens his lids.

"Yeah. Yeah, Smitty. I learned ... I learned to always keep ... keep your phone in your pants pocket. And not ... and not in your coat pocket. Especially on ... especially on poker night. Lot of ... lot of smoke breaks there, Smitty."

Smitty laughs, looking up at Pete, then Deno. He nods with a smile, then looks back down. The water runs off his head.

"You know the worst part, Mack? The worst part is that Stretch was dealing me one great hand after another. I've never been so lucky at poker in my whole fucking life. Could have cleaned up. Both nights I could have cleaned up. But I folded. I lost my stake. I just turned those cards in and let it go. And that hurt. It did. Because I'm a much better poker player than that. Better than you, that's for damn sure. So it hurt. But that's life. Isn't it, Mack?"

They look at each other in the rain. The sky flashes a crooked smile. Smitty doesn't wait for an answer. His voice is soft and serious.

"Here's how this works, Mack. You've seen your last sunrise. Okay? Tonight it ends. Gonna die in the rain. You know it and I know it. I respect you too much to lie about something like that. Only question is whether the lights just go out or whether you feel it to the very end. Okay? Now. We're all going to take a little walk and then I'm going to ask where I can find Suri. You tell me, we make a call or two and check it out. You and I can talk about old times while we wait. We'll get up in one of these boxcars. Get out of the rain. And if it checks out, you get to go to sleep. Like a baby. But if you don't tell me? If you lie to me, Mack? We're going to keep trying until you die very much awake. Is that clear?" Smitty nods. Then he answers his own question. "I think that's pretty clear."

Smitty stands and slicks the water from his face. Silver droplets cling to his beard, refusing to let go. The rail yard booms with thunder.

"Okay then. You start thinking about that, Mack, and meanwhile the boys here are going to get you up so we can go someplace a little more private."

They yank him up as Smitty heads off across the tracks of the Clearing Yard toward the hodgepodge of boxcars, flats and tanks, all quietly taking the rain, like old buildings in a lost, abandoned city. They drag him forward a few steps before Ray goes rigid. They stop. Ray shakes those once mighty shoulders.

"I can walk for myself."

# EIGHTY-FIVE

It's a narrow, steel canyon Smitty has in mind. Long rows of rolling stock on either side. Not much happening in this part of the yard. Sounds won't be a problem. It'll take awhile to find the body.

Smitty's waiting, legs dangling from the opening of a red boxcar, when we cross the last bit of track and round the back end of a tanker car. Pete and Deno let go of my arms.

Not like I'm going anywhere.

The long, rectangular sky above the boxcar canyon walls flashes white. Smitty stops himself from speaking, hand in the air. He wants to wait for the thunder. It rolls over and under and around us, then echoes away in all directions, like the whole world is a bug on a railroad tie just as the fully loaded two-nineteen to Buffalo blows past.

Smitty looks down at me, swinging his legs, fingers drumming the floor of the boxcar. His face is all business.

"So," he says. "Suri."

"What about your nonprofit wife, Smitty? Your tuition-bait boy? They down with all this Big Man crap?"

"What they don't know won't kill them. Unlike you. But thanks for asking. Where's Suri?"

I pretend like I haven't heard him. I can't hear anything over the screaming of my ankle.

"Nice lady, your wife. Erin. She still at the clinic? I remember her from all those charity drives. The nice nurse riding on the blood mobile. Handing out stickers."

Smitty shakes his head and sighs.

He knows. He's trying his best not to show it. Better for him if he can end things without having to consider the truth about what's in my soupy head. But my little neck hairs say he knows that I know. All night he's wanted to believe that retirement has softened me, given me a sloppy tongue or a saggy memory, enough so I don't know one hotel from another. Westin and Westmark.

Now he's up there shaking his head, rethinking who's the better poker player.

Smitty nods to Pete.

Deno is suddenly behind, squeezing both of my shoulders like I'm a tube of toothpaste. Holding me up. Pete unloads his fist into the side of my head. One shot, clean and solid. He puts a spare into my gut. Deno won't let me go and I stay upright. Pete takes a step back.

"Suri," says Smitty, calm and cold.

My ears are ringing. I need to breathe. I need to sit and breathe. I look around. There is no place to sit.

"Want to sit up here with me?" Smitty asks. "Out of the weather? Tell me where she is, Mack. The next time I ask is really going to hurt."

Deno's still holding me in place. I can feel his muscles tense.

"Wisconsin."

"Don't you lie to me, Raymond Mackey."

"Wisconsin."

"Where?"

"Kenosha."

"Where?"

"Hampton Inn. I don't know the room."

"She alone?"

"Yes."

"What name?"

"She didn't tell me. Not after Bloomington. Could try Ginger Turner. But she's not stupid, Smitty. She could be lying about everything. She could ..." It's been coming on since the car. Now it's here. "She could be anywhere."

I get sick in Pete's direction as Deno holds me away from him. I cough and hack and spit until Smitty's had enough.

"So," he says. "Kenosha. Hampton Inn."

"Fuck you, Smitty. Fuck you for making me do this to her. Suri didn't ask for this."

"Better hope she's not lying to you, Mack. Because I can't tell the difference between her lying to you and you lying to me. They're both going to hurt."

"I need to sit," I say.

"So, sit. I forget about your age." He feigns misunderstanding. "Oh, up here? Sure, come on up, Mack."

No way I can climb a ladder up into a boxcar. Not with the bracelets. Not with this ankle. Deno lets go and I let myself drop down into the wet dirt. Everything hurts. Everything seeps. My ankle howls. My ears are ringing.

"Suit yourself." Smitty stands and pulls a cellphone out of his pocket. He dials. Whoever answers already knows who's calling.

"The Hampton Inn in Kenosha. Maybe Ginger Turner. Get behind the desk. Well then, show them a fucking warrant. It's the night shift. Anyone who knows better is in bed and it's not going to take long. Yeah. You know the number."

Smitty reappears in the door of the boxcar. He looks down at me in the mud. He shrugs.

# EIGHTY-SIX

Thirty minutes. They're all still waiting. The storm is on top of them.

Smitty looks at his watch.

Maybe Smitty knows the weather but Pete and Deno weren't counting on rain. At least not like this. They both look miserable, which is the only thing Ray could possibly be enjoying. They're wondering why they all couldn't just wait in the car. Pretty close quarters, and that much more DNA. But it'd be dry.

They take turns up in the box with Smitty, who spends most of the time leaning up against the door, looking down at Ray in the mud. Trying to figure him out.

Ray looks up. He has to shout over the sound of rain.

"Got to say, Smitty, you look good. You know. Fit. You're on your way to ripped. Must work out every day."

Smitty looks down at Pete sitting next to him. Then he shrugs.

"Jimmy's Gym. Convenient, I guess. Right up the street from HQ. Problem is everybody in that place is a cop. Don't you guys ever need a break from each other?"

Smitty takes another look at his watch.

"I mean ..." Ray laughs, at first to himself and then up into the rain. "I mean sometimes I imagine the poor bastards who one day decide to hold up Jimmy's Gym. Jesus Christ. It'll be like ... like Butch and Sundance coming out of that little hideout in Bolivia."

Deno lets out a snort. Ray looks over at him.

"Right? Everybody in the fucking building is strapped. On the treadmill. Free weights. Rowing machine. Locked, loaded and ready."

Good old Ray. He's got them all laughing now. In spite of themselves.

"Except maybe Andy Marx," he adds. "He's not ready. He's not strapped. Andy couldn't find his own goddamned hairbrush if his life depended on it. Am I right? Fucking Andy."

The smile on Smitty's face slowly stretches out, relaxes, and passes away to wherever smiles go when they die. But his eyes keep their focus. Even as they register the sound in his hand and he lifts the phone to his ear.

# EIGHTY-SEVEN

It's not one of those talking phone calls. It's just the listening kind. Smitty pushes the button and slips the phone back into his pocket. It's a rueful look, hiding anger.

"Turns out the Hampton Inn in Kenosha, Wisconsin is closed for remodeling. All summer, Mack."

"The Hampton Inn? Did I say the Hampton Inn? I meant the Hampshire Inn. All these hotels sound the same to me, Smitty."

Smitty crosses his arms as Pete swings his boots out into the downpour and pushes himself off the ledge of the boxcar, landing with a splat. Deno is suddenly next to me, grabbing my arm, yanking me to my feet.

"I gave you a chance, Mack," says Smitty. "This is your choice, not mine."

Pretty clear Pete's going first. He pulls his gun out from behind his back and grabs it tight by the barrel. For some guys, every problem is a nail. Nothing I can do to stop him.

It's my phone that does that.

It's clanging loud and clear through the rain like somewhere in the gloom, sandwiched between two of these train cars, is an old office building that no one has seen, the kind with an open, push-up window and a desk with a big black phone on a stack of files. Looks like some kind of iron, that phone.

Everyone's looking at Deno. Even me. I can feel the blood draining from my head and my knees give up the ghost. I drop and Deno struggles against the sudden weight before letting me go. The phone keeps at it, loud and clear as a church bell. He pulls it out of his pocket.

"Unknown Caller," he shouts to Smitty. "Number Blocked."

"Is that her?" Smitty shouts.

I'm shaking my head almost before he's finished asking.

"It's not her. No, it's not her."

"You gave her a phone, didn't you, Mack?"

"It's not fucking her!" I scream, tapping rage. "Finish it!"

"Ask her where she is, Mack. She's not worth it. You've got another chance. I'm good for my word. Let's be done with this."

He sounds so far away, Smitty. A tiny voice at the end of a long, dark tunnel. All I can hear is the ringing phone. All I can feel – not the ankle, not the face, not the throbbing pain around my chest – all I can feel are the hairs on the back of my neck.

Telling me the truth. Telling me what I know and what I believe.

Pete stoops and grabs me by the arm, yanking hard enough to make the bracelets bite into both wrists behind my back. Deno hands down the phone to Pete, who lays his gun down to take it. Deno pulls out his own piece and jabs the barrel hard into my temple.

The phone only seems to get louder. No one sees me crying. Not in this rain.

Pete pushes the button and mashes the phone against my ear, yanking my arm closer, moving his face next to mine so he can hear.

# EIGHTY-EIGHT

He's broken, this man. Ray. No less than a woman throwing herself from a balcony down onto a steel fence; he's broken himself over the shape of a love that was always much harder than he was. The love is there, without a scratch. But now he's in two pieces. Two Rays.

It's me and him now. It's me and him until it's all over.

Look at him. Crying in the rain. Breaks your heart.

"I'm sorry," he sobs into the phone. Pete's already pulling it away from his face. "I'm so sorry, honey. I should have told you. I love ..."

But that's all he gets. Poor Ray. It was always too late for that.

# EIGHTY-NINE

Deno's gun explodes in my head. The ringing in my ears sounds like an old telephone.

But sound is a slow train compared to a bullet. They say if you can hear the gunshot, then you're alive and the bullet was not the end but only a message. A message that you've still got a hand or two yet to play. A message that maybe you've still got some time to make right whatever you've made wrong.

Movement on my left and right. Deno crumpling away into the mud as Pete reaches.

I don't know how I know. I just do. I make myself fall sideways toward Pete, covering his gun and his straining hand with my body.

A small popping sound from far away. My eyes register Pete dropping as they pass him, climbing their way up to the top of Smitty's red boxcar.

A shape, a man, bends himself down into the opening of the boxcar. Smitty is unholstered and ready for just about anything. Except maybe an upside-down Santiago. But he tries anyway, swinging his arms in a disciplined golf swing. He gets off a shot, but he trades the bullet for a ricochet and two clean holes in the chest.

Smitty pancakes, like his skin is trying to slough away from his bones. The weight of his upper body pulls him off the boxcar and five feet down, face first onto the track. His beard fails to break the fall, so then it's all up to his neck, which doesn't fare any better.

Santiago rights himself, hanging his legs down over the open boxcar door.

Off to my left, down at the far end of the tanker car, Twill stands up out of the shadows. He shakes his head and holsters his gun.

# NINETY

They want him to wait. Stay where he is, propped against a wet iron wheel, rubbing the cuts in his wrists. They want him to wait for the EMTs and a gurney, as the sound of cars arriving accumulates in the distance somewhere behind him. The rain flashes red and blue.

But he's not having it. Not Ray. He wants out of there. Out of the mud and the steel canyon. Out of the rain. He spits blood. A tooth comes out with it.

Ray extends a hand up to Santiago, who sticks a piece of gum in his mouth and looks down at him, dripping, then sideways at Twill. Twill nods.

It takes all three of them working together but he finally gets himself upright. Twill leaves him to Santiago and heads off to caucus with two Chicago PD uniforms looking to define the crime scene. Plant flags and take photos. And figure out what the hell the Chandler IAD Chief has to do with any of this.

"To the back of an ambulance," says Twill, turning. Santiago nods.

"Copy that."

# NINETY-ONE

We round the last railcar and I finally get a line of sight on Deno's Caprice, all four doors and the trunk wide open. A uniform is taking pictures. Not far away there's a white Tahoe getting the same treatment. I can only figure that elsewhere in Chicago, the bad guys are having an easy time of it. All the cops are here at the railyard, looking at cars and trains. Every last one of them.

Santiago takes it slow, holding my arm around his shoulder, letting me step whenever I'm ready. I can hear the ambulance wailing in the distance. Getting closer. It's raining harder, if that's possible. The upside is that I'm no longer hot. I've traded in the heatstroke for a case of shock. My body is shaking.

Santiago steers me to the right.

"Over to that black-and-white," he says. "Let's see if we can get you a blanket."

Counting Deno's Caprice and Smitty's Tahoe, every car out here is either black, white, or both. Every car but one. It so happens I'm in the mood for yellow. I pull Santiago to the left. He obliges.

"You did good, kid. This here's Santiago. We're walking buddies."

Raj looks up at me from inside the idling cab. His eyes are bigger than the hubcaps. He looks at Santiago and then back. He doesn't say anything at first, but when he starts talking, he makes up for lost time.

"Oh my god. Are you okay?" I open my mouth but Raj needs to vent. "Holy shit, Mack. I didn't want to leave the Westmark. I almost didn't. I almost came in. I saw those two guys go in and, I mean, I'm okay in a fight, I can hold my own, but shit, Mack, those guys ... I did what you told me to do. You said stay on him, so I did. I called the number on the card as soon as you guys showed up here. I couldn't get through and then Sergeant Twill had to call me back and I'm sitting out there behind a fucking train thinking no way anybody's going to get here in time and I'm wondering if it's up to me or if I have to stay where I am so they know where to go when they get here ... I mean holy shit, Mack. Are you okay? There's no way that ..."

I reach in the window with my left hand and pat the kid on the shoulder.

"Raj. Raj. Take a breath. Calm down. You did good. Don't suppose you're packing some Old Forester."

I've stunned him with confusion.

"I'll settle for a smoke," I say.

Raj reaches into the cupholder and grabs a pack, knocking out a long, skinny dromedary. He sticks it in his mouth and lights it, then hands it out the window. The ambulance arrives, cutting the siren and coasting to a stop on the far side of Cop Car Lake.

"You good?" asks Santiago. I nod my lie and he heads off to flag down the EMTs. I breathe in the Camel and hold it for a second too long, coughing it out in a wet cloud. Ten seconds and it's already too soggy. I drop it in the mud.

"So tell me, Raj. How long did our boy stay at Bucks after I left?"

"Long time. Twenty minutes. Twenty-five. I started to think there was a back exit."

"Where'd he go?"

"Leonard Park. Fifteenth Street entrance. He's there, I don't know, maybe ten minutes when a Lexus rolls up. Silver. Couldn't get the plates without spooking everybody. So I just sat tight."

"Could you identify the driver?"

Raj shakes his head.

"Tinted glass. They were window-to-window. Five minutes. Then they split. I let the Lexus go and stayed on the Tahoe like you said."

"To where?"

"The Westmark."

"Straight away. No detours."

"No detours. We were there maybe forty minutes before you showed. He was on the phone a lot. Then those two guys showed. Then the Tahoe just took off and I went after him. Led me here. You know the rest. Holy shit, Mack. Are you okay? I mean ..." Raj nods out into the rain. "Is anyone alive out there?"

I know what he means, but I can't get past Marlo. She makes his simple question a lot more complicated. I try to dodge the conundrum, but then I can't get past Suri. I nod my head, grinding the soggy Camel into the ground.

"Yeah. A woman is alive out there. I just don't know where. Nobody does, I hope."

"What can I do?"

"Lots of things, apparently. I'll be keeping that in mind, Raj. Meantime, you can go home. Or to the curb at the Chandler Airport. Wherever you sleep the best. I'll call you for coffee when I can. I'll pay you what I owe you, then I'll double it and buy you a Danish."

Santiago is back with two EMTs and a gurney. They lay me down and strap me in. Raj rolls away with a worried look.

"Good kid," says Santiago. "It've been all over if you hadn't put him in play."

"Don't I know it." I grab his wrist.

"Nice shooting out there, Santiago," I say. "Raj isn't the only one who saved my bacon."

"*De nada,*" he says. "Someone's got to keep feeding your cat. Speaking of which, I gave her some tuna when we went by to clean up your basement. It'll be awhile before you're back home. I can make arrangements, if you need."

"Stop, Santiago. You're already in my will. But there is something."

"Name it."

"Send a unit over to the Chandler Westmark. There's a guy in room 406. He's all mixed up about his age and what it means to be in love. He needs some help straightening that out."

# NINETY-TWO

Long night at Holy Cross Medical. They move at their own pace.

Lying on the bed, tube in his arm, Ray looks old in the vaguely flowered cotton gown. The parts of him that are not red or blue or purple are covered in a pallid, yellowish-gray. And the bandages. He's a mummy in the making, our Ray. Three fractured ribs. Fractured ankle. Concussion. Face lacerations. Missing tooth. Long night.

Santiago stays close until Twill arrives with two uniforms from Chicago PD, dripping wet with rain and a lot of questions pooling around at their shoes. The ER doc is a five-foot-three firecracker with short red hair and an even shorter fuse. She sends them all packing. Santiago comes back later with some dry clothes from a big-box store up the road.

"I need to call Judith," says Ray. "My neighbor. She'll take care of Phil until I get home. Her number's in my phone."

"You're phone's in evidence, Mr. Mackey."

"Call me, Mack. You've earned it. Last time IAD had my phone, things didn't go so well."

"IAD doesn't have your phone. Not Chandler IAD anyway. I'm the shooter times three on this one and Sergeant

Twill's a witness. Chicago IAD is running the investigation. I'm suspended pending. I've got time for Phil."

"I think they're almost done," says Ray. "Guess I'll be home in a couple of hours anyway."

Santiago's own clothes are still wet. He unwraps a piece of gum and chews it with a sad smile.

"Guess again, Mack."

# NINETY-THREE

They decide not to take me in through the front doors. I don't know if it's too much attention or too many steps for an old guy in an ankle brace. I wasn't consulted and I don't care about the reason. All I care about is staying out of the noon sun, which is back in business with a vengeance, baking the concrete and chasing all the water out of the trees up into the air. We wait until someone finds a wheelchair and brings it down to the car.

Not much has changed inside the Chicago PD. It's a lot larger than the Chandler HQ. The floors have always shined a little brighter. The windows hold the light. A lot more money in the budget for public relations. Trust doesn't come free.

I don't recognize anyone we pass. Even if I should recognize them, they sure don't recognize me. Twill on one side, Santiago pushing the chair. I glide through the glassy halls behind two CPD detectives; the comfortably dry, coffee-carrying, well rested, ready-for-business kind. One of them is older and bald; the other has a full head of hair and doesn't like to shave. One of them is patient and reasonable and inclined to believe my side of things, while the other is angry and impatient and ready to watch me twist in the wind. Which one's which, I don't know yet because we haven't started with the questions. But they've already worked all that out.

The people we pass, uniform or no, are all nonplussed at my rolling carnage. Just another victim. I stand out like a suitcase at the airport.

They wheel me into a small room like the kind I've seen a thousand times. The room of a thousand questions. In my experience, I'm the one asking the questions in these kinds of rooms. But not today. Today it's just like the last time I saw one of these rooms. Today I'm not asking anything. Today I'm all about answers. It's just me and Baldy and Stubble. Twill and Santiago get their own rooms. They don't get to ask any questions today either.

We've only just started into what I know and don't know about what went down in Bloomington. My relationship with Goldie. Carl. Suri. The charmer in my cellar. Detective Baldy's convinced I'm dirty and that nothing I say hangs together. Detective Stubble's my new best friend.

The door opens and a mousy gal with a radio in her hand sticks her head in and nods. The boys give me a few reminders, then stand to leave so they can make it to the monitor in the next room. I ask if either of them has a stick of nicotine for my headache. They tell me there's a rule about smoking and I tell them my lawyer says there's a rule for just about everything. Good cop gives a nod and Baldy pulls a pack from his pocket. He shakes one out and gives me a light. It's a Winston but it'll do. I keep his coffee for an ashtray.

Next time that door opens, I'm staring straight into the eyes of history. It looks a lot better than the present and puts the future to shame. History has never looked so good.

"Jesus Christ," she says. Veronica Lodge is not a religious person, nor easily shocked. Her face doesn't quite know what to do with itself. It settles for looking perfect.

"No, just me," I say. "Jesus went for coffee."

The mousy officer gestures to the metal table. Then she leaves with a click.

"Mack." She pulls out a chair and sits, taking in the swollen, bandaged awfulness that is me. "Oh my god, Mack. They said they were bringing you in. I told them I had to see you. I insisted. They said you were banged up but I ... What'd they do to you?"

I wish Winston was a Camel. I let some of it out.

"What'd *who* do to me, Ronni?"

"I ... I ... don't know. More than one from the looks of it. Why are you even here?"

"Same reason you are, I suppose. Friendly game of questions and answers."

She leans in. Her dark hair swings around her shoulders, sweeping her perfume across the table. Her expression is pinched in concern.

"I couldn't come," she says softly. "I was so scared, Mack. You wanted help. I said I would help. But I couldn't do it. I need my job. I like my job. What you were asking ... it was illegal. We both know it. I got what you asked on Rickens. I wanted to ... I know I said I would. But I couldn't deliver. I couldn't show up. I'm sorry, Mack. I'm just ..."

"Might have told me that on the phone."

"It makes me an awful person, I know. I was being watched. I was afraid. I didn't trust my phone. I figured you'd just ..." she switches to a harsh, half-scolding whisper. "Jesus, Mack. I thought you'd just show up and wait and go home." She gestures in uncomprehending frustration at my face. "What the hell happened?"

"Watched by who?"

"What? Oh." She shakes her head. "I can't ... they don't want me talking. You know."

"Yeah. I know. That's why they put us in a room together to watch us on the closed-circuit TV like a bad soap. Who was watching you, Ronni?"

"I can't, Mack."

"Let me guess. Rhymes with shitty."

Ronni cringes. She nods as imperceptibly as is humanly possible, mostly with her eyes. Then she whispers into my smoke.

"Is he ... did ... is that who ... did this?"

"Who, Shitty? No. Shitty didn't lay a hand on me. Your man Pete and his buddy Deno did all the laying on of hands."

"Pete?" She's turned the volume back up. "Pete Phelps?"

"Yeah. You know. Pete. The bad boyfriend. The guy who got you to put the St. Patrick's Day whammy on me so his pal Tony Rickens could take a few pictures from the Westmark parking lot. That Pete. The one with the pointy boots and a note for my wife."

She's shaking her head. Tears are starting to gather.

"Mack. You don't think ..."

"Sure I do, Ronni. I think all the time. Helps me pass the time while I'm getting kicked in the head. Only it wasn't out of jealousy, like you said. And it wasn't for whatever reason Pete told you at the time. Didn't matter what Pete told you, really. It was enough that Big Man wanted it to happen."

"You're wrong, Mack." She sniffs and swallows and pulls a finger beneath each eye. "You're so wrong."

"Sure I am. I'm wrong in all the right ways, Ronni. That's why you picked me in the first place. You can't tell me what you know? Is that it? They won't let you talk? Well, that's fine by me. I'll tell you what I know."

"Mack."

"I know you were in the dark almost as much as I was. You knew they were putting you up to no good. Garden-variety blackmail, I'm guessing. Something to keep Ray Mackey in line. Hell, maybe you didn't even ask. I suppose questions are frowned upon in your line of work."

"You're hurt. You're not being fair."

"You never knew the real plan, Ronni, which was to feed you to the wolves too. Big Man needed a patsy ready to go, just in case the mole hunt ever got too hot to handle. I was that patsy. I was the mole and you were my lover, working in the Records Department, no less. A regular Bonnie and Clyde, you and me. You were already on the payroll, so turning you out would be easy as pie. Putting us in bed got them photos of two rats in a nest."

"Mack ..."

"Big Man knows how to prepare ahead, I'll give him that. This was all about having a plan to cough up a traitor or two to satisfy Internal Affairs or whoever's snooping around. They put it all in place and then they waited to see if the need ever arose. And sure enough, here comes Lieutenant Nutsack on his big white horse, carrying all manner of hot downtown questions about why the task force can't seem to apprehend so much as Lake Michigan or the Palmolive Building. Time to look under all the rocks and find the mole. Big Man was prepared. He knew the day would come, and it did. But a better idea came along first, Ronni. And that better idea had a name. Come on, give it a guess."

Her eyes are chewing the scenery in a beautiful play about brimming emotion disguised as boredom and annoyance. She pulls her purse into her lap.

"No? Cecil Cosmo Green was the better idea, if you can believe it. Cosmo probably never had a better idea in his whole pathetic life and then he *became* the better idea. Better to sacrifice low-rent, jive-turkey, shit-for-luck Cosmo than Big Man's girl up in Police Records. So they decide to put me in bed with Cosmo instead of you. They kept you tucked away for a rainy day. But then what to do with those photos? Can't let them go to waste. Pete tracked down Marlo and gave her a present. Maybe just for shits and giggles. Maybe they thought I'd be an easier mark without Marlo in my corner. Maybe they wanted her out of the picture and a picture or two of me was the way to do it. Turns out she was leaving me anyway."

Ronni's searching the purse with her perfect fingers. Could be that she's looking for a tissue but I know better. I can see her face composing itself across the table. She looks up at me.

"You have another one of those?"

"Yeah, but they've got rules against smoking."

Ronni leans back in her chair and crosses her arms. Her eyebrows are upset.

"So fast forward and I'm in Cosmo's phone and he's in my phone. Like a couple of life-long chums. And then, like some kind of miracle, the task force gets the only bust that had gone right in eighteen months. Imagine that."

I flip the Winston around and hand it across the table. She takes a drag and hands it back.

"Keep it. I'm trying to quit. So Cosmo gets shipped away and yours truly, the sorry widower, gets shit-canned into an early retirement. And not because they didn't have the goods to prosecute. They had more than enough. Enough to at least make a run at it. But they didn't even try. Why, you ask."

I reach for the cigarette. She gives it to me.

"Well I did too, Ronni. Over and over. I did too. Good prosecutors don't fold like that. They don't bargain early. They bargain late. So, why? But then it hits me. They *weren't* good prosecutors. They were pocket prosecutors. Big Man prosecutors. And I'm still the patsy, see. I'm more useful to him out here in the world than I am in the can with Cosmo. I'd have been dead inside of two months wearing a jumpsuit. That's no good. I learned this morning that Cosmo's been dead all of seven hours. Slipped on a bar of soap and fell on a pencil. Can you believe that, Ronni? A pencil."

I hand her back the Winston and she takes it.

"And all because I paid him a visit yesterday. Poor, stupid Cosmo. That could've been me. But I'm no good dead, see? Out in the world, maybe they can use me. Maybe I'm so bitter, I join the team. Or maybe I'm just a bad association they can shake out of the pack and put to good use. You never know how you might use a guy like me. I know a lot of people. I don't like many of them, but I know them. I know where to find them. Like Suri. Like you."

"Everybody knows where to find me, Mack," she says.

"No. Not the real you, Ronni. I'm one of the few. I didn't expect to find you here but now that you are, it all makes sense."

I reach out for the stubby Winston but she's done sharing.

"Oh?" she asks. "And how's that?"

"Been in a lot of interrogation rooms, Ronni. Talked to a lot of criminals hauled in for questioning. And to a person, you put one of those guys at a table like this and the first thing they do is look up at that camera over my shoulder. They can't help it. We all want to know who's watching us. We all want to know who's up there judging and what angle they have on our miserable lives. But you haven't looked at that camera once. Not once."

Well, she looks now. Those two beautiful windows into an ugly life raise the shades. They flit up, and then back.

"So," she says. "And that supposedly tells you ... what, ex-detective. I'm camera-shy?"

"Hardly. You and cameras have a life-long romance. You've got cameras and mirrors fighting each other for your attention, both wishing they were money. No, it tells me you don't feel judged from above. Tells me you haven't been hauled in here as a suspect. Tells me you volunteered to be in this building, Ronni. I think after our little get-together at your place, you called mister rhymes-with-shitty. Told him Tony Rickens was kissing a dump in DeKalb. Shitty tells you to call me with the goods: Rickens was a bad cop in Big Man's pocket. And why not? Rickens is already dead and burned. Why not wet my whistle? Confirm for me what I already know and then tell me there's more. Lots more. Too much to give me over the phone. Documents. Shitty tells you to set up a meet. So you do. The Westmark. Nice touch, by the way. Nothing like nostalgia to get you killed. I bite the hook and you let Shitty and the boys take it from there."

I wait for a response. She doesn't want to give me one. I wait anyway.

"Quite the imagination, Mack."

"Oh, you have no idea, Ronni. See, I imagine people are decent, that's what always gets me into trouble. I also imagine that when you hung up that phone, you realized the shit storm was coming one way or the other. Either I come out alive or Shitty does. Either way, you know too much. And in this world, people who know too much don't get to pass their genes along. But you … you're a survivor. You decide you need to get ahead of it. And so – *I imagine* – you made a call yesterday afternoon. I'm guessing you reached out to your LT first, shared some of your concerns. Your LT told you to bring it up with Chandler IAD, Sergeant Twill, which is fine by you because the more people who know about your concerns, the better. You talk with Twill, probably on the phone. He wants a preview. I imagine you tell him you're concerned about my out-of-the-blue drop-in. You tell him I'm pressuring you for information about a Chicago PD homicide cop named Rickens. You leave out the part about Rickens being dead. You'd like people to think that all this interest on my part is a prelude to me putting a bullet in his head. So – *I imagine* – Twill schedules a sit-down for today. He calls you this morning to tell you there's been a change of venue, Chicago PD instead of Chandler. You're okay with that. You just want to do right. A good employee. A good citizen. How'm I doing so far, Ronni?"

She takes a drag and blows.

"You're a little soft and shooting blanks, Mack. No surprise."

"Cute. So you show up but Twill's not here. You tell your story to Chicago IAD instead. Then they pass you on to homicide, an angry bald guy and a sweet-as-pie detective who needs a new razor." I jerk my thumb over my shoulder. "You've been under one of these cameras all morning. They don't even register with you anymore."

She doesn't look up at the lens. She wants to, though. She's sure thinking about that camera now. I let her think another beat or two. Then I keep pushing.

"They take notes. They fall all over themselves getting you coffee and donuts because, believe me, Ronni, you're the best-looking concerned citizen they'll hear from in a year. Maybe five. The humps in Chandler are all used to seeing you come and go up and down those stairs, but here? They're eating you up. They could talk to you all day and they could look at you for longer. But they've got other plans. These boys know how to walk and chew gum. So when they're done taking down your story, they ask if you'll help put me in a box. They tell you they're bringing me in for questioning. They want to put us in a room together. See what comes out while they listen in."

The eyes want me to believe I was all wrong about the play. It's not a tearjerker, after all. It's a comedy.

"Funny, is it? You didn't ask to see me, Ronni. *They* asked you to see me. They're over there in the next room right now, looking at each other and shaking their heads as they hear these words. You know why? Because they told me the same thing, Ronni. They asked me if I'd help them put *you* in a box. And I volunteered to help, just like you did."

Silence. I wait. She looks up at the camera. The play's really about betrayal. Always is.

"We're the same that way, you and me. Always helping. Difference is I helped myself into a hospital and you're looking to help yourself onto an airplane headed to the land of drink umbrellas. Nothing refreshes like a splash or two of *Contessa* in a short glass on a white beach. Am I right? That'd be about the only way to get clear of Big Man. Time to take a long trip. You've been thinking a long time now about how you were going to spend all the money shoveled your way over the years. I guess staying alive's as good a reason as any. When do you leave? Next week? Tonight?"

"I'm not going anywhere," she says, hanging on.

"Truest thing you've said to me so far."

She has to think for a moment. Her brow furrows. She drops Winston into the coffee.

"The real difference between us, Mack? I didn't do anything wrong."

"No, you did everything right, Ronni. Right up until you told Shitty about the Westmark. Only way he could have known about that plan was from you."

"That's not true." Three little words, bolting past the guard for the exit. Two others are close behind but get their syllables caught in the gate. "You're forgetting. You're forgetting ..."

She doesn't want to say it. She realizes now that maybe the people in the next room, for all the free coffee and donuts and appreciative hormones, are not on her side. I try to fill in the blank.

"You mean I'm forgetting that I met with Shitty personally. That I told him about our meeting. You don't want to say it out loud because there's no way you should know about that late-afternoon drink. Me and Smitty alone in a bar. Sounds like the start to a bad joke. Who told you that joke, Ronni?"

She doesn't respond. She can't. Her mouth is open but there's no sound coming out. If I was a cat, I'd want that tongue of hers too. I make it easy.

"Don't answer that. Get a lawyer and make him earn his retainer before you answer a question like that. But here's the thing about that late-afternoon drink, Ronni: I told Shitty the meeting was at the Westin. Not the Westmark; the Westin. Two big W's separated by the entire city of Chandler. But somehow Shitty Brian Smith knew exactly where to go. How do you think he knew that?"

Ronni shrugs. Her shoulders suddenly seem too heavy to lift.

"Shitty also counted three dead cops when we had our little drink. I figure two of the three died in the Bloomington bullet festival, which leaves the third in a DeKalb landfill with six rounds in his chest and a big nail in his eye. How do you figure Shitty found out about Rickens?"

"I have no idea."

"Sure you do. I told you and you told him. That's a three-piece puzzle."

"You're way off." Ronni pushes back her chair, blinks her dry eyes, and props her magnificence back up onto her heels. "I'm leaving, Mack. Good luck."

I lean back and look up so I can keep her face in the frame.

"Thanks for that, Ronni. Good luck to you too."

She lifts the purse to her shoulder, turns and reaches for the door. Hand on the knob.

"But here's the thing," I tell her. I wait until she's looking again. "They've got everybody's phone but yours. They've sure got mine. Pete's. Deno's. Shitty's. And yours is next. They're going to get the records and see who's been calling who and when. They're going to ask you for consent before you even leave the building. The nice one with the stubble will suggest that if you don't have anything to hide, then you may as well open the kimono. But here's some free advice from a once-upon-a-time cop. Spend the money on this one. And I mean blow it all. The savings, the pension, the works. Get yourself a six-pack of lawyers. Make the boys in the other room work for it. Because from where I'm sitting, Ronni, they could use the work. And because you've got a whole lot to hide."

The door opens away from her, into the hall. I can see her hand squeeze for the knob. But it's already gone.

# NINETY-FOUR

Nothing quite like watching a man in his element. Seeing the shape of him snap so perfectly into the empty space in the puzzle of his own life.

Just look at him. Ray. Me.

He takes a drink, then sets the tumbler back on the desk. Outside the window, the sky is darkening to bluish-pink as the dying sun lights up the contrails like a match to threads of kerosene. Ray reaches forward and pulls the chain on the lamp. He grabs a clean sheet of paper and rolls it down into the Corsair. Behind him, the fan squeaks. The blank page rattles back a greeting. Ray sighs, turning the Old Forester in place with his fingers.

Marlo's sewing room. He won't be here long. For all the struggle to get up those stairs, he's just visiting. The splinted left leg needs more space. If he gives the leg the room it needs, then he can't comfortably reach the desk and the keys of the Corsair. He either has to sit sideways alongside the desk or type in a stiff-armed reach.

That, and the chair back is too rigid, holding his cracked ribs in the wrong position. He's much more comfortable in bed, or downstairs on the couch close to the food.

So he's just visiting. Reacquainting himself with his old life. The one that he was living seventy-two hours ago.

Phil slaloms his legs under the desk, purring and rubbing the white softness of her body against the hard splint, then leaping up into his lap.

"Thought you were going to finish the book," he says. "What the hell've you been doing? Entertaining. Keeping all kinds of company. Redecorating. Can't turn my back on you for a minute."

Phil meows her excuse and waits. Ray dips a finger into the glass. The drop is gone in an instant. Phil pushes her luck and gets another.

"Well." He moves his hand slowly down the length of her body. Phil stretches out. "We'll start a new book. How's that?"

They sit there for five minutes. Ten. He needs to shift. The fan is now advocating on behalf of the cracked ribs. But he doesn't want to disturb her. Not yet. So he only moves his right arm and its index finger, bringing it down on the Smith Corona; once, twice.

*ME*

The sound of a car pulling up outside makes him stretch his torso so he can see over the old desk and out the window. Below, the cab door swings open and Raj steps out into the street. Ray leans back in the chair. Phil is awake now and looking.

"Sorry, sweetheart. Time to go get our car."

Phil meows and leaps to the floor. Downstairs, the front door makes its sound.

Ray reaches forward with a groan to finish what he started.

*MESSAGE IN A BULLET. A Raymond Mackey Mystery.*

# NINETY-FIVE

The Impala is a sight for sore eyes, right where I left it. There's a big red square under the wiper that I can see even as Raj swings the cab into the lot. I don't need to read it. I know what it says.

Raj is worried about whether I can drive. I still look like some version of death so he's still worried about me staying alive. I indulge the concern as best I can. Mostly because I appreciate it. When was the last time someone gave a shit? We make a mutual pledge to stop smoking and seal the deal with a couple of his Camels. He waits until I'm behind the wheel and the engine is running before he takes off.

If Deno had crushed my right ankle rather than my left, I'd have had to make other arrangements. If Santiago had aimed a little high or a little low ... If my phone had not started clanging the moment it did ...

But that's not where the bouncing ball stopped.

I sit and smoke and look sideways at the glovebox. I reach over and open it up and take out the camera. I hold it in my hand. I hold *her* in my hand.

I brush the *On* button, barely touching it. I look at my watch. No time for that which could easily fill another lifetime. I put the camera in the passenger seat on top of the big, red towing threat that was on my windshield. It takes some doing and my ribs don't like it one bit, but I fish the Model 10 out from under my seat with a finger. It goes in the seat next to the camera. I roll down the window and blow smoke in the direction of the Walmart security camera up on its pole, two spaces away.

*Never know who's out there watching, and it's always someone.*

I put the Impala in gear and give it some gas. My right foot works just fine.

# NINETY-SIX

The bar across the room is busy. It's all Doris can do to rush by with their drinks. It's just the two of them in the booth and she looks at Ray with a pained expression. She wants to be Florence Nightingale. She wants to make it better. She can't. The drinks will be free.

Doris puts the glasses on the table, then hands Twill the paper bag and two large Ziplocs. She heads off to take care of business as Twill puts the Model 10 in one of the bags and the camera in the other. He zips them up and labels them with a ballpoint pen. Then he puts both Ziplocs inside the paper bag and sets that down on the seat next to him, out of sight beneath the table.

"Didn't have to bring you either of those things," says Ray.

Twill takes a sip. He's a Pinot guy. Big surprise.

"You want a medal?" he asks.

"Sure, if you've got one on you. I'd like to toss it in the air and see if Santiago can put a hole through it."

"He could."

"No doubt. Keep the medal. What I really want is a flash drive with a copy of the video on that camera. That and a copy of the last photo. Number forty-four. That's all."

"The last photo?"

"Yeah."

"I couldn't make that out. What the hell *is* that?"

"Whatever you want it to be."

"Can I ask what you want it to be?"

"No."

"Okay. Shouldn't be a problem. What else?

"Bloomington," says Ray to his glass.

"Can't talk about Bloomington, Ray. Investigation's open and active. We shouldn't even be having this drink."

"No, we shouldn't. Except you've got a whole lot of questions that you don't get to ask any more because you're a witness and it's all Chicago PD's ball now. But the questions don't care whose ball it is, do they? You're hoping the drink in my hand is going to loosen my cork. And you'd be right about that, Sergeant. Depending on how many times I decide to bend my elbow. I know what it's like to have lots of questions. Mine are about Bloomington."

Twill bends his own elbow. He swallows and nods.

"I had a car on you from the beginning. I handpicked them. Not from Chandler PD. They followed you to Garfield Park. They had eyes on the back of the liquor store. They saw you put a fake body in the trunk. Nice try. We knew she was still inside the building."

"Fooled Deno and Pete."

Twill gives a dubious smile.

"A ... less *discerning* sort, those two."

"Well, they certainly are now. So then I assume your more discerning crew could see that when I left Pulaski Spirits, I had a tail."

"Looked like it but they didn't know for sure. Look. I cared less about you than her, Ray. You, I knew where to find. But not Suri. They called in the options and I had to make a decision. I told them to let you go and stick with her. So they waited. Sure enough, the real Suri emerged and went into a different trunk."

"Why not take her right then?"

"Wish I had. I wanted to see where she was headed. Who she'd meet up with. Figured that would be helpful to know. So they tailed her to Bloomington. Parked across the street from the Lucky Seven Inn and sat on her. Watched and waited." Twill shakes his head. Just a little. "I told them to wait. I could've ..."

Twill takes a drink and holds it. He's up against the part of the story he doesn't like. Worse than that. It's the part of the story that's about as easy to get his arms around as a cactus. Ray knows guilt when he sees it. He leans back and waits.

"The next night, my guys see someone who doesn't look like he's interested in renting a room. A prowler moving along the back of the Lucky Seven. They call it in and I get a bad feeling. This isn't someone looking to talk. So I tell them to intercede. They did."

"And."

"And it turned into a goddamned bloodbath. Either Carl or Suri had an elephant gun and put it to good use. It took out the prowler and then one of my guys."

"What about the other of your guys?"

Twill looks into his glass and gets lost. Ray nods.

"Ah," says Ray. "Good cop, bad cop."

"Friendly fire," Twill corrects, shaking his head. He still doesn't want to believe.

"Oh, that's the very best case, Sarge. Because maybe it wasn't so friendly after all, right? The cannon plugs the mystery prowler. Bad Cop then plugs Good Cop and tries to finish the job that the prowler can't finish because he doesn't have a head anymore. But then the cannon takes care of Bad Cop too."

"That's one theory. Yes."

"That's not a theory, Twill. That's a nightmare. That's a law enforcement network across departments lousy with Big Man vermin. It means one of the guys you handpicked left the stakeout to pee in the bushes. While he was at it, he dropped a dime on Suri's location. Then when things got crazy, he took out his partner to get the job done."

"No. Fog of war. I knew those men, Ray. Both of them."

"Yeah? Well I know a lot of guys I thought I knew."

Ray waits. Twill's nod comes eventually. A concession.

"That leaves the question of Carl," says Ray. "What kind of gun ended Carl? Let me guess. It wasn't the elephant gun."

Twill shakes his head.

"No, because Suri was holding onto that cannon for dear life. Like it was a third arm. Ballistics will sort it out but here's the preview, Twill: It was one of your handpicked guys that ended Carl. And he was unarmed. Because between the two of them, Suri had the gun. That's some pretty serious friendly fire. No one wants those kinds of friends."

Twill pinches his temples between thumb and forefinger. This is one of those topics he can stomach for only so long. He's done. He takes a drink. His face hardens.

"Officer Brian Smith," he says, returning the glass to the table. It's Ray's turn.

"Right," says Ray. "One of those guys I thought I knew. Always thought Smitty was a nice guy. Turns out he was just a Russian with a mile-wide mean streak."

Twill's eyes light up.

"*The* Russian?"

Ray shrugs his eyebrows.

"I've seen the name here and there. The old task force wires. How do you make Brian for the Russian?"

"What's in a name? Cosmo Green. Slappy Gin. Before he left to take a prison shower with a pencil, Cosmo called me Hooch. Seems to be a thing with the Big Man crew. They like their alcohol. Smitty liked his White Russians. Puts a whole new light on the name you think you have for Big Man."

"José Beggamon?"

"Come on, Twill. Five'll get you ten his buddies call him Cuervo when they go out drinking."

Twill snorts out a laugh.

"Doubtful. The wiretaps of his crew are consistent."

"So's the pile under a bull."

"Yeah, so it's a street name. They get that. But the guy's real, Ray. Marco Wolfe. Drug running. Girls. Chicago hauled him in once to shake him up. Nothing current to hold him on. He knows he's under a microscope but that guy's bad news."

"Oh I'm sure he's a real peach. But he's also a patsy, Twill. A patsy in Wolfe's clothing. He's as fake as the tooth I'm going to have to buy."

"You're throwing blind."

"Maybe. But I've got a feeling. It takes one to know one and I'm the biggest patsy that ever was. The task force might have Wolfe in its sights, but they don't have the boss. They don't have Big Man. They're on Wolfe only because that's been the whole plan from the beginning. That's how this crew works. He's a distraction, Twill, tailor-made. Beggamon equals Big Man? Come on. Am I in the wrong class? Is this the first grade? Big Man could be anybody. He's anybody except Wolfe. Count on it."

Twill scratches his bald head, trying to see things that aren't in front of him.

"Need to think about that. Go back through those old wires."

"You do that. While you're at it, look for the name Contessa. That's Ronni Lodge. She's crazy about the stuff. Nothing like a good rum to keep you relaxed as you stick the knife in. They'd probably call you *Pinot*. Maybe *Cabby*. You wouldn't last long, Twill."

"I might not anyway."

"That goes for any of us. If you were on me from the beginning, then you know my routines." Ray tips his head sideways toward the bar. "You knew I'm a regular in this place."

Twill's face apologizes.

"It's just the job, Ray. We needed to find Suri. We figured …"

"You figured I'd know where to look. So you gave Smitty some marching orders. You wired him up, plopped him down in this very booth, and waited for me to wander in. And I did, because we alcoholics like our routines, especially when they involve blondes like Doris. You wanted my old pal Smitty to give me a friendly heads-up. Maybe I'd blurt out Suri's address and telephone number and where she likes to eat breakfast. More likely, you figured I'd head out to meet Suri in person, let her know how popular she'd become."

"There was no wire. You weren't a suspect. Not officially. And Brian volunteered."

"Of course he did. Smitty's always on the team, especially when he's out for himself. Patient too, just like his boss. I'll bet he waited quite awhile for this gig of yours."

"How so?"

Ray shrugs.

"It was your investigation, Sergeant. I'm just guessing."

Twill's eyes cloud with irritation.

"I've been doing a lot of talking so far, Mr. Mackey. My mouth is tired."

Ray leans back and takes a drink. He looks like he's thinking. Weighing his options. But I know better. I know that look. Ray's been counting on this. Twill thinks he has to pull it out of him. But Twill couldn't stop this story if his life depended on it.

"Okay," says Ray finally. "Fair enough. I'm guessing Smitty waited for the bust of some bottom-shelf Big Man soldier. That bust comes soon enough and when it does, it just magically happens to turn up a 50-caliber shell casing with a note inside. I don't know what that note said. But I don't need to know because I've seen one of those notes myself. I'm guessing it had some version of the words *Merriweather Collectibles* at the top followed by something vaguely alarming like *ship not safe*, or *girls not good*, or *don't do drugs*, something to suggest that whatever shipment of whatever contraband Big Man was planning to bring into town is bait. A helpful hint from someone on the inside that the task force is hiding in the bushes, ready to pull the string. How'm I doing?"

Twill's got a long, thin smile.

"I can neither confirm nor deny."

"Boy, you'll go far in this business, Twill," says Ray, emptying his glass. "Ever think about running for office?"

"Never."

"We'll see. So you press Big Man's little soldier. You pull out all the stops and threaten him with everything short of execution and you tell him you're working on that too. And he finally cracks. He tells you he got the message in a bullet from Suri. Suri who? Hell if he knows. Some whore named Suri. He never read the message and was only supposed to pass it up the food chain. If he's told you anything about where the casing was headed, or who he was supposed to give it to, then you can bet it's a lie because he's a soldier, Twill, and one way or the other, soldiers die for the cause. Just ask Cosmo Green."

Doris the mind reader blows by with two more glasses, taking Ray's empty and leaving Twill with a glass and a half. Ray eyes the fresh drink, then pushes it aside.

"Smitty could have come forward right then. He knew who Suri was, even if you didn't. But he doesn't come forward. He waits. That might be what Big Man's crew does best. Better than running drugs or girls or guns. Better than buying cops and judges. Big Man knows how to wait. And Smitty did too. He waits until you're ready for him. He waits until the suits downtown turn up the heat so high that you need a hot mitt to answer your telephone. He waits until you start pulling people into small rooms to play darts with sharp questions. He waits until it's his turn, see. He waits until he's found."

Twill's face is tense. He doesn't like what he's hearing. So much the better.

"That's when Smitty opens up. You're new over there, Twill. You don't trust anybody. So you're asking everybody about everybody just to get the lay of the land. And when you get around to asking Officer Brian Smith about Officer Andrew H. Marx? Well, that's when Smitty's eyes change. He starts telling you about how Andy likes to run his mouth on the treadmill or spotting weights over at Jimmy's Gym. Interesting, you think. You push a little and Smitty gives a little. Maybe about how Andy's been talking about his buddy, Ray Mackey, and what Old Mack's doing with himself in his retirement, like writing books and keeping bad company. And that lit your fuse, didn't it?"

Twill doesn't react. He turns his glass on its napkin by the stem, like he's torturing a flower.

"Oh, come on, Sergeant. Officer Marx in regular contact with the mole that got away? Sure it did. And then when you asked Smitty if the name Suri rang any bells? Smitty scratches his head and says he seems to recall that Ray Mackey had an unregistered snitch by that name."

Twill turns the glass, giving up nothing.

"Come on, Twill. You were orgasmic. Brand new at IAD and you were already pointing up past the scoreboard with the tip of your bat."

Twill takes a drink, then empties the last of glass number one into glass number two. He lets it drip.

"You seem to be enjoying yourself," he says.

"Who doesn't like being right? That's the second or third best feeling in the world. You should try it sometime."

"I'm listening."

"Yes, you are. Because you know that's when Harpo Marx became the prime suspect in the big hunt for the task force mole. Just like yours truly under Nutsack's watch."

"Nosek."

"Right. Him. You've got your guy in your sights and now the game is about gathering evidence. Building a case. You follow Smitty's little crumbs of cheese to Harpo's desk. Let me guess. An identical shell casing or two. A *Merriweather Collectibles* note pad. I know you can't tell me anything. Save your voice. Drink your wine. You make the trip out to West Baker and talk to the owner, Argus Merriweather. Argus tells you that he and Andy are buddies. Tells you Andy's the godfather of his kid. They go shooting all the time. Nothing like killing targets with 50-caliber Nighthawks to take the stress out of the day.

"So you hightail it back to HQ and you get serious with Andy Marx. Smaller room with bigger darts. You put the shell casing on the table. He seems earnest. Too earnest, maybe because Andy's just that diabolical. The whole wide-eyed Art Garfunkel thing is a ruse. He says he doesn't know what the hell you're talking about. Sure it could be his shell casing, but he doesn't know anyone named Suri to give it to. You ask him about me. Yeah, he knew a Ray Mackey in another life. Crappy bowler. Full of opinions and bourbon. But he hasn't seen or talked to Ray Mackey in ages. Ages."

Twill looks up at the repetition. Ray squints back.

"A good performance all around but you're not buying it, are you Twill? No. Your hooks are already in too deep. You can't feel okay about Andy so easily. So you put together a photo lineup. Five officers, including Andy; the picture version of the list you gave me in my living room a few days ago. You go back to that bottom-shelf, Big Man soldier in lockup and you tell him maybe you can go easy on him if he cooperates. What's his street name, by the way? Rummy? Appletini? Jägermeister?" He waits with a wry smile. "Come on, Twill. You can let that little cat out of your bag."

Twill closes his eyes in a slow blink.

"Sidecar," he says.

"Ahh. Right. Did you find him tart and refreshing?"

Twill doesn't answer.

"So you lay out the photos and Sidecar-with-a-twist pokes Andy right in the nose. He says he remembers seeing that very same guy talking to the whore with the bullets. You know … Suri. And then, Katy bar the door, Sergeant, because that did it. Andrew fucking Marx. So now you're on fire, congratulating yourself for being right all along and for not buying the Art Garfunkel song and dance. You suspend poor Harpo and start digging. You requisition his service files. The records officer, one Veronica Lodge, is happy to help. She sends you the records for Andy's time with the Chandler PD and she throws in his Chicago PD records as a bonus. And then there she is, in black and white."

"Who?"

"Come on. Who. Don't play this game with me. Ginger Turner is who. Ginger aka Suri. Arrested and then kicked loose by Officer Andrew Marx for failure to properly Mirandize. *Eureka*."

Twill smiles. He starts to speak but doesn't get the chance.

"No, no," says Ray. "Not yet. So you play another round of darts with Andy. You show him the arrest report. His memory comes back. Oh, *that* Suri, he says. He tells you the street name slipped his mind, but that he remembers the Ginger Turner case because it was so off-the-rails weird. He tells you that your predecessor, Sergeant Nutsack, made a hush-hush, off-the-record request that he kick Ginger loose and take the fall for bad policing. Well, that doesn't smell good, does it? Chandler IAD looking to unhook a Chicago PD vice collar? What's going on there? Andy doesn't know. But back then he was brand new to Chandler PD. He goes along to get along. He doesn't ask questions. Assumes Nutsack's got some uncomfortable connection to the john. So Andy calls the prosecutor in Chicago and says he can't deliver the testimony. Case closed. Suri skates on a good bust. Right?"

Twill doesn't answer.

"Now, I don't know if Andy's story washed with you, but if you're like most cops I know, you don't like to let go of a suspect. That's just petting the fur the wrong way for any self-respecting cop. So you don't let go. You don't. But you've also got this little ... this little ..."

Ray slides the tumbler back in front of him, turning it clockwise in his fingers, trying to think of the word.

"This little splinter in your conscience. Like a voice in your head that won't shut the hell up. Something's not quite right. So you reach out across town to Nutsack. Maybe you even take a meeting. Nutsack laughs it all off. Never happened, he says. Andy's got his wires crossed with someone else. Knowing Nutsack as I do, maybe he shares a not-so-favorable anecdote or two about Officer Marx. Always had his doubts about the guy, that sort of thing. Nutsack slaps you on the back and sends you on your way. Says to call him if there's anything he can do to help. Your job used to be his job, after all. And off you go.

"Well, great. So now what do you do? You think about showing Andy how to properly Mirandize a suspect. But you can't. Not yet. Because even with all you have, you don't have enough. The water's still too cloudy. So you decide you can't pull the trigger on Andy until you find Suri. At least now you know what she looks like and you've got an actual name. Ginger Turner. So you put the word out. All of Chandler and greater Chicago is looking for Suri and Ginger Turner."

"What's her real name, Ray? It's not Ginger Turner. And I know you know."

"I do. I wrote it down so I wouldn't forget. Problem is I forgot where I wrote it down."

"Come on, Ray."

"Oh I remember now. Little slip of paper inside a fortune cookie inside Jimmy Hoffa's pocket. Your problem, Twill, is that Suri wants to be found just about as much as Jimmy Hoffa."

"Like I don't know."

"Right. And so eventually you realize that I'm your best hope. Me. Raymond Mackey. Problem is I'm crazy as a loon and bitter about all things police. At best. More likely I'm pulling Andy's strings from deep inside Big Man's pocket. Either way I'm not likely to give you the time of day."

"Ray ..."

"No, no. Not yet. So you decide you need someone I'll trust. You think about wiring up Andy, but he's too unpredictable and you're not real certain about our relationship. And then, suddenly, there's Smitty in your head, with his hand up in the air. You figure that if I'm dirty, I won't open up to Smitty any more than I'd open up to you. But if I'm only crazy and bitter, well, maybe I'll rant and rave and something will pop out. What do you have to lose? If nothing comes of it, you'll come knock on my door personally and see if I pick Andy's name off a list. Which you did. Ruined a perfectly good hangover."

"You were never officially a suspect, Ray. We just needed some help."

"And you got some. Smitty was Shakespearian. Just a happenstance encounter in an out-of-the-way bar with money on the ceiling. I'm in for my usual nightcap and Smitty's just here working some double-tap, gangland-style homicide of a stripper, waiting for Prancers up the street to start hopping so he can do a little undercover gawking."

"But I suppose you didn't buy it," says Twill.

"Not a word. I asked Smitty why he was going it alone. Smitty says he was breaking in a newbie, fresh off the tree. Two days on the job and the newbie was home sick throwing up his dinner."

"So."

"So when's the last time Chandler PD Homicide plucks from the academy tree? And even if it did, when's the last time two days on the job puts you riding shotgun on a gangland-type murder investigation? Greenies ride a desk for at least a month."

Twill purses his lips, thinking. Ray keeps at it.

"And who lies about a thing like that? Unless maybe everything is a lie because all the world's a stage and I'm the only one eating popcorn."

"The double-tap homicide bit was true, Ray. It's an active case."

"It may be, but there's not one solid lead. Right? *Bupkis*."

"Still too early."

"Smitty wasn't working that case, Sarge. Smitty *made* that case."

"What are you saying?"

"I'm saying you don't really look for a perp if the perp is really you. Smitty did the deed on the dancer, both taps. That or he had it done. I'm guessing he put the dancer on Sluggo's to-do list."

"Sluggo."

"Anthony Rickens. Chicago homicide. I don't know his drink name. Swill. Moonshine. Something unrefined. He's feeding the birds out in DeKalb now."

"How?"

"Suri. She turned him into Swiss cheese."

"Your Suri?"

"No, the one with a fringe on top. Are there two Suris in this thing?"

"Okay. So."

"So I'm guessing the coroner found a lot of skin under the fingernails of your double-tap dancer."

"Maybe. It's not my case."

"Well, it is now. And don't *maybe* me, Twill. Maybe nothing. It's true. The skin under the nails belongs to Andy Marx."

"How do you know that?"

"I don't. But it's true anyway."

"What was Andy doing with this stripper?"

"Defending himself. He didn't know her. Smitty paid her some money to do her worst to his pretty face. So she did and then Smitty gave her the money just like he promised. He just didn't give her any time to spend it."

"Why?"

"Why'd he kill her? Come on."

"No, why'd she scratch Andy Marx?"

"Because they wanted you to see defensive wounds on Andy's face."

"From a stripper? I don't ..."

"Not from a stripper, Twill. From Suri."

"Suri fighting off Marx."

"Right."

"But no one knows where Suri is."

"Right. But the plan was for you to know *exactly* where Suri was. The plan was for you to find Suri in a DeKalb landfill with a bullet in her head and Andy's DNA under her nails."

"You're saying Suri scratched Officer Marx."

"Come on, Twill. Keep up. Jesus H. No more Pinot until you get this part. Did you get the Baggie from the Taurus like I said?"

"Yes. It's at the lab now."

"Good. It's going to come back with Andy's hair in the brush and his blood in the Tabasco bottle."

Ray takes a drink. He swallows and waits. Twill's face starts to sour.

"Do I have to ask?" Twill asks.

"Happy to. Sluggo snatched up Suri and took her out to DeKalb to end her life and do her nails. It was a frame-up, see. Just for you, Twill. Made to look like Andy was feeling the heat and wanted to shut Suri up. He finds her, hauls her out to his favorite landfill, she fights back for all she's worth, scratches his face and catches a bullet or two. Some seagull out at the dump drops a dime and the police come running. Then you get involved and start connecting dots. Presto. That seals the case against Andy Harpo Marx. Not the murder case so much as the mole case. Then you close up shop and Big Man goes back to work until the next time he needs a patsy to take the heat."

"Wait. The hairbrush..."

"Stolen out of Harpo's gym bag. Harpo and Smitty were muscle buddies at Jimmy's Gym along with every other cop in the city. You already knew that, you just didn't think to throw some more darts at that bullseye."

"Okay. And the blood?"

"Smitty's wife works for a health clinic. Erin Smith. Heart-of-gold type. Big smile full of pearls. She was organizing blood drives when Smitty first showed up at Chandler PD. Once a month, the same blue bloodmobile takes up three spaces in the HQ parking lot. And I do mean blue blood. Cop blood. I gave every month."

"Erin." Twill finds a pen in his shirt pocket and clicks it. He flips over his napkin. "Erin Smith."

"Forget Erin, Twill. She's the genuine article. My guess is that somewhere you're going to find a lab tech on the clinic payroll with a bank deposit history that looks like a snake after a big meal."

"Okay." Twill clicks his pen closed. "Walk me through."

"Harpo gets in line at the curb and holds out his arm for a cookie and a cotton ball like everybody else. Then sometime after hours, a handful of dead presidents puts a couple of eyedroppers full of Andy's blood inside an old Tabasco bottle. The bottle finds its way into Sluggo's glovebox for safekeeping, along with the stolen hairbrush. Harpo's already replaced the missing brush with the same make and model because that hair's not going to style itself. He's already replaced the blood in his veins too. And no one was ever the wiser. Not until I saw the new brush in Harpo's bag and the *I-Donated* sticker in his car. Then I was the wiser." Ray points. "Now you're the wiser. We owe all this wisdom to my movie date with Harpo and Doris' cocktail napkin."

"What?" Twill's pen clicks back to life like it doesn't understand.

Ray reaches across the table and flips over Twill's napkin. He taps the glass with the celery straw. *Bloody Hot!*

"But they didn't count on Suri, see. Kid's got grit. No one ever figured she'd put Sluggo down. But she did."

"So now everybody wants her," says Twill, like he's reading a headline. "Us and them."

"Right. Luckily the wind found her first. Blew through Bloomington and took her away."

Twill scratches his head again. The itch is getting worse.

"So the messages. In the shell casings."

"Meaningless. All the world's a stage, Twill. How hard is it for a couple of crooks – a mole and a goon – to have a quick conversation, back-to-back in a café? Window-to-window in some parking lot. They don't need to go through the elaborate message-in-a-bullet crap. Those messages were never for Big Man. They were for you. Or for whoever might've had a mind to hunt for a mole on the task force. A bullet casing is just a bunch of brass wrapped around a bunch of nothing. The bullet has left the building. It either hits you or it doesn't and that's the only message worth a damn. Whatever's left inside the casing is for chumps."

"Guess I deserve that," Twill says.

Ray shakes his head.

"I'm no one to talk about getting played. Took a jailhouse chat with Cosmo Green for me to realize Smitty was the one who brought me down. Smitty picks up a burner phone and waits for the right time. The right time turns out to be a couple of marathon poker games at Stretch Wilson's place. Just a friendly game of cards with a bunch of cops making sure I didn't eat my gun for losing my wife. Stretch doesn't abide smoking. Got to go outside on the stoop to do that. Smitty played the big loser and spent a lot of time outside those nights. Turns out he took my phone with him to keep him company."

Ray tightens his lips and pushes the air through his nose. I know what he's thinking.

"I had the dates and times of those calls. The poker games were my alibi. Me and a bunch of cops. But, of course, I took smoke breaks too, most of them alone. And all those guys watched me step outside and come back in again. In and out. In and out. All night. Nutsack hit that point hard: I made the calls during my smoke breaks." Ray looks across the table and shakes his head. "You know, people always said smoking's bad for you. I always thought they meant cigarettes would kill you with cancer. Never considered they might help frame a guy as a mole."

Ray looks away again. It's Twill's turn to keep quiet and let the other guy roll in regret.

"And the thing is, Twill … The thing is the answer was always right in front of me. I just never looked at it. It was Smitty. The goddamned Russian himself. He got the burner number inside my phone. Right outside on Stretch's stoop, cigarette in his mouth. His right hand called his left hand. Then he slipped the burner phone to Slappy Gin, who got it to Cosmo, per the norm. Cosmo's got no idea he's the sacrificial lamb. Next night Smitty loses big on a good hand, slips outside again to smoke and play with my phone. Makes a call to Cosmo, pretending he's me. Cosmo calls him back on my phone. The next day Cosmo shows up at a surprise party with my number in his phone. And his number in mine. The rest is history." Ray looks across the table. "So I'm the last person that can judge you as a chump."

"Ancient history," says Twill. "It's dead, Ray. Let it stay dead."

"Not possible. Read your Faulkner. 'The past is never dead; it's not even past.' But Smitty's dead. Guess I'll settle for that."

Twill holds up his glass. Ray nods and they toast.

"This one's for you, Santiago," says Ray. And he means it. "You and your waterproof nerves and your twenty-twenty night vision."

They both swallow and think and fondle their glasses. Across the room, Doris holds up a bottle with a question on her face. Ray shakes his head.

"Here's what I don't get," says Twill finally. "If the plan was for Suri to get picked up so she'd finger Officer Marx as the mole, the guy with the bullet casings, then why take her off the street? Why kill her? Isn't it better if she's around to testify that she got the messages from Andy?"

"Sure. I'm guessing that was the plan. But plans change, Twill."

"Don't they though. And what, exactly, changed these plans?"

"Dry cleaning."

Twill looks like maybe he misheard.

"Come again?"

"Dry cleaning. Sluggo really knocked Suri for a loop. Beat her up bad as a signing bonus into this whole racket. Suri never takes to the hard sell, Twill. Like I say, the kid's got grit. She went along with the program for awhile, but then he tuned her up again, and just for the hell of it that time. You know what the word *suri* means in Japanese?"

"Hard to find? Invisible?"

"No. Means *pickpocket.* After that last beating, Suri went pocket fishing when Sluggo was in the can. She got some loose bills and a dry cleaning ticket came out as a bonus."

"And?"

"Back at the hospital, I gave Santiago a phone number."

Twill hesitates. Then he nods.

"Yes."

"Has he run it yet?"

"Yes."

"Let me guess. Came back to the office of His Honor, the Mayor of Chicago."

Twill is quiet. Thinking about whether he should answer.

"Yes," he says. "Part of a block of fifty reserved numbers."

"It's his. It's the mayor."

"How do you know?"

"Because S. Royce was the name on the dry cleaning ticket. The dry cleaner uses phone numbers as account numbers. The S doesn't stand for Sluggo. Tony Rickens took that name to the landfill. No, the S stands for Samuel. Samuel Trenton Royce."

Twill closes his eyes.

"Hold it." They open again in fresh confusion. "Let's assume, for a second, that that's ... Can you tell me what Sluggo ... what Anthony Rickens is doing with the mayor's dry cleaning ticket?"

"No. No, I cannot."

They look at each other for a long second. Someone at the bar is laughing.

"Okay," says Twill. "So. Suri."

"Like I said, Suri doesn't take too well to being beaten up. So, with her face swollen like some Macy's parade balloon and thinking Sluggo's last name is Royce, Suri gets herself loaded on cheap rosé and lets her fingers do the walking. She calls the number. She leaves an impolite message. She's not working for Big Man, she says, no matter how many rapes and beatings she has to take. She says they can all meet in hell and Ray Mackey's going to take them there."

"Oh."

"Yeah. Not the kind of message the Mayor of Chicago likes on his voicemail, I'm guessing. The whole plan for Suri to finger Andy-the-mole had to change at that point. I became a liability then, too."

"You're telling me ... Jesus, Ray. You're telling me ... that the Mayor of Chicago ..."

Ray holds up a hand.

"I don't make you as being simpleminded, Twill. Bald-minded, yes. Skinny-minded, maybe, to go along with the rest of you, but not thick in the head. I'm not saying the mayor's in Big Man's pocket. I'm saying his dry-cleaning ticket was in Big Man's pocket. You've got to figure out the rest. I'm not police anymore."

Twill stares like he's someplace else. Ten seconds of silence bleed into twenty. Thirty.

"Would you like to be?" he asks.

Well, now. Our boy Ray is not easy to surprise. He covers well enough. But I can tell. It hits him in the chest.

"Sorry, Twill," he says. "I'm sworn to serve and protect the Southside Mall."

"Think about this, Ray. Last night was quite a haul for me. When the dust settles, three bad cops are off the payroll."

"Four," says Ray. "You're forgetting your handpicked guy out in Bloomington. He should count for something."

"Fine. Four. Point is, downtown my stock is headed uptown. I've told them I want my own team. They don't like it but it's a reasonable request. They want to see how I make out on my own. When Chicago IAD closes this investigation, I'll be renewing the request."

"Come on. You can't sell that. My name is something you want to scrape off a shoe."

"Your record's clean, Ray. No charges. Retirement with a pension. You afraid of not being liked?"

"No. I'm used to that. I prefer it. Fewer surprises that way."

"IAD's not an easy beat. I need good people with thick skin. People who don't mind cold shoulders and sharp looks and eating lunch alone. I need some people I can trust."

"Oh? Think I trust you, Twill?"

"No. But I'm used to that."

"What about Santiago?"

"He's thinking about it. He likes where he is. But Property Crimes is wasting his talents and I'm tired of borrowing."

"You do know I'm crazy, right? My psych eval is required reading."

Twill nods and lifts his eyebrows.

"Depersonalization-Derealization Disorder. Garbage, Ray. You're as crazy as I am. And I'm just floating it out there for now. I don't need an answer."

"Well, you have one anyway. That way it's there and waiting when you do need it."

"Sleep on it, Ray."

"Thanks. I've got a couch and a backseat for that kind of thing."

"Okay. But something tells me you're dreaming about dry cleaners and bad people looking for pickpockets who don't want to be found."

Ray's got nothing. Twill smiles a little, then turns the page. He reaches into his back pocket.

"Meantime, I suppose you'll be wanting this."

Ray brightens. He takes the phone like Twill's a good Samaritan returning a lost pet.

"That was fast."

"You said to see if I could expedite. I asked for a favor. Chicago PD has all the data. You can have the stupid plastic back. Speaking of which, you really need to upgrade into the twenty-first century, Ray."

Ray slips the phone in his pocket and drains his glass.

"I know. I'll make the leap when they make a phone that can pour me a drink and give me a light." Ray struggles out of the booth and upright. "Meantime, I'm enjoying being smarter than the thing in my pocket." He sticks out a hand. Twill looks up and takes it. "Call me Mack."

# NINETY-SEVEN

I leave Twill at the table, nursing his Pinot and the kind of headache that comes with a lot of questions. Doris meets me at the end of the bar. She reaches out for me, her eyes ahead of her hands.

"Oh, Mack," she says. "Are you ..."

"I'm fine, Doris. Stop worrying. I'm going home to sleep for a week and make up with Phil. You won't see me again until ... well, until about this time tomorrow."

"That long?" She lends me the smile that Buck fell in love with and betrayed. "Thought you were going to be asleep. For a whole week, as I recall."

"Think I can't find this place with my eyes closed? You haven't been paying attention. And don't go thinking it's about the booze. I've got plenty of that at home. It's all you, Doris."

I hobble my way outside and stand on the sidewalk. The air is dark and hot and wet, like stepping out of a cool bar you love and into someone's mouth. A horn sounds off. Up the street, Prancers flicks its neon tongue. I don't have a Camel to my name. I know that, but I pat my shirt pocket anyway, just in case I've lost my mind. Which I have.

I walk the other way, toward the corner and the square of pavement where I parked the Impala. Too many people are in my head all at the same time. Twill. Santiago. Harpo. Smitty. Pete. Deno. Ronni. Sluggo. Nutsack. Suri. His Honor Samuel T. Royce and his dry cleaner. They all want my attention. It's like the floor of the stock exchange at the opening bell.

My head's too soggy to sort them all out. The ER docs said to think about laying off the booze and cigarettes until I've cleared the concussion. I do my best thinking with a drink in my hand and an ashtray nearby.

But then someone inside my head flips a switch and everything goes quiet and still.

There is only one of them left, now. Maybe two.

Marlo. Coming out of the dark, toward the opening door, flying eyes, arms wide.

Marlo. Across the street, sticking a photo in the crack of Victor Roby's front door. A photo of Victor bending into the passenger window of a car. He can't see her on account of the light inside his cozy room. I'm watching it all from across the street, through a lens as big as a telescope. As if from some distant planet. Marlo turns. Smiles for the camera. Her lips move but the sound is out of sync. *Time for Victor to get a view from outside his bubble of light.*

And then there's me. Raymond Mackey. I'm in there too. As a grab bag of light and shadow pretending to be a picture. Like any of us. Me wrapped in a white, make-shift turban, bent into the passenger side of a dead man's car. Holding the camera that took the picture. One man's opinion.

I keep hobbling. Feels like I'm being watched. But it's not the cops or Big Man's goons. It's not my instincts. It's the

*Triple-D*, my old friend. That familiar presence I've come to accept, like someone's tied a helium balloon to my belt loop with a long string. I can see myself down here, hobbling in my splint for the corner. I can see the parking lot and the street and the moonlit rooftops. I can see all the way home, where there's a white cat on a beat-up desk next to an old typewriter, looking out the window. Waiting.

*Triple-D*. That's never going away. And maybe I don't want it to. Maybe I need the company.

I turn at the corner and step into The Bodega. Rocky lights up like a Roman candle.

"Mac-a-doodle!" he exclaims, throwing open his short little, fire-hydrant arms. But one good look at me and the Roman-candle face fizzles and drops into a puddle. "Jesus, Mack. What the hell happened to you?"

"Sleepwalking," I tell him. "Woke up at Wrigley Field in time for batting practice. Can you hook a guy up with a Camel?"

Rocky turns and gets up on his stepladder, reaching and talking.

"Don't get me going about sleepwalking, Mack. Got a cousin in Hoboken who does that. Two weeks ago his wife finds him up on the friggin' roof goin' on about the dolphins. Dolphins! Leapin' around in the sky. And my cousin's up there cryin' because of all these dolphins. He's like worried or some shit. So she gets the guy back in bed, right?" Rocky comes back down and slaps the pack on the counter. "And the next morning ... what do you think, Mack? Finish the story."

"He can't remember a damn thing," I say, pulling out a twenty. Rocky points.

"Wrong. Remembers every friggin' thing, Mack. He's just amazed that she didn't see any dolphins. How fucked-up crazy is that?"

Ray takes the Camels and the change.

"Careful with that word, Rocky. Never know who might be crazy. Maybe we all are."

"Yeah, but come on, Mack. This is flying-dolphin crazy I'm talking about. This is not knowing the difference between dreaming and being awake."

My phone rings. Not quite as loud as usual but enough to get our attention.

"Maybe there's less difference than we think. Maybe this is the dream, Rocky. Ever think of that? Ever think that maybe when you die, you wake up?"

"You mean like in another life?"

"No. Another dream, Rocky. Just one dream stacked above another, see? Each one bigger than the last. Like a ladder or a staircase."

I knock out a Camel and fire it up. The phone in my pocket keeps at its old-fashioned ringing.

"What do the dead dream about, Rocky? That's what I want to know. Maybe they dream of us. Maybe *we* are the dream of the dead. We're the dolphins. And maybe they worry about us. Maybe they forgive us."

Rocky's mouth is open.

"Now I'm starting to think *you're* crazy," he says. "Jesus. You going to answer that thing?"

"No need," I say.

I turn and head for the door. An El Camino rattles past, dragging a muffler. Across the street, there's only one working streetlight to cover the entire parking lot. It flickers. I take a drag and raise a backward hand, stepping out onto the sidewalk.

"Watch yourself, Mack," he says.

I let the smoke go. It floats up toward me in a cloud.

"Thanks, Rocky. Always do."

A Preview

The Russian Doll
A Raymond Mackey Mystery
Book 2

# CHAPTER ONE

The bedside clock is a branding iron. My retinas take the news about like you'd expect. I close my eyes again, but that turns out to be pointless. I can still see the numbers floating in the dark: *3:00 AM.*

I pull back the covers and get myself upright. I get dressed in yesterday's clothes and go downstairs, Phil at my heels meowing for attention. My head is still sloshing from the Old Forester. Coffee would be nice but there's no time for that now, so I wake up the Camels and shake one free, patting my pockets for a light as I step outside on the stoop and close the door. I have to stop to set the flame, cupping the tip of the cigarette against the hot wind in my face. I drop the lighter back in my pocket and look around.

She's already waiting at the curb.

"You're late," she says. I close the door and lean my head against the back of the seat.

"Stop talking nonsense," I say. "It's way too early for me to be late."

She watches me with the lie on her face that we're in no kind of hurry. Like we have all the time in the world.

"Those things'll kill you, Mack."

I let out the smoke and bend forward, feeling around under the seat.

"What, the Camels?" I ask as my fingers finally find the Sig Saur. "Maybe." I sit up and nose the gun into my shoulder harness where it belongs. "But they'll have to get in line and wait their turn. I'm betting they never make it."

She pulls away and we ride without talking. I want to sleep. I close my eyes and the time once again glows red in the dark, throbbing with my pulse: *3:00 AM*. I try to ignore it, feeling for the black space between the numbers, looking for anywhere my bourbon-soaked brain can curl up for a nap. Her car is plush and quiet. The city moves beneath me in soft thumps and rumbles. She smells like forest beneath fresh snow.

"Want to tell me where we're going?" I ask.

"You'll know when you know," she says. "Maybe try being a big boy detective and figure it out for yourself."

We ride in silence. I can't keep my eyes open. Beneath me, Chicago is a city of muted vibration, mumbling up through my bones in rhythms of villainy and hope. All the buildings have eyes, and they watch us pass. Hard not to feel the conspiracies of malice, burning cold florescent inside. I don't need to see the proof. I know it's there. Just like I don't need my eyes open to feel the moon up in its pocket of muffled light, begging to be untied and set free.

The Camel smolders between my lips. The Sig burns next to my heart. I don't want to be here, sitting upright in a car next to a beautiful woman, packing a loaded gun under my arm. I want to be home. Lying down next to a beautiful woman and uncorking a loaded bottle. Forget the gun.

And then, finally and all of a sudden, we are still.

"Let's go," she says, opening her door. I lean forward in the seat, peering through the windshield. The headlights wash the end of a building on the far side of a hundred feet of gloom.

"Where is this?" I ask. "What is this?"

"You'll know when you know," she says. She reaches down and pulls the thing that pops the trunk. "Get to it."

I push open my door and step out into a warm wind blowing in my face. I drop the Camel and walk around to the back of the car. I close my eyes. This part is never easy. I have to prepare myself. I lift open the trunk with a finger.

It helps that she is so tightly wrapped. Her body is easier to lift. Easier to manage in my arms. Easier to bend over my shoulder like a long sack of flour.

It's a tough walk around to the front of the building. The snow is black without the headlights. Like I'm plowing through ash. The hot night air in my face is relentless. I look back to see if she's still by the car, but then I can hear her in the dark up ahead of me.

"Getting old, Mack," she says with a smile I can't see. "Back in the day you could carry one of her on each shoulder."

When I finally reach her, she's leaning up against the front of the building. My shoulders and knees are starting to feel the weight.

"Here?" I ask, looking. The door is metal and black. The next door down is red. And the one after that too. They keep going off into the gloom.

The number on the front isn't a number. It's a word I can't read. I look a little closer.

"What is this place?"

"You'll know when you know, Mack. How many times do you want me to say it? I'd unwrap her face before you knock. Don't make them do it."

I prop the body up against the door, glad to have her off my shoulders. I yank the sheet down off her head and we both look at her for a few seconds in silence. I want to arrange her hair and clean up her face. Smith & Wesson did her make up like they were in a hurry.

"She'd have hated looking like this," I say. "She was tough, but Suri cared how she looked."

"Then maybe you shouldn't have pulled the trigger," says Marlo. She's right and we both know it. My heart weighs more than all three of us put together. "You're out of time, Ray. They know we're here. Knock already."

But I don't have a chance to knock. The door starts to open on its own, and Suri starts to fall away with it. I let her go, wanting to protect Marlo from what's coming, but Marlo is gone now. All over again she is gone. I pull Sig from the holster. No time to aim. I stiff-arm the thing into an opening darkness that is like a sideways jaw, a fetid maw looking to swallow me whole, and I start shooting, firing blind, the muzzle flashing a burnt orange into the void.

The noise is deafening and sets my ears to ringing.

It sounds like a telephone.

Register at https://www.OwenThomasLiterary.com for advance notice regarding the release of Book 3 in the Raymond Mackey series, *The Big Dream,* and for purchase discounts available only to Owen Thomas Literary subscribers.

## For Your Consideration

Independent writers and publishers, deprived of the reach and resources of their gold-plated, establishment relations (by a difference that requires astronomical telescopes and laser technology to calculate), live and die by the reviews of their readers, or the lack of such reviews. The same astronomical tools and laser technology is necessary to measure the depth of gratitude the author feels for those who, having now finished this novel, are willing to leave a review on Amazon to either encourage other readers or warn them away. It takes just a moment and you will have made a tremendous, even if incremental, difference in the lives of those who read independently published books and those who write them. Also, Heaven. You'll go to Heaven. Eventually. Thank you.

Reviews at: https://amzn.to/3sYehAt

Visit Owen Thomas at his author website for information on upcoming books, photos, videos, excerpts, interviews, purchase links and to register for updates: www.OwenThomasLiterary.com.

## ABOUT THE AUTHOR

Owen Thomas is a life-long Alaskan living on Maui because life is too short for long winters. He has written six books: ***The Lion Trees*** (which has garnered over sixteen international book awards, including the American Writing Awards, the Amazon Kindle Book Award, the Eric Hoffer Book Award, the Book and Author Book of the Year, the Beverly Hills International Book Award and, most recently, a finalist in the Book Excellence Awards); ***Mother Blues***, (a novel of music and mystery set in post-Hurricane Harvey Texas, Finalist for the American Writing Awards and the Book Excellence Fiction Award, and collecting a Bronze in the Readers Views Reviewers' Choice Awards); ***Message in a Bullet: A Raymond Mackey Mystery***, (the first in a series of detective novels, shortlisted for the Best Mystery Book of the Year by Forward INDIES Book of the Year Awards and collecting a Silver from the eLit Book Awards); ***The Russian Doll: A Raymond Mackey Mystery*** (the second book in that series, Book Fest Awards Silver Medalist and Finalist for the American Fiction Award); ***Signs of Passing*** (a book of interconnected short stories and novellas, and winner of fourteen book awards, including the Pacific Book Awards for Short Fiction, the Indie Reader Discovery Award, the Great Southwest Book Festival, has garnered placements at the Paris, London and Los Angeles Book Festivals and was also named one of the 100 Most Notable Books of the Year by Shelf Unbound Magazine); and **This is the Dream**, (a collection of stories and novellas that explore that perplexing liminal distance between who we are and what we want; Finalist for the American Writing Awards and the International Book Award in short fiction, and collecting a Bronze in the Readers Views Reviewers' Choice Awards).